An abandoned airplane hangar—heat and humidity mixing with the musty smell of cheap cologne, the sweat of nervous and anxious men. They knew how violently this could end; a wrong move, a spark—a shootout:

Crime Scene Techs, paparazzi-like cameras flashing like bolts of lightning showing the dead—their bloated and leaking bodies sprawled like marionette puppets—strings abruptly cut.

Bold newspaper headlines: DEADLY SHOOTOUT IN MIAMI AIRPORT HANGAR posted just above: KIM K WOWS IN SKIMPY BLACK DRESS.

No way we're all making it outta here . . . no way.

* * *

From the authors of *Beachside PD: The Reluctant Knight* and *Beachside PD: The Gypsy Hunter* comes a prequel to the series, *Beachside PD: Cities of Sand and Stone.*

Angelo Tedeschi was forged by his father's fists, his mother's love, and shaped on the streets of Brooklyn. Tempered by his friendship with Danny Phillips and Jay Gardner, he survived to eventually work for mob boss Eddie "Mambo" Salerno.

From the stone city of Brooklyn to the sand city of Beachside, Angelo Tedeschi's story is one of constant betrayal. If you are a reader who prefers realism along with hard-hitting action and savvy dialogue, then you'll enjoy the third novel from this father/son writing team.

D1521008

Beachside PD: Cities of Sand and Stone
Printed by CreateSpace/August, 2012

This is a work of fiction. Names, characters, incidents, and places are a product of the author's imagination or are used fictitiously. Any resemblance to actual events, business establishments, locations, geographic areas, or people, living or dead, is entirely coincidental.

Contact the author at www.beachsidepd.com for information about special discounts for bulk purchases, promotions or to bring the author to yourevent or reading.

Cover design by David A. Yuzuk

ISBN-13: 978-1478215103
ISBN-10: 1478215100

Library of Congress Control Number:
2012913316

Cities of Sand and Stone

A Beachside PD Prequel

By

David A. Yuzuk

&

Neil L. Yuzuk

From David:
In Loving Memory of Edward F. Soldiviero
December 20, 1965 — October 22, 2010

From Neil:
In Loving Memory of Jack Jay Allan Yuzuk,
but we called him, Jackie
March 18, 1952 — April 14, 1977

FOREWORD

In the beginning, my full-time police officer, part-time actor and writer son, David had an idea for a screenplay that would be "Schindler's List" with cops—a story of excess and redemption. We went back and forth and came up with a script that mirrored the story, eventually told, that started the Beachside PD series. The original title was "Suicide By Cop" and then it evolved to "The Reluctant Knight."

After taking Robert McKee's four day STORY seminar, I decided to turn the screenplay into a novel and the first book in the Beachside PD series was born. A town and more characters were created, along with back stories and a foundation for the future. The original story tripled in size. This third book in the series is a prequel, as David has explored the childhood of Angelo Tedeschi, and if it is reflective, in part, of the Brooklyn and Long Island club scene of the 1970s and 1980s—so be it.

Although my name appears as a co-author, for the most part, this is David's story to tell—his vision. Angelo Tedeschi, as he appeared in "The Reluctant Knight," certainly appeared as a rather simple and reactive character. But, underneath that facade is a complex man driven, for the most part, by his childhood demons. His closest friend, Danny Phillips, described him as ". . . a vicious thug certainly, a psychopath probably, and yet caring to those very few he loved." Angelo is a fascinating creation and I have a feeling that this is not the last we will hear of him. There are more stories to tell about him and we still need to bridge the ending of "Cities of Sand and Stone" to "The Reluctant Knight."

Of all the stories in the book, the only one that David will admit to being true is the one about SWAT member Jason Youngblood. "What he did, was the most heroic thing I've ever seen."

The fourth book in the series, "Beachside PD: Undercover" is in progress and should be published by the end of December, 2012. I am hoping that two more Beachside PD books will be added in 2013. They are tentatively titled, "Beachside PD: A Captain's Story" and "Beachside PD: Special Weapons."

Neil L. Yuzuk
June, 2012

For your convenience, we've included a glossary of some of the military and police terms in the book.

Military/Police Glossary

AED	Automated External Defibrillator
A.S.A.	Assistant State Attorney
Baker Act	Florida State statute 394.462 states that if a person becomes a danger to himself or to others and refuses medical treatment he will be taken into custody and transported to the nearest health facility for treatment. To "Baker Act" someone is to invoke this power.
Boat Space	A seat in a military vehicle
B.O.L.O.	Be On the Look Out
C.I.	Confidential Informant
C.O.C.	Combat Operations Center
Dbol	Dianabol, a steroid
Drank	Liquid Vicodin/Hydrocodone mixed with Sprite
E-Club	Enlisted Club
F.D.L.E.	Florida Department of Law Enforcement
Finocchio	Offensive Italian-American term for homosexual
GHB	Gamma-hydroxybutyrate, AKA the "date rape" drug
HGH	Human Growth Hormone
I.A.	Internal Affairs
I.E.D.	Improvised Explosive Device
I.O.J.	Injury On The Job
KIA	Killed In Action
LZ	Landing Zone
Made (Man)	A Organized Crime description for a man who has murdered and gone through initiation into a crime family
MRAP	Up-Armored Humvee
P.T.	Physical Training
PFC	Private First Class
RPG	Rocket Propelled Grenade
SAW	Squad Automatic Weapon
T.H.I.	Traffic Homicide Investigator
Triggerfish	Cell phone tracking technology
U.C.	Undercover
Vikes	Vicodin, a semi-synthetic opioid

PROLOGUE

Inside the abandoned airplane hangar the humidity was sweltering. Hanging in the air was a musty-smelling cloud of cheap cologne mixed with the pungent aroma of anxious, sweating men. The men all knew how high the stakes were and how violently their lives could end.

Shootout: The dead sprawled like marionette puppets abruptly cut from their masters' strings. Fat cops standing over bloated, leaking carcasses. Flashbulbs popping from the crime scene tech paparazzi. Cold, pale bodies on aluminum slabs. The Medical Examiner pretending he's Zorro carving his Y incision with one hand while holding a grilled cheese sandwich in the other.

The newspaper headline: **DEADLY SHOOTOUT IN MIAMI AIRPORT HANGAR** posted just above KIM KARDASHIAN WOWS THE RED CARPET IN SKIMPY BLACK DRESS.

No way we are all making it out of here today . . . no way.

Angelo Tedeschi, forty years old, tall, solidly built, with dark hair showing the beginnings of gray, felt the beads of sweat flowing down his back and onto the .45 Caliber Glock handgun concealed in his rear waistband. He remembered some scorching days in Brooklyn where they'd had to break open fire hydrants to cool off but never anything this merciless. The air was so heavy with moisture that just breathing it exhausted his overworked lungs. With every beat of his pounding heart, images flashed in his mind. *Home, Bora Bora, Alaska, anywhere but this fuckin' shit hole.*

Facing Angelo was the heavyset fifty-two-year-old Russian, Viktor Matyushenko. A bear of a man with cold, blue eyes and a protruding Neanderthal-like brow ridge that added to his brooding appearance. He was sweating profusely and constantly tugging on his shirt; praying for just a wisp of fresh air to reach and cool his body. His pasty, flushed face was just starting to show signs of heat exhaustion. Viktor and his partners were the new kids on the mobster block in South Florida and they were already creating a deadly wave of crime.

Scattered behind Viktor were three Cuban thugs dressed in oversized button-down linen short-sleeved shirts known to the locals as a Guayabera. Although they were still relatively new students of Viktor's business training, they were already all highly proficient in the tactical use of weapons and each concealed a deadly arsenal on his person.

Positioned next to Angelo was his boss: the always-intense Michael Frakes. At forty-eight years old, with thinning light brown hair, and medium height, his athletic build was concealed under a large Marlins baseball jersey. The oversized shirt was sticking to his body like shrink-wrap plastic, making just standing there highly uncomfortable. As a Florida native, Michael was used to this type of heat, although this night was definitely up there with some of the worst he could remember. *I should have called this off . . . it's too late to turn back now.*

Standing off to the side of the group, and bathed in vertical shadows, was one of Angelo's oldest friends, forty-six-year-old Joey Salerno. Built like a mix between bulldog and a concrete pillar, Joey was known as a man to fear . . . and that was before people learned he was a card-carrying member of the New York Mafia. Concealed behind his back, he tightly gripped his Sig P226 handgun. *Let's get this shit over with,* he thought with his typical Sicilian impatience.

"Show us what you got?" Angelo calmly asked Viktor, while wiping the excess sweat off his face with the back of his hand. His grizzled old mentor flashed into his head, giving sage advice. *Ange, never let the palm of your hand get wet when you're doin' a deal, 'cause not for nothin', what if you need to grab your piece? MING-YA! You don't want your fuckin' hand to slip!* Viktor paused, and without taking his eyes off Angelo, he motioned to his guys and ordered,

"Bring it out."

Two of the muscular Cuban men walked over to a white van parked inside the hangar. They opened the rear doors and carried out a large wooden crate with U.S. military markings stenciled on the side. They heaved the heavy crate onto a rusty metal table and it groaned under the weight. One of the men pulled open the lid and Angelo walked up and peered inside. It contained two .50-caliber Barrett sniper rifles, packed neatly.

"Where's the rest?" asked Angelo, as he turned back towards Viktor.

"Call your money man and I'll show you."

Angelo motioned to Michael and said, "Go ahead and tell him to come in."

An older model brown sedan drove up to the front gate of the hangar. A fiercely-bearded Russian guard in a wrinkled suit motioned the vehicle to stop. The guard was cursing under his breath about the oppressive heat as he checked the car. The driver—Bobby "Dee" Ochoa, thirty-seven years old, with a wiry, muscular build and heavily tattooed arms—took notice of his Russian rival. *Very nice: an AR-15 neatly concealed under your jacket, I probably would've missed it if your shirt wasn't sweat-soaked with its imprint against your stinking body.* After checking the car's interior and trunk, the guard picked up his radio and said something quickly in Russian. He waved Bobby inside the complex and pointed toward the hangar. *Later, hijo de gran puta!* Bobby pulled the vehicle into the hangar and parked it next to a white van.

Bobby exited the vehicle holding a bulging gym bag. He scanned the room, noting every threat, and placed the bag on the rusted metal table next to Angelo. Angelo unzipped the bag, exposing its contents, and showed the large bundles of cash to Viktor. Without warning, the youngest and most inexperienced of the Cuban thugs pulled out his gun and started shooting toward Michael and Angelo. With that, the other two thugs whipped out their firearms and started blasting away. Unnoticed in the initial chaos, Joey shifted further to the side, seeking cover behind a concrete wall.

For Michael the scene became surreal. Even before the first Cuban reached into his waistband for his weapon, he sensed impending danger. It was as if an electrically-charged static filled the heavily laden air. His senses sharpened and he achieved a heightened state of awareness he'd experienced only once before. He saw with perfect clarity the unshaven stubble and the open, sweating pores on the pink faces of his adversaries. As the first Cuban wrenched his gun from under his shirt, Michael could almost make out the etched serial number on the rusty slide mechanism of the 9mm Beretta. In a painstakingly slow arc, the gun reached its peak and aimed directly at his face. The last thing he remembered before the blackness enveloped him was, *how beautiful the colorful muzzle flash of the weapon's discharge was, - popping amber flashes mixed with streaks of burnt sienna dancing before his eyes.*

Chapter 1

October, 1956 was a momentous year. The New York Yankees had regained their throne on the top of the baseball world led by Mickey Mantle's Triple Crown year; President Eisenhower handily defeated Adlai Stevenson for a second term in office and in New York Harbor, an ocean liner docked at a closed Ellis Island and a fourteen-year old Rosario Moretti walked, head held high, down a gangplank.

The Immigration Service had scrambled to find a safe harbor after smallpox had been discovered among the steerage passengers and they quickly set up cots and tents in the Great Hall, along with medical services for the lower-class passengers. The upper-class passengers were allowed to remain on the ship enjoying its comforts.

After a full medical examination, Rosario Moretti was declared disease-free, but he was held in quarantine for five days, just in case. In the emergency, the ship's manifest and other papers were mislaid, so when young Rosario declared his name to be Rosario Tedeschi, his new papers reflected his odd name change and no one was the wiser.

Charles Moretti, known to most as Chuck, was a soft-spoken, hard-working building superintendent in Queens, New York. One night, without notice, he received a knock on his door. Standing in the doorway was a disheveled young boy, cap in hand.

"Can I help you?" he said.

"Io sono il tuo cugino Rosario," was the reply, as the boy pushed an envelope at him. Chuck opened the letter. It was from his aunt begging him to take in his young cousin due to family problems. *The obligations of family*, he groaned inwardly. He knew he could not refuse the request; his aunt had helped him leave Italy all those years ago before he could be caught up in the German hunt for Italian partisans fighting the occupation. Chuck knew there was more to the boy's story than just a family hardship, but he decided not to pressure Rosario for the truth. He knew if he stayed patient, either the boy would tell him on his own or the mystery would eventually reveal itself.

Despite Rosario not being able to speak a word of English, Chuck was able to enroll him in the local public school. During the enrollment process, Chuck got another surprise. Rosario insisted his last name was not Moretti but Tedeschi. The boy refused to discuss further his reasons. *Well, that's just another clue to my cousin's curious past.* Rosario's school days, however, would be short-lived, because only three weeks later the principal expelled the fiery-tempered young man due to excessive fighting.

Without schooling, Chuck provided the next best thing and taught Rosario handyman work. In the beginning it worked out well for the overworked and underpaid superintendent. Unfortunately, the assistance Rosario provided was quickly nullified by his hair-trigger temper. When he started beating up the kids in the neighborhood, Rosario became public enemy number one. Sometimes he fought because he was teased, while at other times he would snap at an unintended or imaginary slight.

Always the opportunist and tired of apologizing to parents in the neighborhood, Chuck decided to encourage his little cousin's pugilistic ways and introduced him to his first boxing gym. Rosario took to the boxing like a duck to water and was soon catching the attention of several prominent coaches. The boxing training kept the tenacious teenager mostly out of trouble throughout his adolescent years. Many of his coaches also acted as surrogate fathers to the highly emotional and sometimes unstable young man.

While at a neighborhood Labor Day block party just after his twentieth birthday, Rosario met his future wife, Theresa Russo. Despite Theresa being seventeen years old, the two hit it off and were married only five months later when she turned eighteen. After their wedding, against the advice of those close to him, Rosario quickly signed a lucrative three-fight contract with his manager and turned professional. Rosario had another motivation for signing, over and above the fact that he and his wife lived in a tiny one-bedroom apartment: only four months after their marriage, Theresa was pregnant.

With the thousand-dollar advance his manager gave him, Rosario moved with his expecting wife to an expanding new neighborhood in Brooklyn called Mill Basin. They had fallen in love with the neighborhood after visiting Theresa's older sister Loraine, who had already been living there the past two years. Living only three blocks away from her older sister gave the still-young Theresa a feeling of security.

Rosario's worst times began when he received word Chuck had died of a heart attack. Like most, his biggest regret was that he never told Chuck throughout the years how much he appreciated all he did for him. In the following weeks, he slid into a dark world of negativity. It severely hampered his training and started the first rift between him and his wife.

Fighting as a professional was much tougher than Rosario had ever imagined, and he ended up losing his first two fights. With one fight left on his contract, the pressure was mounting, and another loss would mean his manager would not re-sign him. To add to his problems, one week before the fight, his son Angelo was born prematurely, severely underweight and with several health complications.

Rosario lost his last fight, along with his manager, and was forced to quit boxing. Somehow, he formulated the idea that Theresa and Angelo were responsible for sabotaging his once-promising career. He returned to handyman work, hating every boring and tedious minute of it. *What kind of fuckin' life is this . . . ? Theresa shut the fuck up and take that whining little bastard back to his room. Slap! Don't you ever fuckin' disrespect me, not in my house, you ungrateful bitch.* The slaps, punches and kicks would begin with the uneven pattern of raindrops, but when a severe storm blew in and the skies opened up, Theresa and Angelo lived in a world of pain. Years later, Rosario's condition would have been fairly easily diagnosed as bipolar disorder, and he would have received proper treatment. In 1961, that wasn't the case, and Rosario started self-medicating his ever-worsening condition with alcohol.

In order to keep a roof over their heads, Rosario moved the family into a smaller and cheaper two-bedroom apartment in the blue-collar neighborhood of Canarsie. Over the next few years, his cruelty steadily increased as he sank deeper into the murky darkness of his mental illness. Every day, the voices getting louder, "Your mother is a whore, you half breed son of Satan! You don't belong here, Tedeschi, you should have fled in the night with your coward father." *He is not my father, I have no father!*

Theresa could have left Rosario and taken Angelo to her sister's house, but being the perfect victim she remained like a deer in the headlights. She knew the signs of when the sickness would grab hold of him: the pasty chalk spittle forming on his lips; the increasingly manic speech patterns. She believed the answer to her husband's sickness somehow encompassed the mysterious childhood he refused to speak about.

Living in that hellish environment caused young Angelo to suffer numerous anxiety disorders himself, including trouble controlling his bladder. Inside the apartment, Angelo constantly clung to his mother for any type of protection she could offer. This behavior only served to further infuriate Rosario, who constantly reiterated how ashamed of and disgusted he was by his crying, weak son.

Chapter 2

As Angelo got older, he escaped the insanity and dysfunction of his household by spending most of his time on the street. He loved his new neighborhood because, on his block alone, there were at least ten kids his age he could hang out with. Just when he thought his luck was changing for the better the new school year started. On Angelo's first day of elementary school after class, a kid from the sixth grade forcibly ripped his jacket off his back and refused to return it. Angelo immediately ran home in the cold weather and, in between tears, told his mom what had happened. Rosario overheard the conversation and forbid Theresa from intervening in any way.

"If he can't handle some fucking punk kid from school, then too bad for him, let him fucking freeze for all I care."

Although the jacket incident certainly wasn't the worst thing that ever happened to Angelo, over hearing his father's cruel words and knowing that he had no one to rely on pushed him over the edge.

The anger and humiliation built like a festering boil and one week after his jacket was stolen, Angelo waited patiently after school behind a large metal door where the bully always exited. As the bully stepped outside, Angelo without hesitation swung a large rock and bashed the back of the kid's head, making an audible thump. The bully collapsed and fell, face forward into the ground. Angelo took out years of anguish by pummeling his now defenseless tormentor with a flurry of punches and kicks. It was an unbelievably intoxicating feeling as the adrenaline coursed through his veins. After the beating, he stood above his vanquished enemy, savoring every brutal, bloody second of payback. Roughly, he grabbed a thicket of the semiconscious boy's hair, lifting his face off the concrete. The bully's eyes were glazed as syrupy thick, copper-colored blood ran down his scalp. Angelo looked into the boy's eyes and said, "Know that this is just the beginning."

Before releasing the boy's hair and walking away, Angelo hocked up a wad of his vilest saliva and spat thickly into his victim's face. Next day at school, a friend of the bully returned the jacket, no questions asked.

Once Angelo learned the power and benefits of violence, he started exerting his will over the other kids at school and in his neighborhood. The streets were now Angelo's real home and he ran roughshod over anyone who got in his way. He formed a small gang with a group of boys several years older and began to extort his fellow students, and eventually the local storeowners. If the owners didn't pay protection, his gang would start fights in the stores, causing more damage than the extortion payment cost.

At twelve years old, he got his first real job as a matboy in the Flatbush Terrace Sun and Swim club. The idea came to him after he started breaking into the lockers at school and found it profitable. He figured the scores would be even bigger at a pool club because the members would keep their wallets and other valuables in the locker rooms as they lounged in the sun and swam in the pool.

In the middle of urban Brooklyn, the swim club was an oasis for those unable to afford the hefty prices of joining a real beach club in the Rockaways. No sand, no fancy cabanas, no canoes or boat docks—just a huge pool surrounded by concrete, with paddleball courts in the rear and a large upper-level sundeck. Hundreds of its blue-collar members joined each year to escape the summer heat with their families. All the lounges for the guests were made of wood, so they required a padded mat. Due to the climate, the hundreds of mats couldn't be left out overnight, so they had to be put away at the end of every day. As customers entered the club, a matboy would grab the best mat he could find from a storage room and carry it to the lounge for a tip. On a busy weekend, a matboy hustling could make as much as twenty five dollars for two days' work. With his aggressive approach, Angelo quickly established himself as one of the top earners that summer. Even the older thirteen-year-olds would steer clear of him after he demonstrated how vicious he could be with an uncooperative coworker.

Several weeks after Angelo started working at the club, the manager hired another young kid around the same age. No one cared to learn the new kid's name, so he was given the nickname "Bones" because he was so skinny. The one thing Bones had going for him was the gift of gab, which he used with great prowess. Before Angelo knew it, most customers began to request their mats from the ever-popular Bones.

When Angelo saw his tip jar was almost empty, he decided it was time to straighten out the new kid. Inside the storage room, he grabbed Bones by his scrawny throat, shoved him up against a wall, and said, "Here's the deal. If you don't quit by the end of the day, you're gonna catch a serious beatin'." Bones wasn't fazed by Angelo's tactics and calmly looked him in the eye. As Angelo tightened his grip, Bones said, I'll tell you what. Meet me after work at six o 'clock on the upper level sundeck and let's have ourselves a fight."

"Why should I wait till six and not beat your ass now?"

"'Cause if we fight now, the manager will just fire us both, but if we wait he always leaves at 5:30."

Angelo agreed, even though he figured the kid would chicken out and dip out the back door.

Six o'clock came and Angelo knew the fight was on, because Bones stayed and worked the whole day. As Angelo climbed the steps to the large sundeck, he was shocked by what he saw. Waiting on a makeshift line on the stairs were a group of kids he recognized from the neighborhood. At the top of the stairs were two of the other matboys, collecting money from kids as they entered the sundeck. He pushed his way past them and was surprised to see at least fifty more neighborhood kids clamoring on the deck. Standing in the middle of the crowd was Bones, who didn't appear to be too concerned about the fight. The crowd parted as Angelo approached Bones.

"What's going on? This was supposed to be a fight," asked a confused Angelo.

Bones finished giving instructions to another pool employee and turned to Angelo.

"Yeah, exactly, so let's give them a good fight."

Bones turned his back on Angelo and calmly removed a gold chain from around his neck. He handed it to a friend in the crowd and uttered something about "making it a minute." Angelo had never fought in front of a crowd and was a little hesitant at first, but that unending reservoir of rage was always easily accessed. Especially since, standing in front of him was the kid who was robbing him of good money. As soon as Bones turned around to face him, Angelo clocked him in the head with a big looping punch. For the next several minutes, Angelo beat on Bones, knocking him up and down the sundeck. All the while, the crowd screamed with enthusiasm as they watched the two mini gladiators go at it. Although Angelo was badly thrashing him, the scrawny runt never gave in and even tried fighting back several times. It wasn't until Bones could no longer protect himself that the crowd intervened and finally pulled Angelo off, who was still swinging for the fences.

Twenty minutes later, Angelo was eating pizza across the street with two of his friends, laughing it up about the fight. To his surprise, Bones strolled into the parlor, with a ripped tee shirt and bloody lip. He sauntered right up to Angelo and coolly said, "I want to talk to you. Why don't we step outside?"

Angelo couldn't believe the balls of this kid, looking to

fight him again after catching such a beating. Angelo and his two friends jumped at the challenge and started to move.

Bones looked them over and said, "No one else this time; just me and him, one on one."

Angelo looked at his friends and said confidently, "Wait here, 'cause this won't take long."

As Angelo followed his opponent out the door, Bones turned and walked into a side alleyway. At first, Angelo thought he was being set-up, but decided to follow anyway because, well, *Angelo Tedeschi ain't afraid of anyone or anything.* As he entered the alley, he saw Bones waiting alone.

Without waiting, Bones said, "Okay, good job out there, we really made out well. Here's your cut of the take."

He handed Angelo forty dollars in cash. Stunned, Angelo took the money and said, "I don't understand."

As cool as a used car salesman, Bones answered, "You think we should have fought for free? I promoted the fight all day long and charged every kid three dollars to watch us fight. I then bet some money on me lasting over a minute with you. There were several times I almost blacked out, but when I thought about all the money I would make, there was no way I was going to quit."

Angelo shook his head in disbelief and couldn't stop himself smiling. Although he'd won the battle, this skinny little kid had won the war. He extended his hand and grinned.

"Angelo Tedeschi. Nice to meet you."

Bones shook his hand, and said, "Danny Phillips . . . although I was starting to get used to people calling me Bones and it was a pleasure doing business with you today."

A thought popped into Angelo's head and he asked, "Can you do this every day and help me make more money?"

Danny put his arm over Angelo's shoulders and said with a big smile, "Ange, my boy, this may be the beginning of a beautiful friendship."

After that day, Angelo and Danny were inseparable and their legendary scams started to grow with increasing profits.

From sports book betting pools to loan sharking, Danny was the brains while Angelo provided the muscle.

Angelo also started spending more time at Danny's house, especially around dinnertime. Danny's mom was an excellent cook and she loved to watch the intense little Italian boy eat. Danny's father Samuel Philikowski was a police officer who worked at the 69th precinct in Brooklyn. Although Samuel was a large, intimidating man — especially in his uniform — he also had a heart of gold. Several times he interceded on Angelo's behalf and saved him from going to the Juvenile Hall.

One of those times was when Angelo witnessed his father in one of his usual tirades, screaming at his mother in the living room. When Theresa didn't immediately capitulate to his dominance as she normally did, and then had the audacity to talk back, it sent him over the edge. Rosario immediately escalated his aggression by slapping her open-handed several times in the face. The blows jolted her head, like a child's balloon hanging outside the window of a moving car. A frail woman, Theresa was almost knocked unconscious by her husband's heavy hands. His cruelty still not quenched, he dragged her around the room by her hair bouncing her off several pieces of furniture.

Angelo ran into his bedroom and grabbed the first thing he could find — a baseball bat. Holding the heavy wooden bat with both hands, he raced into the living room. Out of the corner of his eye, Rosario saw Angelo coming towards him with the bat slung over his shoulder. The only emotion Angelo could read on his father's face as they made eye contact was utter disdain. *Look at this, my cowardly son who pees in his pants and cries on his mother's skirt thinks he's a man now. You don't have the fuckin' balls to raise that bat to me!* Angelo's first swing shattered Rosario's cheekbone and fractured part of his skull. After that first hit, the rush of endorphins flooded Angelo's brain, giving him an amazing high. The rest was all a blur.

The neighbors, who were all too familiar with the constant fighting in the Tedeschi household, heard the blood curdling screams coming from Theresa and called the police. When the cops arrived, they found Angelo still clutching the bloody baseball bat and standing over his unconscious father. Theresa was sitting on the floor in the corner calmly straightening out the creases in her dress, as if she were in church. Rosario had to be transported to the hospital and Angelo was arrested on scene for aggravated battery.

If it weren't for the intervention of Danny Philips' old man, Angelo would have been convicted. Samuel had known the judge for years and testified on Angelo's behalf. He told the judge that Rosario was a sick, abusive bastard who'd had it coming to him for a long time. Inside the courthouse, Danny's mom and Angelo's Aunt Loraine also offered their support. Theresa couldn't bring herself to attend the hearing and asked Loraine to stand in for her. The judge released Angelo into Loraine's custody and he stayed with her for the next several months until Rosario healed and cooled off. When Angelo eventually moved back home, father and son—oddly enough—never discussed the incident again.

Danny had a beautiful younger sister named Rina who Angelo was really attracted to. Having been raised in the streets, Angelo knew the rules of being a stand up guy, and rule number one was that you never dated your friends' ex girlfriends or sisters. Sometimes, it was hard to be in the same room with her, but Danny was his boy and he would never betray his friend. Danny was the only person Angelo trusted enough to know the truth about his mother. Theresa's alcoholism became so devastating that by the time he was fourteen, she could no longer function at any level. Early in her illness she would only leave the house to go on errands, but when her alcoholism and depression worsened she would spend most of her day in bed.

Angelo's aunt Loraine went through her own tragedy when her husband was killed in a car accident. Without her husband, Loraine spent even more time with her sister. Over the years, Loraine took on more of the responsibilities as a mother to Angelo. To avoid embarrassment over Theresa's worsening condition, Loraine even posed as Angelo's mother for school meetings and other functions. After enough time had gone by, every one of Angelo's friends except Danny believed Loraine was his actual mom. Loraine, a devout Catholic tried to keep Angelo away from what she called "the Devil's path." She felt Rosario could not be saved but the boy still had a chance. By the time Angelo was in his late teens, however, she became completely discouraged and gave up all hope of him ever walking the righteous path.

If it wasn't for Danny and all the school-related scams they had going, Angelo would have skipped going to school entirely. But business was good, and Danny needed Angelo's presence every day to keep all their so-called sheep in line. In sixth grade, Angelo had a history teacher named Martin Senigal. "Marty," as he was known to his students because he didn't believe in titles, was the first teacher Angelo respected. Marty besides being an ex-pro football player was an avid world traveler and would mix his history lessons with tales of his exciting journeys. Angelo saw Marty as a heroic character, sort of a Brooklyn version of Indiana Jones. For a kid living in a small apartment in a home full of misery, Marty's adventure stories took him to a better place.

The lesson one day was about 17th Century British explorer, Captain James Cook. After the lesson, Marty wheeled out his old slide machine that projected pictures onto the classroom's big movie screen. He showed his students his trip to Tahiti and the island of Bora Bora. When the kids heard the funny name Bora Bora, they all laughed, thinking Marty was just making it up. Not only did he prove the island existed, but he also showed them that it was one of the most beautiful islands in the world. When Angelo looked at the images of the emerald blue lagoons with perfect white-sand beaches, he was sure he was looking at paradise. His mind soared with an ecstatic rush of excitement and purpose because there was no other place in the world he wanted to live.

Over the next few months, he became obsessed with learning as much as he could about the magical island. Every day after school, he would take two city buses to the Brooklyn public library and read several books about the tiny island over and over. He stared at the pictures and maps of that tropical paradise so long and intensely that each color and shape was burned into his memory.

A vision started to form in Angelo's imagination. The image was of he and his mother walking on pristine beaches, living a beautiful and normal life. *With Danny's help I can make enough money to move with my mom to Bora Bora. I can save her from that sick bastard.* The money would come from his schemes with Danny. They now had ongoing betting pools, protection service to students, and a newspaper delivery route that they out-muscled from the competition.

When Danny first heard the plan, he thought Angelo was just kidding and pulling his leg. After seeing he was serious, Danny quickly stopped smiling. Danny knew that deep down under all that toughness, Angelo was a dreamer. He also knew that Angelo didn't have any real concept of money, of how costly this trip would actually be. Although he knew Angelo's dream would not be happening anytime soon, he didn't have the heart to tell him. Instead, he told Angelo that every week they would start putting money on the side for his big trip. Angelo's motivation to make money dramatically increased and he started getting reckless. Many times, Danny had to slow him down because he didn't want to see his best friend go to jail or blow all their ongoing scams.

Angelo never got the chance to rescue his mom or go to Bora Bora, because later that year she succumbed to alcohol-related chronic pancreatitis. At her funeral viewing, he placed the best picture he could find of Bora Bora inside her coffin along with tears of guilt for not being able to save her. With her death, Angelo threw away his silly childhood dreams of Bora Bora and focused more on his limitless hatred of his father.

Chapter 3

Danny Phillips—A.K.A. "Bones" or "Houdini," depending on whom you were talking to—grew into a tall, well-built young man with movie-star good looks. While Angelo continued to muscle his way through life, Danny's charm and appeal only increased, allowing him to obtain things a lot easier. Danny's goals were always money, power, and stature. Growing up wearing second-hand clothes and watching his father struggle each week to pay the bills gave him his motivation to want the finer things in life. In his head, Danny despised his father, Sam, for his honesty as a cop. Danny swore that he'd never be like his father. When Sam was killed in the line of duty, Danny was torn between mocking him and loving this man who saw life so clearly.

Women were constantly fighting for his attention and Danny played it to the hilt. As a teenager in the nightclub scene, Danny had a knack for hooking up two or three times a night with different girls, and then taking them out to the parking lot for a good time in his Chevy Monte Carlo. He always bought the drinks those nights because, after seducing them, he would convince the lucky ladies to lend him money. He would use any excuse to swindle the money—from leaving his wallet at home to claiming he'd had his pocket picked while waiting in line. When asked why he would scam these beautiful women, Danny would grin mischievously and answer, "You know I have to get paid for my services!"

Later in life, Danny used his charisma as an investment

consultant for J.P. Morgan and began to make a fortune. A few years later, he opened his own office in downtown Manhattan as a financial advisor. The expansively decorated office was complete with a large mahogany desk and a curvaceous knockout blonde as a secretary. Together they fleeced the wealthy with get rich schemes and for Danny it was blondes, bourbon and success. And yet, even though he achieved the lifestyle he'd always dreamed of, Danny Phillips always wanted more.

Chapter 4

Jay Gardner always stood out when he hung out with Angelo and Danny. At 5 feet 4 inches tall, with a thin build and unassuming looks, Jay had to utilize his intellect to get along. The thing that surprised people the most about Jay hanging out with Danny and Angelo was that he was the only black guy amongst their friends. Which just happened to be the reason behind how they met. Jay was one of a handful of African-Americans who attended the predominately all white Italian school, Roy H. Mann Junior High.

One day, while walking home from school, Angelo and Danny watched Jay get jumped by a group of white kids. Angelo was upset because he didn't like the odds and always hated people who were afraid to fight one-on-one. Danny, whose real last name before he changed it was Philikowski, knew what it was like being on the receiving end of a racist beating. They interceded on Jay's behalf and the three became good friends ever since. In return for the comforting protection of Angelo and Danny, Jay always helped them with scholastics and, later on, with business ventures. Somewhat ironically, Jay eventually became a criminal defense attorney, which Angelo and Danny always joked they would someday need.

In those days, Jay gravitated to hanging out with the more easygoing Danny. "Danny, you know I love Angelo, but when he gets around those crazy friends of his . . . " This lesson couldn't have been any truer than the one night he did hang out with Angelo and his friends without Danny. Jay was twenty-two years old and was attending N.Y.U. law school in Manhattan. One night, he stayed late on campus so he could finish up an overdue paper. He also had plans to meet up with a very pretty classmate later the same night in order to do some studying and, hopefully, a little more.

As he left the school, he crossed through Washington Square Park and headed up 5th Street. Walking briskly in the cold November night, he heard someone calling his name. When he turned, he saw Angelo with a group of his raucous friends inside an old Buick. Jay walked over to the car with a little trepidation; although he knew Angelo was his boy, his buddies—especially that really muscular guy, Joey Salerno— were nuts. Besides Angelo and Joey there were two other guys in the car, who he later learned were Jimmy Castaldi and Tommy Lesner. Angelo invited Jay to come out drinking with them and Jay politely declined, explaining he had a date. But the other guys insisted and despite his earlier trepidation, Jay figured that maybe one night on the town would be fun— *what could possibly go wrong?* If things started getting rowdy, he would just pack it in and call it an early night.

Jay jumped in the back seat of the old car and they headed to their first destination: happy hour at the China Club. At the bar, they pounded shots of Patron Tequila and chased them with bottles of Heineken. Jay was just starting to relax and have a good time when a large Latin guy got into his face. The guy accused Jay of grabbing his girlfriend's *coolita*. Jay figured that was probably the Spanish word for ass and that meant things weren't looking good. Before he could even answer to defend himself, a blur of motion closely whizzed by his face and smashed into the Latin guy's nose.

Over the loud music, Joey Salerno hadn't heard what the guy had been saying to Jay, but he could tell by his body language that the guy had a beef and had been about to start a fight. The Latin guy's nose was shattered instantly by Joey's sledgehammer fist and he rolled on the floor, writhing in pain, his nose leaking like a faucet. Joey and Jimmy, who were both on probation, decided it would probably be for the best if they all immediately headed for the exit. Amazed at how quickly things could get out of control, Jay decided it was time to call it a night. Again, the guys — now more drunk and belliger-ent than ever — insisted he finish out the evening with them. Jay realized he was being given the proverbial offer you can't refuse and despondently followed the inebriated band of merry men out of the bar.

Once inside the Buick, the new plan was to drive back to Brooklyn and hit a more familiar bar named TJ Bentley's. Angelo, exhausted from working his bouncer job at night and his construction job during the day, passed out in the back seat next to Jay. As they pulled onto 3rd Avenue in Bay Ridge, Brooklyn, Jimmy, sitting in the front passenger seat, hurled a beer bottle at two guys walking on the street. Why Jimmy did it nobody had the *slightest fucking clue*. Later on, Jimmy explained that he knew those guys didn't belong in the neigh-borhood and it pissed him off. The bottle hit a huge blonde-haired Viking looking guy. The Viking's smaller companion who just missed getting hit in the face with the bottle sported a spiky red Mohawk hairstyle.

After getting struck with the bottle, the giant Viking stalked towards the Buick, which was now stopped. Hoping for another chance to hit someone, Joey jumped from the back seat and into the street. When he got about three feet away from the agitated behemoth, the guy reached into his waistband and pulled out a Forty-Four Magnum handgun. Joey imme-diately grabbed for the gun and a struggle ensued. During the struggle, the giant unknowingly pulled the trigger. Fortu-nately, the hammer got caught in the skin webbing between Joey's thumb and forefinger, and the gun didn't go off.

While this was happening, the guy's friend sprinted to the corner and flagged down a cop car that was stopped at a red light. The two cops who were relatively new on the force exited their car and headed towards the fracas. Halfway down the block, they spotted a very muscular male subject holding a gun above a large blonde man, who was sprawled on the pavement. The more inexperienced of the two cops pulled out his weapon and started firing wildly down the street. Joey, who was able to disarm the guy, heard the shots and dove into the Buick, still clutching the gun.

Tommy floored the car and took off straight past the two bewildered cops. The cop who hadn't fired his weapon screamed at them to halt and pointed his gun at the fleeing car. When it was clear the car wasn't about to stop, he fired several times at the back of the Buick. Only one of his shots hit the car, striking the rear window inches above the still-sleeping Angelo's head. Jay was hunkered down as low as he could in the rear seat in an utter state of panic. *Please, Lord Jesus Christ as my savior, get me out of this alive.*

The rookie cops in the street radioed in the B.O.L.O. on the fleeing armed suspect vehicle. Due to the overlapping shift change around that time, there was twice the usual number of patrol cars in the area. Ten blocks away from the initial incident, Tommy raced down a one-way street. Waiting for him at the end of the block were at least five patrol cars, creating a formidable roadblock. Despite Joey's insistence on ramming them, Tommy knew they were trapped. Before placing the car into park, he spotted several more patrol cars in his rear view mirror coming up on them fast. *Man, these cocksuckers look pissed!*

The scenario: Felony Police Take Down. Midnight shift Sergeant asleep at the station. *Let him sleep.* The scene: Guns pointing in all directions, disregarding all safety rules of cross-fire. An unruly mass of blue uniforms surging forward sans pitchforks and torches. Subject vehicle swarmed as if it were a caterpillar trespassing on a fire ant nest. Red-faced cops shouting louder, loudest. It was time to give the devil his due and tonight he was collecting.

"Get your fuckin' hands up! Let me see your motherfuck-ing hands!"

"Don't move! Don't even fucking think about it."

"I will blow your fuckin' brains out!"

Jay was already working on Psalm 23:3, *He guides me in paths of righteousness for his name's sake . . .*

Before ever being asked, all the Buick's occupants had their hands raised in the air. The only exception was the still-sleeping Angelo. It wasn't until one of the cops yanked open the rear door and viciously kicked Angelo in the thigh that he even woke up. Jay would never forget that moment the rest of his life; when Angelo finally opened his eyes and saw the screaming cop's gun in his face, all he did was smile.

Except for Jay, the Buick's occupants fully understood what was going to happen next. To them, it was as simple as having to pay the check after an expensive meal. They'd run from the cops and now the ass-kicking toll at the end of the road needed to be paid.

Jay watched in horror as Tommy was yanked through the vehicle's open window and dragged face first over the pavement—"road rash style"—for quite a distance. *Oh Lord, even though I walk through the valley of . . .* When it was Jay's turn to be extricated from the vehicle, he was shaking so severely that even the nastiest of the adrenaline-pumped cops couldn't find it in him to rough up the little guy.

Inside the back of the paddy wagon, Angelo never complained, or said a word, or even asked what was going on. After finding a comfortable position, he dozed off with his head on Jay's shoulder for the entire ride to the police station.

At the 68th precinct, veteran detectives Holbrook and Erben interrogated Jay and his new friends. They were all informed that they were being charged with attempted homicide, fleeing and eluding, and possession of a firearm. The detectives went on to explain that because Joey shot the victim in the leg, they were all accessories to the crime. The victim, whose name was Robert Myers and lived in Georgia, was in town visiting his old college roommate. Myers was currently at Coney Island Hospital in stable condition after having a bullet removed from his leg. For the detectives it was a slam-dunk case, because not only were they aware of Joey and Jimmy's heavy criminal pasts, but they had excellent witnesses who were actually willing to testify. Thanks to this over-confidence, they failed to conduct a full initial investigation.

Jay was the only one to waive his Miranda Rights and speak to the detectives. He offered an excellent account of the night's events worthy of his future occupation as a lawyer. He was so adamant and convincing that lead detective Holbrook decided to investigate the case a little deeper. Holbrook responded to the hospital and was surprised to learn that the doctor actually removed a bullet from Myers' leg. At that proximity, he thought the .44 Magnum round should have gone clean through the victim's leg, leaving a huge exit wound. When Holbrook examined the round, he immediately knew Jay was telling the truth, and his case had now turned into what detectives refer to as a leaky bag of shit or a major clusterfuck.

The spent .38-caliber bullet was fired from a Smith & Wesson Model 10 revolver. Apparently, the rookie cop who initially called in the fleeing vehicle forgot to mention in his supplemental report that he fired upon the two subjects he'd seen fighting in the street. When Holbrook later interviewed Myers in his room he learned that the .44 Magnum revolver did indeed belong to him. Myers was also surprised when he learned who actually shot him. He was convinced he had been shot by his own gun during the struggle and had even provided that testimony to the on-scene cops before he was transported to the hospital.

After being locked down for seven hours in the precinct's dingy holding facility, the guys were finally released. Once again, Angelo had to be violently shaken awake from his deep slumber. All charges were dropped, except for a citation of reckless driving issued to Tommy Lesner. Tommy was more than happy to sign for it after initially looking at a felony fleeing and eluding charge. Jay thought his biggest victory of the night was when he provided an articulate argument clearing Joey of the possession of the firearm. He argued that Joey had to remove the gun from the scene in self-defense.

For his part, Myers' admission that the gun was his could have seen him charged with the unlawful possession of the firearm. Detective Holbrook, however, decided to cut him a break. Holbrook was so relieved when Meyers refused to press charges of battery on Joey—thereby allowing him to close out the case and relieve him of this mess—he just called it all a wash. Jay's new best friends were so appreciative of his efforts that they promised to take him out the following week. This time, Jay politely turned down their offer and never hung out with Angelo again without Danny's presence.

Chapter 5

Angelo's late teens and early twenties were his best years by far. His love for nightclubs and bars started in his second year of high school. Danny was easily able to obtain fraudulent driver's licenses, making them both twenty-one years old. The boys then hooked up with Peter Diamond, the first guy in the neighborhood to own a car. Peter had an older brother who would give them advice on all the best clubs, not just in Brooklyn but also Long Island and New Jersey. Angelo loved the thrill of the night life, especially when they walked into a new, anonymous club in some far-off location. The boys felt like explorers, sometimes driving for hours to check out a new spot where no one would know them. Those nights were a series of drunken, wild adventures during which Angelo completely forgot the misery of his household.

By his senior year in high school, he got his first job as a bouncer in a nightclub called Speaks. Through the years, Speaks had enjoyed a long history of being one of the most popular clubs on Long Island. Although Angelo was only seventeen-years-old when he was hired, he was already a big kid and was always down to throw some hands. The first night he came to work he was given a white buttoned-down short-sleeved shirt and a red Members Only style jacket. He later learned why it was red — because of all the blood that accumulated on it nightly.

Joseph Riggs was the head bouncer — a huge blonde haired guy with a flat-top haircut. After handing Angelo his jacket,

Riggs sat him down and explained the rules. *Rule one: if I see you on your back doing the turtle during a fight, you're fired.* This was twenty years before Royce Gracie with his Brazilian Jiu Jitsu made it cool to fight off your back. *Rule two: if you're going to get a blowjob, make it quick and have someone cover your area. And lastly: whatever scams you come up with to hustle money from the customers that you think I won't find out about, think again, and you better give me half.* Riggs stood up to his full height of 6 feet 7 inches, held out his huge paw-like hand, and Angelo shook it. *Now, go stand on the stage overlooking the dance floor and handle any problems that come up.*

Working the stage on the opposite side of the dance floor was Joey Salerno. Nineteen-year-old Salerno was also relatively new as a bouncer and was the shortest guy in the club by almost a foot. It was because of being "vertically challenged" that he was given the nickname "the exception." Joey's father Eddie was rumored to be a high-ranking mobster and responsible for getting Joey the job, despite his physical shortcomings and lack of experience. What Joey lacked in height, he definitely made up for in strength and aggression.

Joey was the master of the full nelson hold. It was a move he learned in his high school wrestling days, where he would pin a guy's arms above his head. In the club, he used this technique to run unruly customers—their arms trapped up in the air—headfirst into metal poles located throughout the interior. Sounding like an aluminum bat hitting a coconut, the collision could be heard over the club's blaring music. Like Angelo, Joey used those days working in the clubs as a further education for violence. It always surprised Joey how much punishment a human body could actually withstand. Angelo and Joey were like two long lost brothers finally reunited and their unholy friendship caused a lot of bloodshed to all that got in their way.

On his nights off, Angelo would hit the other nightclubs on Long Island, along with Danny, Joey, and several of their buddies. Their favorite nightspots were spread out throughout the week. Sundays in summertime, they would hit the huge outdoor Channel 80, Wednesday nights were Uncle Sam's or Club 231, and on Tuesday nights they would always head to the home of the New York Guido, Metro 700. Those were the days Angelo would describe later as all night drinking that ended with banging some hot broad in a car or getting into a huge fuckin' brawl.

No matter how many times they were offered, Angelo and Danny never got into using drugs. Not that they were against people using; they just both felt drugs would work against them. Danny knew his charisma and brains were his way out of lower middle class and didn't want to mess with his meal ticket. Angelo, who boxed and exercised all his life, didn't want to poison his body with drugs, although he made up for it with the drinking. Their drinking did get out of control occasionally, but it was an almost unavoidable aspect of the lifestyle they were living at the time.

Joey, on the other hand, liked to take a few blasts of cocaine every now and then. He was extra cautious about anyone knowing about it, due to his father's zero tolerance for drugs. Many a night he heard his father threatening to "fuck up" anyone around him who played around with "junk." Ironically, his father didn't have a problem with the thousands of dollars a month he spent on steroids. Joey, who would also sell steroids or "juice" on the side, was able to make enough money to pay for his monthly consumption. His dad actually liked the idea of his son starting to learn how to run a business and become independent.

Chapter 6

While Angelo and his buddies fought in what they believed were the dangerous parking lots of Long Island nightclubs, twenty-four-year old Michael Frakes was also doing some fighting of his own. United States Marine Corps Staff Sergeant Frakes was leading his platoon on patrol in Northern Iraq during Operation Desert Storm. After Michael's dream of becoming a major league baseball player was derailed by a shoulder injury, he decided to follow his next dream: to become a Marine, like his father.

John Frakes had been killed in action while serving in Vietnam. Michael's only clear memory of his dad was the time they had been lying together on the couch listening to an old Don McLean song. He could never recall the song; it remained lost like an unnamed computer file in his memory banks. All he knew was that it was a sad song, which was appropriate for the moment because he'd heard it when his father informed him he had to "leave for a while." Later, Michael did manage to meet several soldiers who'd served with his dad and they all expressed the highest admiration for Sergeant John Frakes.

Just before shipping off to Iraq, Michael married his long-time girlfriend, Susan McEvoy. Susan was a student at the University of Miami where she was studying to become an occupational therapist. Susan and Michael were complete opposites, and because of that, they perfectly complemented each other. Michael was a hard-driving, Type-A personality perfectionist, while Susan was more into exploring her spirituality and going with the flow.

For their honeymoon, they went camping in Yosemite National Park. Susan thoroughly enjoyed how well thought-out her new husband's plans were of their vacation. It reminded her of an operational plan formulated in order to take over the park in a swift military maneuver. After pitching their tent on the first day, she donned the hidden army outfit she'd purchased at the second hand store. Michael, to his credit, quickly got the joke and thanked her for reminding him of how serious he sometimes took things.

Michael returned the favor the next day when Susan attempted to feed a mother Grizzly bear and her two cubs. Michael, who was at least three hundred yards away from Susan, quickly went into action before the huge bear became agitated. He jumped into his pickup truck and raced towards her. Susan, who thought the bear would pick up her peaceful vibrations and welcome her as a fellow creature, was shocked when it reared up on its hind legs and charged. Honking the truck's horn and bouncing wildly across the rocky, hilly field, Michael was able to distract the bear and turn it back. Frozen in fright, Susan needed to be carried back into the truck. After which, she appreciated her overzealous and highly cautious better half more than ever.

Chapter 7

Sometimes monsters are born and other times they are made—the argument is endless; nurture versus nature. Either-or, or why not both?

Laid out in triangular form in 1773, the town of Gzhatsk was built on the road west from Moscow. In 1968, it was renamed Gagarin for the Cosmonaut Yuri Gagarin, who was born in the nearby village of Klushino. Yuri, however, wasn't the only person of interest to hail from that small village. In the winter of 1960, in a dilapidated one-bedroom cottage, a new scourge to society was born: Viktor Matyushenko.

Viktor stood in the filthy hospital room looking down upon the pale, fragile body of his anemic little sister, Misha. Each painful rasping breath she took caused her protruding ribcage to strain against her paper-thin translucent skin. The years of malnutrition had caused her to suffer from all types of wasting illnesses, but today was apparently the day her little body and spirit could fight no more. She died that cold winter night, as Viktor looked into her beautiful arctic-blue eyes for the last time. As waves of sadness contorted his body in spasms, he swore to exact his revenge on fate and take all the spoils of life by any means necessary.

Viktor couldn't remember a time when he wasn't robbing or stealing. His father Sergei died when he was only six-years-old, and his mother never made enough to keep all her children properly fed. Viktor was always hungry, and even on the rare occasions when he would eat a decent meal, he would still feel the hunger pains that would stay with him for the rest of his life.

Growing up in the poorest section of town, he quickly learned what he needed to survive. At fourteen-years-old, he opened up a little wooden fruit stand on the corner of the main street. He would either steal his produce the night before or trade some other items he'd stolen earlier in the week. When a competitor opened up across the street, Viktor firebombed it with a modified Molotov cocktail. After the distraught owner went after Viktor with a large hunting knife, he became the first man Viktor killed, and certainly not the last.

With his insatiable drive fueling him, Viktor fought his way up the chain of local street gangs. For even the most hardened Russian hoodlums, Viktor's inhumane tactics went way beyond anything any of them had ever seen or heard of. When an accomplice in a jewelry robbery failed to give Viktor his cut, Viktor left the man alive but forced him to watch as he mutilated the man's wife and children in the most horrific of ways.

Those wanting to join Viktor's gang were put through a brutal initiation. Not physically but mentally, because Viktor demanded extreme loyalty.

"I want to join you," said Alexi, a violent teenager who wanted to be in the one gang all others feared.

"Are you tough enough?" Viktor asked casually.

"Put your toughest man in the room and I will show what I can do."

"You are very brave and tough my friend. I already spoke to people who know you, and they all say the same. Being tough is just one of the qualities I look for. But I can pay any animal on the street to rough someone up. The question is, will you do anything I ask? That is what I need. Come back tomorrow night and I will put you to the test."

Alexi was sent out the following night with two of Viktor's men to accomplish a simple task. All Viktor asked from the new prospect was that he bring him an ear. Alexi had killed men before, and an ear was nothing. He decided he would show Viktor what he could do and bring him the whole head. Alexi was taken to an abandoned factory on the outskirts of the town by two of Viktor's men. Before entering, the accomplices pulled ski masks over their faces and gave one to Alexi. Hardly able to control his excitement, Alexi quickly donned the mask.

Once inside, Alexi saw a man handcuffed to a chair with a dirty burlap sack over his head. The man was shaking in fear. Above him stood another gang member, also wearing a mask. Alexi was handed a pair of rusty shears and told to hurry up and get this over with. Full of confidence, Alexi approached the man, enjoying the rush of adrenaline that flowed through his blood. Violently, he ripped the sack off the terrified man's head while lifting the shears toward his intended target. Horrified, Alexi jumped back, dropped the shears, and fled the factory.

Viktor never heard again from the brash wannabe gangster, Alexi. *All I asked was a simple task of loyalty. Any fool could cut a stranger's ear off, but what if the victim was his brother? Are you mentally strong enough to do that for me? All men who follow me must be that loyal. Tough times require tough tests.*

Viktor's criminal activity was put on hold when he failed to bribe the proper government officials. He was sent to a Gulag, a Russian labor camp worse than any American jail. In that hellhole, the prisoners were introduced to the rehabilitative "benefits" of forced labor. For Viktor, however, the Gulag wasn't all bad, since he made many new contacts and learned the tricks of the trade from the more experienced prisoners. After getting his education and deciding he'd learned enough, he bribed his way out of jail using the same officials who'd put him there. He also had to make a promise to his financial backers that he would head to the United States and help carve out new territory for the Russian mafia.

Initially, he was sent to Brighton Beach, Brooklyn, and placed in the low-level tier of a mafia gang or "Bratva"

(Russian for brotherhood). In the 1970s, a gang of con artists and thieves from Odessa, Russia, were the first to move to the Oceanside Brooklyn territory. They became known as the "Potato Bag Gang," after one of their earliest scams, which involved selling victims bags full of supposed antique gold rubles. After sales that sometimes reached into the thousands, the bags of rubles were deftly switched for bags of potatoes. For the next several years, Viktor honed his skills and worked the streets, biding his time for the big opportunity he knew was coming.

Chapter 8

When Angelo was in his early twenties, he received a phone call from his older cousin Lorenzo, who lived in Miami. Although they'd only hung out a couple of times, he'd always had a real liking for the guy. Lorenzo told him that Rosario had been hospitalized and diagnosed with a rare kidney disease. He also explained that Angelo's father was already on dialysis and would require a kidney transplant.

Rosario was on the list to receive a kidney, but doctors believed that unless a suitable donor could be found quickly, he would probably die on that list. Despite numerous phone calls by other family members, many that he'd never heard of, Angelo refused to help. For years, he'd dreamed of killing his father, he also knew that he could never go through with it. Although he couldn't kill the bastard, he sure wouldn't do anything to save him. Rosario Tedeschi died five months later, alone in the hospital, weighing half his normal weight and looking far older than his age. The nurses who treated him remembered that in his semi-conscious state before he died, he constantly called out the names of Chuck and Angelo.

Fifteen years later, Angelo Tedeschi descended the carved stone steps of his brownstone home into the warm, golden sunlight. He lived just off 86th street, in Bensonhurst, Brooklyn — the neighborhood named after Arthur W. Benson, the former president of the Brooklyn Gas Company who had purchased it as farmland. In the 1950s, the area experienced a large influx of Italian immigrants and it quickly became known as the Little Italy of Brooklyn. It also had the reputation of being a haven for the Italian Mafia. On April 13th, 1986, after leaving a social club, reputed mobster Frank DeCicco was killed by a car bomb explosion on Bensonhurst's famous 86th street. The hit was alleged to have been ordered by Genovese family boss, Vincent "the chin" Gigante. The intended target had apparently been John Gotti, who had not been present when the bomb went off. Numerous high level mobsters called Bensonhurst their home, including John Gotti's under-boss Sammy "The Bull" Gravano.

Angelo moved to the neighborhood when he took a job as head of security for an area nightclub. It was only open three nights a week, so on his days off, he did some side work with a connected guy that Joey introduced him to. Most of the work was acting as muscle to intimidate delinquent gamblers who fell behind with their bookies. He could only recall a couple of occasions when he'd actually had to hurt some of the more reluctant deadbeats. It wasn't anything he was proud of, as they were mostly pathetic degenerates down on their luck, but the money was good and business was business.

Angelo needed to go back to his earlier style of muscling people for money because his buddy Danny Phillips was busy doing his own thing on Wall Street. Not having Danny around, he couldn't come up with any intricate schemes that actually worked. He needed to continue to make good money because, over the years, his taste for the finer things in life had dramatically increased. In his routine trips to Vegas he could drop up to ten grand in a week. While in Vegas, he liked to go by the name Angelo Ferris because as he so often said, *I might be a regular guy in Brooklyn but when I'm in Vegas I'm a big wheel like Mr. Ferris.*

It was the first week in May and spring in Brooklyn was a rebirth, especially after a winter filled with snow, sleet, and freezing cold. The air took on a jaunty scent as the trees, sprouting new leaves, came back to life. Even in this city of stone, flowers burst forth in a riot of colors made more dramatic after the drab winter months. Even the smell of the water coming off of the bay invigorated the joggers, cyclists, and the sun worshippers who filled the parks along the ocean-front. Rejuvenated New Yorkers welcomed the spring with an intensity people living in the warmer states could never appreciate. A New York spring was magnificent—Angelo once heard a quote about comparing a real rose to a plastic one, and he always thought it expressed the same sentiment as a New York spring. The quote to the best of his memory went something like this,

> *The reason we find a real rose more beautiful*
> *than a fake one is because the real rose isn't forever,*
> *it eventually dies, and its value and beauty,*
> *therefore, is in its impermanence.*

For a guy who thoroughly enjoyed beating people up and watching Ren and Stimpy cartoons, he did on rare occasions have some deep thoughts.

Angelo was dressed in his usual black Puma jogging sweat suit and white tank top, along with his radio headphones. After a quick warm up stretch, he started his daily routine of a seven-mile jog. He knew the secret to winning fights was having good cardio. When he first started boxing as a teen-ager, he learned this lesson the hard way because the only times he was ever scared in a fight were when he had no wind or stamina left and couldn't lift his arms. Ironically, his father never watched him train or fight, and that was just fine with both of them.

His jog started towards Gravesend Bay as he slowly dodged the traffic on 17th Avenue. Once across the Belt Parkway Overpass, he turned east and picked up his pace. As he passed Bay Parkway, he remembered the old Caesar's Bay Flea Market, now gone. Sometimes, Angelo had acted as a middleman in selling off items that "fell off the truck," and he'd had several booths in the flea market that were always willing to unload the stolen items.

Eventually, he jogged onto the boardwalk that ran alongside Coney Island Beach and amusement park. Past the old Parachute Drop ride that stood abandoned, a silent and forlorn symbol of bygone days when Coney Island's Steeplechase had been New York's playground. All that remained were rubble-filled lots and the ghosts of laughing children.

Although he was a block away, he could already smell the hotdogs and fries from the famous fast food restaurant, Nathan's. The aroma always triggered memories—of the few and rare good days he'd had with his dad at the park: riding the rickety old Cyclone roller coaster to driving the Disco Room bumper cars. The best part of the day had been the hotdogs and tantalizing french-fries at Nathan's. But that was a lifetime ago and he tried not to dwell on the past. There were many times during his day that some unrealized stimulus would trigger vivid flashbacks, despite his reluctance to face them.

Abruptly, he did a U-turn, heading back the way he came. Instead of cutting his jog short, he continued on to the Verrazano Bridge. As he passed under it, a white four-door Cadillac pulled over and the passenger—an older Italian man—jumped out and shouted, "Yo, Ange, Mambo is lookin' for ya."

Angelo gave him a stern look and the older man realized the danger of calling his boss by that nickname. The man quickly recanted, saying, "C'mon, you know wadd' I mean. Eddie is looking for you."

"Did he say what he wants?" Angelo asked, while jogging in place.

"Nah, he wants you to come in." Hating to stop his routine, Angelo nonetheless relented, saying, "Ah shit . . . give me a ride back to my apartment I gotta shower and change."

The hour-long drive to Eddie's house gave Angelo some time to go over in his mind why Eddie might want to see him.

Shit. With Eddie, it could be almost anything, so fuck it, why worry? I sometimes think he calls people in for no reason, just to keep everyone a little off balance and to show his authority.

The traffic on the Belt Parkway into Long Island was always heavy, so the driver took the shortcut through the Rockaways, Flatbush Avenue and over the Gil Hodges Bridge. As he drove through the pothole-laden roads of the Rockaways, he approached the Atlantic Beach Bridge. It always amazed Angelo how, by the crossing of one bridge from Far Rockaway to Atlantic Beach, the changes on Long Island could be so drastic. Only a mile separated people from poverty-stricken apartment buildings and Atlantic Beach million-dollar homes. It was as if the bridge was an invisible barrier that kept the classes separated. The driver made the right onto Kings Avenue and then pulled up to the large automatic gate in front of Eddie's recently-rebuilt house. He punched in the security code and when the gate opened, he drove up the large, paved driveway.

As he knocked on the front door, he remembered all the times he'd passed out drunk on those front steps. It was hard for him to believe that twenty years had passed since he called this place his home. In actuality, the original, drafty old house with no air conditioning had been knocked down in order for Eddie to build this new, modern mansion. On the second floor, Eddie had even built a secret room hidden behind a bookcase only a few people knew about. As an avid reader, Eddie had a liking for old mystery novels with their "whodunit" murders and hidden rooms.

Joey Salerno answered the door of his dad's house with his usual chocolate protein shake in hand. He drank at least five a day and he attributed them to helping him keep his muscular size at the ripe old age of forty-one. The shakes, along with a cycle of steroids thrown in every now and then just for good measure, were also part of Joey's regimen. It was hard to argue his point, when at 5 feet 9 inches, he still weighed two-hundred-and-forty-five pounds of lean muscle. After giving

Angelo a rib-crushing bear hug at the door, he stepped back in order to do his usual assessment of Angelo's build.

"What's up, cuz? Looking good, brother, looking good. I see you're still keeping in shape."

"I'm tryin' to keep up with you. What's up, Joseph?"

"How come you haven't been around? I never see you no more."

"Brother I ain't wealthy like you. I got to be out there hustling and earnin' a living."

"Shit, my dad's hooked you up with work more times than I can remember."

"Obviously, cause I'm so handsome and smart. Where's Mambo?"

"Only you can get away with calling him that. He's out back. You know the old man always misses you. Try to come by a little more often."

"Thanks, cuz."

Eddie "Mambo" Salerno, 62-years-old, silver haired, but a large man thanks in part to years of working with his hands, was standing by the lit barbecue drinking a beer. He gave Angelo a hug and several heavy slaps on the back. In his deep booming voice, he asked, "My boy, Ange! How ya doing, kid?"

"Good, good, Ed. You know, layin' low and staying out of trouble. How you doin'?"

Flipping several burgers with the precision of a pro, Eddie answered, "This morning I sat down in my kitchen, read the paper, and ate my breakfast like a gentleman. I then grabbed my coffee, sat down on the porch, and saw the most beautiful sunrise. What more could a man ask for, except maybe a few more bucks?"

Angelo quickly added, "Well, I'm workin' on a few things that'll hopefully make us a few bucks."

Eddie turned away from the grill and gave Angelo a friend-ly pat on the shoulder and said, "I appreciate that, but I have something more important for you right now."

"Whatever you need, Ed."

"First things first, what did I tell you about that temper of yours?" Before Angelo could answer, he continued, "I told you over and over that you always got to use your head. So what do you do, you put your hands on Carmine's cousin, Nicky."

"Ed There's no way I would have touched him if I knew he was a made man. I thought he was just connected."

"C'mon Ange don't give me that shit. You knew he was Carmine's cousin and you touched him? Nicky is still in the fucking hospital peeing through a freakin' tube."

Eddie stopped what he was doing at the barbecue and looked Angelo in the eye with that intense stare that always made him nervous. He put his big hand on Angelo's shoulder, and said, "Don't worry, I already know the real story, that he was banging Joey's girl, and I appreciate the fact you kept your mouth shut and didn't tell Joe. Jesus . . . if he knew Nicky was tagging his girl, he would have started a fucking war! Over a freaking broad! Ange, you can't do that shit, you should have come to me first. Now there's a lot of pissed off people. You know if you came to me I would've seen that Nicky was punished severely for that offense. We can't have guys coveting other guys' wives or girlfriends; it's just not done. Listen, I can smooth it out but I need you to lay real low, right or wrong. Ange, you broke the rules, and that's serious. In my day, you would have already been gone for putting hands on a made man, but then again, these are different times."

"Not a problem, I'm already layin' low, I haven't been out on the town since."

"No I mean serious; like, I need you out of town."

"But Ed, I . . ."

Eddie cut him off and said, "There's another reason I need you out of town. We got a guy in a small beachside town near Miami, a police Lieutenant named James Hagen. He's a 57-year-old degenerate gambler, and he's into me for close to seventy-five grand. I let him pay me off monthly and I don't kill him with the vig. In return, he feeds me info, which I either sell or use to my advantage.

"Last time I was in Miami, he cried on my shoulder his whole life story. He comes from a long line of gamblers in his family and he said he once hit a jackpot on a Vegas slot machine for 100,000 dollars. Within three months, this bozo not only lost all the money but he also went into the hole another fifteen grand trying to recover it. His third ex-wife bet their marriage on him going and completing a Gamblers Anonymous program. Hagen lost that bet and his wife, too."

"Sounds like this loser could be your golden fuckin' goose."

"He could be, but the problem is, this degenerate fuck is gambling with all types of local scumbags down there and he's going to get himself hurt, despite the fact I already put a claim in for him. The locals don't understand how things are done and that's why I need you to go down there and be my representative and protect my golden goose."

"How long?"

"It could be a while. Oh, and the last thing is, when you get down there, you're going to be a cop."

The normally stoned-faced and composed Angelo almost fell down with disbelief, and said with a grin, "You gotta be shittin' me, are you serious? You want me to be a cop?"

"Listen, they have been killing our business with these Goddamn RICO laws, our own guys' rather rat than do time, and then they're planting their guys inside our world. That's not to mention the Russians are grabbing a lot of our territory, along with the South Americans. Old man Ragano is now looking at doing life on his last pinch, and I still have the South District Crime Squad crawling up my ass. Here's my chance to plant one of my guys in their law enforcement world."

Angelo, in deep thought, asked, "How come Joey isn't doing it?"

"I love Joe more than anything in the world, but you know him, he's not ready yet for that type of responsibility. He can't think on his feet as well as you can, or make his own decisions. You have also been real lucky, with the help of your buddy Danny's dad, to have been popped only once with a felony arrest as an adult. Ange, when I took you in all those years ago, I saw a kid with a lot of potential. Problem is, you take one step forward then three back."

"Whatever you need me to do, I will. Shit, you're the only guy who ever told me I had potential and that I'm worth something. I'll never forget that. One thing, though: how are you going to erase my record?"

"Hagen's taking care of all of that. In return, I'm waving fifty of the seventy-five thou he owes me. Ange, this is an expensive investment, so that means you need to keep your temper in check and not do anything reckless. Also, I know your degenerate cousin Lorenzo is down there with his strip club, so don't be losing your fucking mind banging strippers all day."

Angelo couldn't stop himself breaking into a big smile.

Eddie immediately got hot and pointed his big finger in Angelo's face, shouting, *"Ange, I'm fucking serious! don't fuck this up!'* He paused, caught his breath and continued, "Here's a chance for you to go down there and start new. You could really open up a lot things for us. Think of the valuable inside info you could supply us with. But you need to get rid of those demons inside your head and work on that fuckin' temper. Your old man couldn't let go of his demons and look what happened to him—he died alone in that hospital room."

Angelo nodded in agreement with Eddie, but inside, he never wanted to even think of making comparisons between him and his father, not now and not ever.

Chapter 9

After the barbecue, Angelo headed back home to Brook-lyn. His mind was reeling with all the changes he would soon be making. During the toughest times in his life, Eddie had been one the few people who'd actually given a shit and helped him. One night, after another big fight with his father, Rosario had thrown him out of the house. Over the next several days, he'd ended up sleeping in the back of his friend's old Econoline van. During the day, he would go to the Jack LaLanne Gym where some of his other friends worked, in order to take showers. Although he knew he could have asked Danny's family for a place to stay, he'd been too embarrassed to impose on Mr. Philikowski again for yet another favor.

When Joey' heard his good friend Angelo was homeless, he immediately spoke to his dad. Eddie had only met Angelo a few times but there was something he liked about *the hard-headed crazy fuck*, as he thought of him, so he'd summoned him to the house. Once at the house, Eddie had sat Angelo down and told him the story of when he was a teenager and also got kicked out of the house. He'd offered Angelo a temporary room in his basement, then read him the riot act about the rules of his house. After his speech, he'd pulled a thousand dollars in cash out of his pocket and placed it in Angelo's hand. The cash wasn't a gift or charity; he would eventually have to pay him back, one way or another.

Angelo was only 20 years old when Eddie asked him for a

favor. The favor was for Angelo to help Joey talk to a neighborhood guy named John Pomorico. John was one of the very few men that actually walked away from the wise guy life. John grew up on the same block as Angelo, and as kids, the two were good friends. John was also one of the most stand-up guys Angelo knew from the old neighborhood.

There was the time when Danny Phillips got roughed up by a group of guys from a neighborhood in Sheepshead Bay. Apparently, Danny got jumped by a bunch of guys while leaving some neighborhood girl's house. The girl's brother wasn't a big fan of the smooth-talking Canarsie kid known to some as Houdini. The brother heard that Houdini was at the house, so he gathered some friends for a good ole beat down. Immediately after the incident, Danny went to Angelo, who was playing handball at the park with John Pomorico. When Angelo saw Danny walking up to him, all beat up and disheveled, it reminded him of their little encounter all those years back. Danny gave Angelo and John the Reader's Digest version of what just occurred. Angelo immediately called for revenge, and jumped into Danny's car to go look for the guys. Without being asked, John got in his car and followed them into Sheepshead Bay.

Danny figured Angelo's plan would be that once they found the guys, they would call for back up, since there were at least seven of them, including the angry brother. After driving down numerous streets, they finally spotted the group of guys standing in front of a newsstand. As soon as Danny pointed them out, Angelo jumped out of the car like a maniac and rushed towards them. Danny was running right behind Angelo, as John was pulling up in his car. John was also under the impression that they were just going to locate the guys and then call for back up. Although he didn't really know Danny, John leaped out of his car without hesitating, and sprinted towards the brawl.

That day, John took one of the worst beatings in his life. At first, the neighborhood guys were caught so off guard by

Angelo's audacity and aggression, they initially hesitated in fighting back. Angelo was able to knock out one of the first guys he encountered, but the numbers were on the neighborhood guys' side, and both Angelo and Danny were quickly overwhelmed. They found themselves under a pile of bodies getting kicked, kneed, and punched.

As the last man to run across the street, John clearly saw what was happening to Danny and Angelo. At that point, he could have stayed out of it and retreated to his car. But he didn't, and as the last man into the fight, he got the worst of it. After being kicked to sleep on the sidewalk, his body continued to be pummeled by a barrage of vicious blows. The beating put John into critical condition for almost two days. His brain took a little over a week to heal from the swelling.

John's uncle Louie was a made man out of Mulberry Street and immediately wanted all the facts. John stood up to his uncle, the police detectives, and his other friends, and refused to talk about what occurred. All he would say about the incident was that he deserved it and took his beating like a man.

Angelo had a tremendous amount of respect for John and owed him big time on that one, knowing full well it was his own quick temper that had gotten John into trouble. When John was a few years older, he started to work more with his uncle, learning the family business. On a few occasions, he even crossed paths with Joey Salerno. He and Joey, along with several other guys, worked a scam together in which they would help people who couldn't make the payments on their cars and wanted to cash in on the insurance. They would set the location for the owners to leave the car, which gave them all a good alibi. They would then take the cars and either strip them at a chop shop or send them to the port, where they would be sold overseas.

At around that time, John got married to his high school sweetheart and his wife gave birth to twins. He loved his family so much that he felt he had to change his life. In his line of work, he knew he would eventually have to do some jail time or worse, take a bullet to the back of the head. He watched this scenario play out too many times to the neighborhood guys he grew up with.

One day, he made the decision that the mob life was no longer for him. He went to his uncle, who was very understanding, and got the rare blessing to leave the life. His uncle hooked him up with a legitimate sales job in upstate New York and John jumped at the chance. Ironically, his uncle was later gunned down by one of his own men that year, for some type of rule infraction. Walking away from the life and not having his uncle around didn't leave John feeling too easy, but he hoped that his years of being a stand-up guy would put everybody at ease.

Two years later, with mounting pressure from insurance companies, a joint force task unit between the New York D.A.'s office and the F.B.I. was created to target the rising tide in insurance fraud. An NYPD detective who was already on Eddie Salerno's payroll provided Eddie the information that his son was a person of interest in the case. For Eddie, that information was enough to seal John's fate. In Eddie's mind, he broke it down like this:

One – John did the unthinkable, and although he wasn't a made man, he knew too much to leave the life.

Two – John's uncle Louie was gone, so there's no need to ask for permission.

Three – Everyone told Eddie how much this guy John loved his wife and kids; in Eddie's world, that made him the weakest link in the chain. The guy might try to cut a deal with the District Attorney to avoid a lengthy prison sentence in order to be with his family. Eddie had seen it happen too many times and wasn't going to take the chance.

Eddie summoned Angelo in and sat him down with Joey. He explained that because Angelo knew John so well and John trusted him, he needed Angelo to go with Joey to make sure things went smoothly. Eddie made it clear that the plan was to feel John out, and if he seemed at all weak, then they needed to whack him immediately. Angelo stood up for John and assured Eddie that John was no rat or stool pigeon.

"Well, Ange, if that's the case, then your boy John has nothing to worry about because we just need to be sure of his intentions."

Angelo felt conflicted about his loyalty to a good old friend and his loyalty to his father-like mentor. Eddie had never asked him for a favor before, and he knew this was important to him. He also knew that if he didn't go, John would eventually catch wind of Eddie's intentions and then go on the lam. The fact that John trusted Angelo would probably be enough for him to hear out what they had to say. The problem for Angelo was that he wasn't sure Joey would follow Eddie's plan. Joey sometimes made decisions for himself and as he once told Angelo, "I'd rather ask my dad for forgiveness than ask for fuckin' permission."

With that, Angelo put in the phone call to John, and they all decided to meet up at a diner close to where John lived. In contrast to Brooklyn, John's new home in upstate New York was very rural and wooded. The meeting went down exactly as Angelo thought it would. John hadn't changed much in the last ten years and he made a very compelling argument that all was good, and that Joey had nothing to worry about. His reputation as a stand-up guy was stellar, and he felt the D.A. would probably never find out that he worked behind the scenes with Joey. Joey decided that, although he believed him, the risk was too high and he wanted John out of the country.

Joey wrapped it up with saying, "John, forget about it, 'cause this is a win-win situation for you and your family. Because of the respect my father had for your uncle Louie, the best arrangements were made for you. We own a safe house on the beach in Mexico that is a fucking mansion. It's over five miles away from the nearest house. I stayed there two years ago and didn't ever want to leave. You go down there first and then we'll make arrangements for your wife and kids to follow, 'cause time is not on our side and we need you unavailable for the prosecutors. Listen, if our guy on the inside says the D.A.'s got nothing, then you come right back and you had one hell of a fuckin' vacation on us. Like I said, John, it's a win-win situation."

John asked for two weeks to get his things in order and Joey gave him two hours. The plan was for John and Joey to start driving to Mexico that night and to get him across the border as quickly as possible. Joey told John to leave his car there and they would drive him back to his house to quickly grab some things and explain to his wife what was going to happen. As John started to protest, Joey cut him off, and said, "Cuz, this is my fucking ass hanging out in the wind, and I'm staying by your side until we get you deep into Mexico."

Angelo was about to give his two cents, but knowing that arguing with Joey was pointless, he decided against it.

As they walked up to the car, Joey motioned for Angelo to get in the back so John could sit in the front. They drove about a mile, with John giving directions through the rural streets. Joey pulled the car over to the dimly-lit side road to make a quick phone call. As he reached into his jacket to grab his phone, out came a .22 Caliber Taurus revolver. He put three shots point blank into the top of John's head before he could even react. Joey intentionally angled the gun down, keeping the bullets from exiting John's skull and shattering the window.

Instead of hearing the ultra loud crack a .22 caliber makes, especially in such a confined space, John's brain must have dampened the sound because Angelo heard only slight muffled thumps. He knew all along that Joey had been lying about taking John out of the country because they'd never discussed that option the whole four-hour ride upstate. Angelo knew what Joey was going to do, but he had no choice; this was the life they all chose. *Well, except for John,* he thought. *He was the first and only guy I knew that had the balls to say it's not the life he wanted anymore. Rest in peace, my friend.*

Many times, Angelo contemplated an aspect of this life-style you never saw in any of those mafia movies or T.V. shows: what these types of killings really do to the people involved. He knew several old timers who would talk about the real mafia life, how it was all smoke and mirrors and bullshit. There were no rules, no loyalty; it was only about the money and power. This came from men who'd had to kill people they had no beef with, and sometimes the targets were their best friends. It's the sort of thing that scars a man so deeply that even if he tries to bury it in his mind, it always finds ways to seep out. For such men, it causes those night-mares in which they wake up in pools of sweat, eaten at by the guilt and remorse with which they then feed other neuroses and addictions: gambling, drugs, and alcohol.

Chapter 10

After his tour in Iraq, Michael Frakes returned to his wife Susan in South Florida. After graduating college, Susan opened a non-profit organization that utilized horses for physical therapy. At first, she used the therapy for children with autism and Down syndrome. Once her business started to grow, she expanded her treatment to all types of neurological and psychosocial diseases. Michael immediately started pitching in and helped his overwhelmed young wife as the business continued to grow at an astounding pace. He also found working with the horses and being on the ranch had a therapeutic effect. It eased some of the anxiety of the posttraumatic stress he'd brought home from the war. Although the business was now booming, Susan refused to take a salary any larger than that of an average occupational therapist. Instead, she always assigned the money that came from donations and grants back to the company.

Later that year, Michael and Susan became proud parents of a beautiful baby girl named Amanda. Although Michael loved working on the ranch with the children, he knew that in order to provide for his family, he would need a full-time career. He decided his future might lie in law enforcement, and was subsequently hired by a fairly new department in the city of Beachside. He also remained in the Marine Corps as a reserve. Michael's attention to detail and his enthusiasm for the job quickly got the attention of Beachside P.D.'s administration. They rewarded his professionalism by promoting him to several different specialized units, including plain-clothes work and the SWAT team. Michael responded by working even harder and winning numerous awards for arrests and acts of bravery.

He did, however, get a reputation among some of the guys as an ass kisser and a goodie-two-shoes. Besides being highly motivated, Michael was also a stickler for doing things by the book. This rubbed a lot of the older veteran cops the wrong way. His eventual placement in the internal affairs unit further lowered his popularity among his fellow officers. Even his staunchest critics had to admit that, although they disagreed with his tactics, they did indeed respect him. As a Marine Corps reserve, his career also flourished and he received a promotion to the rank of Master Gunnery Sergeant, which was a rare promotion for someone so young.

Following his latest promotion, his unit was activated and mobilized in support of Operation Iraqi Freedom. Seventeen years after leaving Iraq, Michael was back on its familiar desert soil. After tearful goodbyes with his family, his new journey began with a three-month work up at Marine Corps Base Camp Pendleton, in California. He then caught a "bird" to Landstuhl, Germany. From Germany, he flew in a C-130 to Kuwait, and in Kuwait his battalion was airlifted in CH-46 Chinook helicopters to Forward Observational Base Saint Michael in Mah-Muh-Diyah, Iraq. During the flight, the Iraqis welcomed Michael back with heavy small arms fire and occasional RPGs. He was originally scheduled to be in-country for only six months, which soon extended to three more.

As he exited the helicopter, the first thing to hit Michael was the familiar smell of burning garbage. It was the primary way the Iraqi's disposed of their refuse. The cities and towns looked far more dilapidated than they were during his first tour. Michael's new home for the next nine months was an old chicken factory that had been converted into barracks for his battalion. The bathroom port-a-potties were conveniently located at least a hundred yards away from the barracks, and many a soldier would be "Smurfed" after returning from their bathroom breaks. Smurfed was the term used because the blue chemical solution at the bottom of the port-a-potty had a nasty habit of splashing back up on the hapless G.I.'s backsides.

As a Master Gunnery Sergeant, Michael would accompany the battalion commander and his personal security detachment, which was composed of six MRAPs or up-armored Humvees on patrols. After being in-country for eight months and seeing no action except for a few paper cuts, he requested via chain of command to go on a mission. Operation Phantom Fury had just started, and Michael wanted at least one mission in the area known as the triangle of death. His request was denied, and Michael decided to ask a favor from his old friend, Marine Corps Lt. Colonel Harvey "Mad Dog" Freeman. Michael and Harvey's friendship went back seventeen years when they served together in Desert Storm. Freeman had only been a Captain back then, but everyone had known he would quickly climb the ladder. Freeman was a hard-charging, hands-on, lead from the front type of Marine, and his men loved to serve under him. Freeman approved Michael's request and then loudly cursed the fact that he couldn't accompany him.

At 0200 hours, Michael responded to the briefing at the combat operations center. He learned that he would be attached to Echo Company and convoy en route to Golf Company in order to provide fire cover and support. That morning, he carried on his person his M-4 rifle, 9mm Beretta, eight extra magazines for his M-4, four extra magazines for his 9mm, radio, flex cuffs, knife, gas mask, camelback, and 550 cord rope. He was given a boat space in a Humvee and after leaving the line of departure, they headed toward their objective.

Only twenty minutes after their departure, the Humvee in front of Michael's was hit with an IED. Michael's Humvee, along with several other vehicles, immediately surrounded the damaged vehicle with three hundred and sixty degrees of coverage. Before they could even get to the wounded men, the convoy started taking heavy amounts of small arms fire. Michael, along with two other Marines, exited their vehicle and attempted to locate where the rounds were coming from. The insurgents were firing rounds from AK-47s from several rooftops approximately two-hundred yards away.

As the highest-ranking officer, Michael could have taken charge of the firefight, but he deferred that role to Gunny Mario Estrada. Michael understood that being a good leader sometimes meant stepping aside. He also knew Estrada would be more familiar with the men in his platoon and their capabilities. Estrada called out on the radio "contact left," meaning the insurgents' fire was coming from the left side. The other Humvees immediately walled off the left side and started laying down suppressive fire.

Three of the casualties in the damaged Humvee were conscious and stable, while the fourth man, who was the driver, was in critical condition. Gunny Estrada continued coordinating the counter attack while also requesting a Black-hawk to evacuate the seriously wounded soldier.

Despite the heavy suppressive fire Michael and his fellow Marines were pouring onto the rooftops, the rate of the insurgent's incoming fire kept increasing. A nineteen-year-old PFC next to Michael was hit in the chest with a round, and went down without making a sound. As soon as he saw the downed man in his peripheral vision, Michael immediately grabbed him by his backpack and dragged him to the other side of the vehicle to assess his wounds. Even before he opened the young man's vest, he knew he was a KIA. The soldier's face was already chalk-white, and his eyes were frozen in anguish. Michael learned later that the first AK-47 round the soldier took severed his aorta, causing instant death.

As Michael was getting back in the fight, Gunny Estrada called for a tow bar for the damaged Humvee and ordered the convoy to move out. The damaged Humvee, its axle broken, would be dragged out of the area. They would move the LZ to a safer area before allowing the Blackhawk helicopter to come in. The convoy would then return back to base and another platoon would be sent to support Echo Troop. Only forty-five minutes had passed since the troop had left their base and now they were limping their way back home. Michael was drenched in sweat and exhausted from the adrenalin dump. He placed the dead soldier in the rear seat beside him and policed up all the extra magazines, in case the convoy got hit again. He also didn't want to leave any extra ordinance for the enemy to utilize.

As Michael looked over the young faces of the men beside him he was very proud of this new breed of Marines. These new jarheads who referred to the Corps as "the suck" were just as proficient as any of the men he'd served with seventeen years ago.

One month later, Michael's Battalion was shipped back to Camp Pendleton for their final two weeks of paperwork known as demobilization. On the last night at the Camp, the battalion had a raucous going away party at the base's enlisted club. As Michael sat nursing a hangover on his last flight home to Miami International Airport, he already missed the brave young men he'd spent the last nine months with.

Chapter 11

When Angelo broke the news of his impending departure for Florida to his friends, Danny decided to throw him a going away party. Angelo didn't tell them the real reason he was leaving, as the less people who knew the better, a rule that applied even to his closest friends. All he told Danny and Jay was that he got into a fix with some big time made man who called himself "the Don of Carol Gardens," and it would be better if he skipped town.

Danny picked up Jay and Angelo in his new black BMW 750IL. He was dressed immaculately in his finest Hugo Boss suit, Tanino Crisci shoes, and Invicta Signature Diamond Pave Diver watch. He parked the car down the street from the club because he never trusted the valet guys with his baby. Before they exited the car, Danny pulled out his old flask that the guys hadn't seen in over twenty years. Danny had obtained the flask in high school when he and Angelo were working a World Series betting scheme. When one of the students couldn't pay up, the kid stole his father's flask and gave it to Danny in lieu of payment. The flask was made of stainless steel and was engraved with the name "Steve," and below the name was a picture of a Labrador Retriever. Danny never pawned it and he and Angelo would cut class and drink cheap whiskey out of it in the stadium bleachers while watching the cheerleaders practice.

Danny wanted to have one drink and make a toast with his close friends before they entered the club. Danny lifted the flask and said, "We wish you luck, happiness, and prosperity in your new life, and if doesn't work out, fuck it, and come back to your good friends!"

All three men took a swig from the old flask, and had a good laugh when Jay complained as usual about the whiskey being too strong and cheap.

As they walked down the block towards the club, Jay and Danny talked about maybe heading down there in a few months for a weekend vacation. Jay had also been talking recently about buying a condo in South Florida as an investment. Before they walked into the club, Danny pulled Angelo to the side and said, "Well Ange it's no Bora Bora, but Miami is tropical and loaded with hot broads!"

The statement wasn't made out of jest, but one of a shared bond between two old friends. When Danny thought about the meaning of Bora Bora, it sometimes brought him almost to tears, but Danny Phillips was a man's man, and real men don't cry . . . at least that was what Angelo preached.

As Angelo walked inside the nightclub, he was shocked to see some of the old timers he hadn't seen in years. The first to grab him inside the club was Stevie Kirsch, A.K.A. Dogballs. Stevie was one of the wild men he'd hung out with in his teenage years. Stevie always went by the motto of "when in doubt whip it out." There was that one Halloween party when Stevie paid a Polaroid picture girl in a nightclub to photograph his illustrious exposed lower half from numerous angles.

He then went around the club the whole night and displayed his photographs to various women. Stevie earlier explained to Angelo the method to his madness: when he eventually found the one girl who wasn't disgusted by his photos, she would be the perfect one to buy a drink for.

Standing at the bar downing shots were Joey Salerno and the Castaldi brothers, Jimmy and Jack. The Castaldis owned a large construction company and both were known for their wild partying reputations. Angelo went to Las Vegas a few times a year with either brother and he would always remember the one time he thought he lost Jimmy. They were hanging out in the Crazyhorse Strip Club when Angelo saw Jimmy leave the club with one of the dancers.

For three days straight, Angelo couldn't find or get in touch with Jimmy and he started to get genuinely worried. He knew at some point he would need to call Jack, who was in Brooklyn at the time. The problem was that Jack would think that Angelo had either set his brother up somehow, or whacked him himself. Luckily for Angelo, Jimmy came strolling into their hotel suite on the third day, wearing the same clothes Angelo had last seen him in. He told Angelo that he'd partied with the girl and her friends for the last three days, and that Angelo was too much of a pussy to keep up with him. Jimmy then demanded Angelo make him a drink and proceeded to call an escort service to have them send a girl up to his room.

Standing next to the Castaldis was a buddy of theirs, known to Angelo only as "Ralphy Lump-em." Ralph was another interesting character due to his "thing" for highway tolls. For some reason only known to Ralph, he completely refused to pay them. Before he'd even turned eighteen, Ralph's bizarre behavior resulted in his license being revoked numerous times. His next trick was to get into more car accidents than a Hollywood stunt car driver. Why he would purposely crash his cars, nobody knew, but not many people would ever take a ride from "Ralphy Lump-em."

The going away party was starting to heat up and the drinks were flowing. Once again, Joey and Jimmy were busting Jay's balls about when he was going to hang out with them next. All of a sudden, Angelo saw his night come to a screeching halt. His ex-girlfriend of a stormy ten-year relationship walked into the club with a group of her friends. Mia Lavalle looked as good to Angelo as she had ten years ago, when he'd met her at the Arios restaurant where she'd worked as a waitress. Mia was the most popular waitress back then because not only was she one of the most beautiful women in Brooklyn, but she somehow didn't seem to know it. She was petite with long, black hair and stunning green eyes. Her exotic looks came from her mixture of French and Thai heritage. During that time, she was living with a boyfriend who she'd dated since high school.

She always thought Angelo was different from all the other guys who came into the restaurant and hit on her. He was a little more aloof and always had a dangerous confidence about him. He was the kind of guy who didn't need to tell people he could handle himself because he seemed to naturally exude it. Back then, all the wannabe Italian Stallion *guidos* with their one liners didn't interest her. There was something about Angelo and his imperfections that gave him a more real and honest feeling. While some women weren't interested in a guy who had a nose that had been broken a few times, along with a couple of scars, Mia thought it gave him character. She once admitted to him that although Danny was real nice to look at, she felt Angelo's ruggedness made him much more appealing. She also realized later on that the most important asset Angelo possessed was his ability to make her feel protected.

Although Angelo had a steady girlfriend back then, he would still go to the restaurant a few times during the week. He would stay till it closed and walk Mia to her car. She came to work one night and, although she tried to hide it, Angelo knew something was wrong. She ended up confessing her ribs were sore as a result of her boyfriend's increasing violence. After months of being friends, and despite the fact she was very private about her personal life, she finally opened up to Angelo and told him about her problems.

The next day, her boyfriend received a visit in his office from Angelo. Angelo was able to convince him it was not only in his best interest to keep his hands off her, but it would probably be the best for both of them if they broke up. Within two weeks, the now single Mia moved in with Angelo.

Those ten years for Angelo were full of highs and lows. Their relationship would always be pushed to the brink by

Angelo's reluctance to get married. After almost ten years of being off and on, and despite the fact she loved him deeply, she'd finally had enough and left him. Angelo never talked about it to any of his boys, but they still knew how much it hurt him. He seemed unable to get the childhood demons out of his head. Without his knowledge, they affected all his adult relationships.

Even with Angelo's baggage, he never raised his voice or hand in anger to Mia or any of his other girlfriends. His problem was always one of trust. The constant years of cruelty and neglect numbed him and didn't allow him to let down his guard. Most people knew him as a man with many friends, but the people who were really close to him knew him as more of a loner and would probably always be that way.

Angelo watched as Mia and her friends approached the bar. She still hadn't seen him and he figured it would be best to keep it that way. He told Danny he was going to the bathroom and slipped unnoticed out the club's back door. Just like that: no goodbyes to his buddies or confrontation with Mia. For a man who had no fear and loved to fight with his fists, he was never comfortable in arguments. Danny and Jay would understand his unnoticed departure because they knew that avoidance was always his way of handling emotional situations. When it came to conflict, Angelo could either be a freight train or a ghost but he could never operate in between.

Chapter 12

Undercover Beachside P.D. Detective Michael Frakes and his partner Bobby "Dee" were conducting surveillance of a known drug house. Bobby was finishing the lunch his wife had made him, and Michael couldn't help glancing over every so often as his partner ate. Bobby had a strange eating habit: he didn't like the food to touch his lips, so he would curl them up and try to stretch his teeth forward. It provided Michael the only entertainment in a boring all-day surveillance. They were parked under a large palm tree in order to grab a little shade from the beating August sun. Michael would intermittently stretch his right shoulder over his head in order to prevent it from stiffening up on him. Many were the times he thought about the day he'd ruined it by sliding head first into home plate in his first game of the season in the minor leagues. The resultant shoulder dislocation caused his rotator cuff to completely rupture and since then, he'd never had a pain free day.

A B.O.L.O. crackled over their police radio frequency: "B.O.L.O., Attention all units ATF agents are advising that at 0500 two military crates were stolen from the homestead air force base. The crates contained 20 SAW machine guns and 10 FN M203 grenade launchers. The suspects may be driving a 2007 to 2009 white Ford van with government license plates. There is no suspect description at this time."

Michael said in disgust, "You gotta be freaking kidding me!"

Trying to stay hydrated, Bobby downed his third Gatorade

and tossed it into the backseat, and said, "A damn military base can't secure its own weapons. If the Uzis and AK-47s weren't bad enough, now we got to deal with grenade launchers, ain't that some shit! Mike, why do we gotta sit on this house? I told you my C.I. will give us a sworn affidavit stating that he already made the buys, that's more than enough for Judge Schwartz."

All Michael could think of was all the cops he'd come up with who'd been fired, arrested, or had completely ruined their careers. These new kids had no idea how easy it was to get jammed up. A short cut here and a short cut there and next thing they know they're a subject in an internal affairs investigation. It's the old simmering frog theory: if you place a frog in a pot of hot water, he will jump right out, but if you put him in warm water and then slowly raise the temperature, by the time he realizes it's boiling, it's too late.

Michael, who was usually very controlled, had been losing his temper a lot more than he would like, and he now ripped into Bobby, "How many god forsaken times do I have to tell you guys that I'm running the show now, and I don't cut corners or take shortcuts? If you want to stay in my unit, you will always do things by the book."

After a few minutes of uncomfortable silence, Michael realized that he lost his cool, and added, "Bobby, I'm sorry about that, I didn't mean to yell. I just want to do things the right way, that's all."

Bobby took his time to formulate his thoughts, finally saying, "Listen Mike, I know you don't like to talk about this, but I know Susan ain't doing so good, and me and the guys want you to know whatever you need, anything at all, just ask."

"Thanks Bobby, and thank the guys. She's such a fighter and she never complains, but I know she's in a lot of pain."

Bobby looked Michael in the eye and with utter conviction, said, "She has all the prayers and support from everyone at the department."

Michael nodded his head, and said, "I know, I know, and please tell everyone thanks for their prayers and support."

As Michael tried to recall the last two years of his life, it all seemed like a blur. The only crystal clear days were the ones on which the doctors informed him his wife's cancer had spread into her lymph nodes, and that her prognosis did not look good. The other was when he'd had to tell their daughter that her mother was not going to recover.

Chapter 13

The waves were lapping up on the beautiful private beach, ten miles north of the famous South Beach. Angelo was sprawled out on a chaise lounge chair with a mojito in hand. Next to him was his cousin Lorenzo Russo, forty-two years old, 5 feet 6 inches tall, with dark wavy hair, and a heavy tan from years of relaxing and playing in the sun.

Lorenzo grew up in Staten Island, New York, where his dad worked as a jeweler. After his dad got robbed of his jewels at gunpoint in his home, he decided to move the family out to California. California wasn't Lorenzo's speed, so at twenty-years-old he moved to Miami and worked as a bartender in a nightclub owned by an ex New York mobster. Within a year, he was promoted to general manager, and under his sharp eye, profits went up. When the right opportunity opened up for a partnership in a dilapidated strip club, Lorenzo borrowed the money from his dad to make the purchase. Within three years, Lorenzo built it up to one of the highest grossing clubs in the area.

Angelo downed his Mojito and slapped Lorenzo on the back with his big rough hand and said, "Shit if I knew my little cousin was livin' this good, I would have moved down here years ago."

"Ange, I tried seven years ago to cut you in on this strip club deal but you wanted no part of it!"

"You know me. I'm like an ant. I like to follow the same path every day. Movin' down here seven years ago would've

been too much of a change for me. You know, not for nothin'
I never saw myself leavin' Brooklyn."

"Well, better late than never. Did you really put Nicky
Ferrozo in the hospital?"

"It's a long story which I'll tell you some other time. Bottom
line, I was looking out for Eddie Mambo's best interests."

As they talked, three beautiful women in scantily-cut bikinis
walked up to them; Latinas, with brown skin and curves that
could stop a man's heart. Lorenzo made the introduction,
"Ladies, I would like you to meet my cousin Angelo."

Angelo held his drink up as a toast to their beauty, and
added, "This place can really grow on you." The girls smiled,
walked up to Lorenzo and kissed him on the cheek. Angelo
checked them out as they walked away, showing off their
assets and heading into the calm, blue water.

Lorenzo nodded towards the girls and said, "They work
for me at the club, and we'll be seeing them later tonight after
our dinner with your guy."

"Good, you found out where he hangs out. I can't wait to
see what this character is all about."

"Like I said, Ange, I can find anyone anytime. Miami is my
town."

After the beach, Angelo drove back to his leased penthouse
apartment. The apartment's owner, a Venezuelan man named
Pietro, was asking $2,500 a month for the prestigious three-
bedroom apartment with views of the city of Beachside and
the ocean. Angelo cut a deal with him where he would pay
$1,200 by check and $700 in cash on the side. Pietro would
routinely fly back to Venezuela for real estate deals every two
weeks, and liked the idea of cash.

Angelo decided to get rid of his white 1984 mint condition convertible Cadillac Eldorado. He took Eddie's advice on
starting new, and decided to lease a brand new black Cadillac
Escalade SUV with leather and all the toys. The Eldorado was
a big part of his life and identity. *Shit, if that car could talk, it
would have some unbelievable stories to tell of all the insanity and*

nonsense that went on inside of it, especially in the backseat.

His best memory of the car occurred only a month after he bought it. He was twenty-one-years-old and was shopping at the Kings Plaza mall. After exiting a clothing store with his new pair of black Z Cavaricci pants and tight fitting Chams de Baron shirt, he ran into a group of guys he'd had a beef with at the nightclub he was working in, two weeks earlier. The four guys were about to jump him right there inside the mall when a couple of cops on their way to eat walked by. With the momentary break, Angelo told the guys that he would meet them on the top level of the parking garage and fight them all one at a time, if they had the balls to go.

The four morons fell for it and went to the top floor of the garage. Ten minutes later, in the empty parking lot, Angelo appeared in his new Cadillac. He then proceeded to run over three out of the four guys. Unfortunately, one of them rolled up the hood and cracked his front windshield, but better the windshield than his own head, Angelo thought. Never in his wildest dreams did he think he would ever leave Brooklyn or, for that matter, become a cop. With the strange turn of events that led him to South Florida, he figured it was time to at least try to change his old image, starting with his beloved Cadillac.

Angelo wasn't the kind of guy who thought too deeply about his past, but he did realize he was at the halfway point of his life and needed to make some changes. What Eddie had said to him before he left, about his mistakes, was true. Every time he made a score or was mildly successful, he would somehow blow it, and usually thanks to his volatile temper. As Eddie used to say, the problem was that your balls and heart can only get you so far but it's your brains that will take you all the way. Could a leopard change his spots? Angelo wasn't sure, but he was going to at least try to make the most out of this opportunity, and give it his best shot.

Angelo and Lorenzo walked into the upscale Palme d'Or restaurant, located inside the prestigious Biltmore Hotel of

Coral Gables. The city of Coral Gables—also known as The Rare Pearl of South Florida—was founded in the 1920s by the son of a reverend, Mr. George Merrick. Mr. Merrick's dream was to create a city with the aesthetic style of poets and artists. The world famous Biltmore Hotel, built shortly after the city incorporated, was a prime example of the Gables trademark Mediterranean style architecture. The restaurant's Maître d'—tall, silver haired, and distinguished—appeared to embody the elegance and sophistication of the hotel's motif. After warmly greeting Lorenzo and Angelo, he escorted them to the best table in the house. It was situated in the corner on a slightly raised podium and overlooked the entire restaurant. Several curious diners peered over their shoulders, trying to figure out who rated high enough to get the best table in the house.

Lorenzo's attempt at impressing his cousin was short lived when Angelo immediately advised him that they had to move.

"What's wrong with the table? It's the best in the house," argued Lorenzo.

"No fuckin' way am I sitting here under that big fuckin' vent above my head," answered the now-agitated Angelo.

"Ange, are you fucking with me?"

"No, I ain't fuckin' with you! Everyone knows that a vent blowin' cold air on your head will make you sick, and I ain't fuckin' sittin' here."

Lorenzo still thought Angelo was messing with him until he saw how upset Angelo was quickly becoming, so he got the Maître d' to move them

When Angelo was in his early thirties, he started getting chronic sinus problems. Although the doctor told him it was probably due to allergies, Angelo had his own theory. He thought the years of boxing and, more specifically, the numerous times his nose had been broken, were the main cause of his sinusitis. His close friends quickly learned how he hated any type of breeze, wind, or draft he claimed he could feel irritating his sinus cavity. He also made outrageous claims that his sense of smell was now super sensitive, and he could tell if someone lit up a cigarette or joint from blocks away. On numerous occasions, Angelo either walked out or refused to sit in restaurants or movie theaters because of his theory.

The new table they were moved to happened to be directly across from Lieutenant James Hagen. Hagen was sitting with a small wiry guy whose hair looked as greasy and unkempt as the rest of his appearance. Despite the fact he was sitting, the small man was in constant motion. His twitching and rocking gave the appearance of a second grader who desperately needed to use the bathroom.

The restaurant manager, a short Latin man with a cheerful smile, approached Lorenzo's table and greeted him warmly, "Whatever you need, Lorenzo, I'm at your service."

"Miguel, I would like you to meet my cousin Angelo, he just moved down here and I'm showing him around."

"Angelo, el placer es todo mio, it's a pleasure. I know Lorenzo for almost ten years, and he's a first class gentle-man. If you need something in Miami, please don't hesitate to ask."

Lorenzo looked at Angelo with his usual grin, turned to Miguel, and said, "Actually, Miguel, I need your help with a little matter tonight."

At the next table, Tommy Amerosa was so jittery as he talked to Hagen that he could easily have been confused for an ice cube bouncing in an empty blender. Hagen struggled to keep his composure, completely disgusted by the little man's erratic drug-fueled movements. Talking with a mouth full of bread, Tommy leaned into Hagen, and said, "Here's the deal. I will waive the ten you owe me, but I want assurance that your cops won't be anywhere near the Highlow Marina when my fast boats come in."

I can't believe how stupid I am. Just three weeks ago, I was totally in the clear with all my bookies . . . well, not all my bookies, but most, and now I'm stuck listening to this twitching scumbag.

"Listen, Tommy, I might put a few dollars down on a game here and there, but I don't mess around with those types of things. I'll get you your money, but you got to give me some time."

Tommy laughed out loud in a spasmodic fit that reminded Hagen of a coughing goat. Tommy then spit out in a mocking tone, "Time's up; either you do this deal, or I will go on record with your department and reveal all your dirty little secrets."

Twenty years ago, Hagen would have beaten up a dirtbag like this, then cuffed and stuffed him down to Dade County Jail. On the drive down, he would have had to slam on his brakes every few miles to avoid a cat, dog, or squirrel that mysteriously kept jumping in front of his car. Unfortunately for the handcuffed rear passenger, this defensive driving would have caused him to head plant into the Plexiglas rear-seat divider. Hagen's old temper started to return, and he snapped, "And why shouldn't I lock you up right now and hit you with a shit load of charges?"

With a big smile, Tommy answered, "No problem, 'cause I don't give a rat's ass about jail, I will just bond out and then go talk to the D.A. and work out a deal on helping them bag a corrupt Lieutenant. Why don't you think about that, Jimmy-boy, while I go take a leak."

Tommy got up and, just to rub it in, patted Hagen on the head as if he were a dog. With a shit-eating smirk on his face, he headed towards the bathroom in the rear of the business. As soon as he was inside the bathroom, a busboy quickly walked over to it and put an Out Of Order sign on the door. As if on cue, Angelo got up, winked at Miguel and walked into the bathroom.

Tommy went straight into a stall and used his magical silver bullet, his pet name for his little silver bullet-shaped cocaine dispenser. He let the coke burn into his dry, red, swollen nasal cavity and waited for the pleasurable waves of energy to ignite his body and mind. Once, there'd been a time when Tommy had thought cocaine was for partying on the

weekends, but now he knew the truth: it was a daily necessity, and allowed him to think better and faster than he did
without it. It also gave him the sense of confidence he always
lacked.

After relieving himself in the toilet, he went to the sink to
wash his hands and check under his nose for excess powder
residue. As he looked up into the mirror, he noticed a big goon
standing behind him, staring straight at him. Back in the old
days, guys like this made him nervous but not any more, not
since he found his powdered God. He placed his hands on the
sink and sneered at the goon, "What the fuck are you looking
at?" Using his toughest voice.

Angelo sized him up for a few seconds then asked, in a
matter of fact tone, "You're from the Bronx, no? I thought
I knew you from somewhere. You're Tommy, Mike the
mechanic's son. You guys ran that chop shop."

Tommy hesitated, starting to lose some of his confidence.
Shit, I knew I should have taken a bigger silver bullet hit.

"Who are you?" he asked, in a voice drained of some of its
bravado.

"At first I didn't recognize you, 'cause you lost so much
weight. Man, you look like shit. I heard the stories that you
became a fuckin' crackhead. You ratted out a bunch of your
dad's guys just to get out of some bullshit pinch."

Faking it now, Tommy puffed out his scrawny chest and
walked over to Angelo."Well, pal, I don't know who you are,
but let me tell you who I'm with . . ."

Without any hesitation or anger, Angelo slapped Tommy
open-handed in the face so hard and fast that he was knocked
off his feet, and his head bounced off the side of the porcelain
sink. Angelo raised his voice slightly, "I don't give a flyin'
fuck who you're with."

He grabbed Tommy by the throat, lifting him easily off
the floor and smashed the back of his head into the mirror,
shattering it. The blood immediately started flowing, but
Angelo knew from years of practice that he hadn't hit him

that hard. *It's because the scalp tends to bleed easily, and a lot of times all that blood could fool you into not giving a guy a good enough beating.* Angelo's rule of thumb was that, until the pool of blood matched the person's body size, it was still okay to keep beating them without killing them. He warned Tommy, "If I ever see you anywhere near Hagen again, I will fuckin' bury you."

Angelo followed that up by throwing him back down to the tiled floor. He then started stomping on Tommy's head with the heel of his shoe. A lot of people kick guys with the point or toe area of their shoe, but Angelo knew better. He knew from experience that it not only scuffs up your shoes — especially if you hit some teeth — but it could also end up damaging your own toes. The best and most efficient form was definitely the heel stomp. He also liked to time his foot stomps in order to highlight and punctuate his most important words. He then added, "*Everyone* was already put on notice that Eddie Mambo put a *claim* on him. Your *stupid* ass doesn't know that, 'cause you're a dumb fuckin' *crackhead* and all your contacts are *gone*. You will now tell all the other *junk-ies* . . ." Here, 'junkies' received a double stomp . . ."and wannabe tough guys, to stay away from my guy Hagen, because he belongs to Eddie."

Tommy was trapped in a corner, lying in a mixture of urine, water, and old toilet paper. As the kicks bludgeoned his head and torso, he adopted the universal sign for "Help, I'm getting the shit kicked out of me," the full fetal position. He attempted to roll with some of the kicks but didn't have too much luck. He cried and sputtered, "I'm sorry, I'm sorry, I didn't know I didn't know."

Angelo walked over to the sink, shook his head in disgust and shame for the once neighborhood guy who'd turned into a piece-of-shit drug addict. He casually washed his hands while watching the sniveling, quivering lump of excrement on the floor. He fixed his hair and walked out of the bathroom, wiping his hands with a paper towel and neatly disposing of it in the elegant wooden wastebasket. As always, he used the paper towel to grab the door handle because he feared the germs from other bathroom users who didn't have the class to wash their hands. As he exited, he calmly strolled over to a waiter and said, "Hey boss, not for nothin', but you got a drunk guy that fell and hit his head in the bathroom. I think he needs some help."

Angelo strolled back into the main room and saw Lorenzo at the bar, drinking and laughing with Miguel. He walked over to Hagen's table and, without asking, took a seat.

Ah shit, soon as this Tommy gets up, now I got another debt collector sitting with me, and this one looks real nasty.

"Can I help you?" Hagen asked, with as much nonchalance as he could muster.

"No, but I can help you."

"Who are you?"

"Your guardian angel," said Angelo.

"Guardian angel?

At that moment, Hagen spotted two waiters carrying the bloody, limp body of Tommy, as discreetly as they could, out through a side door.

Hagen smiled, extended his hand, and said, "You must be Angelo, New York Eddie's guy."

Shaking Hagen's sweaty hand, Angelo answered, "You got it and don't worry about that guy. Your business with him is over. He's not coming back."

"I don't get it. Just like that, it's squashed?"

"Let me put it this way: you, me, and Eddie are sort of business partners now, and Eddie and I will always protect our investment."

"Partners. Remember, once you start as a cop, you will technically be working for me. I'm putting my ass on the line to erase your past and get you in. I mean, you guys are getting the better end of the deal. Matter of fact, that reminds me: I need you to talk to Eddie, 'cause in order for me to erase your record, I'm going to need some extra funds to grease the wheels."

In a blur of speed, Angelo grabbed Hagen by the throat. Customers sitting nearby stopped eating and stared at them, while an older couple, sensing trouble, got up and walked out of the restaurant. Angelo rasped, in a threatening whisper, "Listen, you degenerate gamblin' fuck, you don't try to shake us down, we shake you down. At any time, we can terminate this agreement and that means I'll put a fuckin' bullet in your head without hesitating, got me?"

Hagen coughed a few times, and finally got his breath back. He took a sip of water, smiled at Angelo, and said, "Take it easy, take it easy. I'll figure out another way to get you in. Geez, you crazy New Yorkers get worked up for nothing."

A broad smile appeared on Angelo's face, and he laughed out loud. It always amazed him how efficient random acts of violence were. He would have wasted so much more time trying to articulate and convince Tommy and Hagen of his point of view. But with violence, the universal language, everything was so much quicker and more efficient. *Not for nothin' it's the one language all people comprehend and respect.* With a friendly pat to Hagen's shoulder, he added, "Good, now we understand each other. Listen, this place is a gold mine for a guy like me. If I start makin' some moves and get ahead, I will throw some of it your way. The last thing I want you to understand is this, with me down here, nobody except Eddie is going to take any action with you. As of now, your gambling days are shut down, and I'm sure that last guy, little Tommy boy, will also help spread the word."

Chapter 14

After years of paying his dues by working the streets of Brooklyn, Viktor decided he needed a change. He had worked hard learning the language and customs of his new country, new skills were combined with the old and he knew he needed to branch out. Sometimes, the Russian bear thought of himself as a shark that had to keep moving forward . . . or die.

He'd outgrown the constraints of the heavily Russian-controlled territory where he had, as he moved up the chain, started to bump heads with the top-tier Russian money-makers. Although he was living very comfortably in his three-bedroom, penthouse duplex that overlooked Brighton Beach, those pangs of hunger once again kicked in.

He was sitting in a nightclub on Coney Island Avenue with a group of Russian mobsters eating blinis and caviar, and washing it down with peppered vodka. The talk bounced from business, to women, to sports, and back to business. His ears perked up when one of the men mentioned that he'd bought a condominium in the town of Sunny Villas.

Sunny Villas was the latest Miami city to incorporate and break away from the County for municipal services and have its own autonomy. It was located on the east coast beaches about five miles north of the town of Beachside. The city was in the midst of a building boom, with a new high-rise condo going up every week replacing the old mom and pop motels that had once littered the beachfront. South Americans and a

small group of Russians were gobbling up the high-end properties.

Viktor's decision was made right there at the table—he
was going to either take over the entire territory or die trying,
Viktor never asked permission from his peers to open up shop
in South Florida, and one week later he headed south to the
wide-open territory in Sunny Villas, Florida.

Chapter 15

The Miami Dade Police Academy was nothing like Angelo had imagined. The other guys in his class were, for lack of a better phrase, all nut jobs. Although he was one of the oldest, the other cadets weren't exactly spring chickens either. The physical training was a joke. They started with one-mile runs that caused the out-of-shape class to almost revolt in protest.

The guy who sat in front of Angelo in class, Double C as he called himself, was some piece of work. Another transplanted New Yorker, Double C hailed from the Bronx, where he claimed the toughest guys in the world lived. Double C reminded Angelo of every crazy bastard he grew up with, which was a good thing, because he laughed his way through the academy.

The instructors were also pretty cool and, for the most part, never busted his balls. Only once in the academy did Angelo have to give an overzealous instructor an attitude adjustment. After two weeks of the twenty-eight-year-old ex Marine instructor's nitpicking, Angelo asked him for assistance in defensive tactics training. The instructor was unable to return to the academy for over a month, due to the concussion he received from Angelo's hands. After that, the academy was smooth sailing.

Two months after graduating from the police academy, Angelo was sitting in the roll call room inside the Beachside

PD station. Roll call was the system where basic information was passed on from the sergeants to the road patrol officers, before turning them out to the road for their shift. Forty-eight-year-old Sergeant Jimmie Burke was one of those guys who never seem to age. He was tall, well built, and had a look in his eyes of either great intensity or insanity, depending on whom you asked. There are people who are known for being very animated by talking with their hands, but Jimmie took that activity to a whole new level. In a heated verbal conversation, Jimmie's wild erratic hand gestures could be outright dangerous to himself and those nearby. On this occasion, he was finishing up his daily briefings standing at the podium at the front of the roll call room.

In a loud, authoritative voice, he continued his speech, "So, make sure the Zone Three units tonight do area checks of the construction site, because that's two weeks in a row it's been burglarized. Folks, also remember officer safety; the A.T.F.'s last report has Miami getting real busy as the new black market for high-powered weapons. Finally, I would like to welcome to midnights our new officer, who just completed his field-training, officer Angelo Te-de-schi. I expect you guys to help him out with report writing and anything else he needs. Check in to service, 'cause they're already holding calls for new crew."

The uniformed officers walked over to Angelo and introduced themselves. With one of his frantic waves, Burke called to Angelo, "Tedeschi, come with me."

Angelo followed Burke into his tiny office that was littered with all sorts of martial arts memorabilia and books on scuba diving.

Manically, Jimmie said, "Dude, shut the door and have a seat."

"You got it, boss."

"Aren't you a little old to be a rookie cop?"

Uncertain whether he was joking or not, Angelo shrugged it off without saying anything.

"Here's the deal, mids is either for the cops who can't hack it on the busy shifts or the ones trying to hide from the administration. That basically leaves me in charge of a bunch of useless fucks. I also got more females on my shift than anywhere else in the department. Most of my guys here are so afraid of liability and getting written up that they hide like roaches and do no proactive police work. Last month I had three officers injured by violent subjects and you know what happened to the subjects? Nothing. They didn't even have to go to the damn hospital. Dude, seriously I hope you ain't a pussy. Can you handle yourself?

Enjoying the speech and thinking to himself that Burke's herky jerky arm gestures reminded him of an orchestra maestro on speed, Angelo answered, "I think I can hold my own."

Burke shook his head in disgust at the thought of what this once-noble job had turned into. He then started to sift through the mountain of paperwork he had to complete every night. Not looking up at Angelo, he ended the meeting with a curt, uninterested, "Well, we'll see . . . that's all."

Chapter 16

With the price of Oxycontin rising on the black market in South Florida, Dennis Del Rosario couldn't afford to feed his increasing habit . . . even after all the items he'd stolen from his air conditioning repairman job and sold at the flea market. *I remember talking to that fat guy, what was his name, shit it was . . . I got it, yeah, it was Weiser or Weezer, the one from that stupid court-ordered drug rehab program.* He met Michael Weezer, a fellow Oxycontin addict, at his first mandatory meeting, and the two of them had a lot in common. After the meeting, Weezer asked Dennis to help him out and act as a lookout for his ongoing series of armed robberies of small drug stores. According to Weezer, it was always an easy score because most drugstores had in-house policies not to call the cops till after the robber left. Apparently it was easier for the pharmacist and staff to just hand over the money and prescription drugs than get into the middle of a shootout with desperate drug addicts and over-zealous cops.

While sitting in the drugstore parking lot at one thirty in the morning, while smoking a joint with his overweight new partner, Dennis reflected back on his life. He had trouble believing that, before his injury, he had been a regular family guy who, as far as he was concerned, had been doing pretty good. Although he'd always used a few recreational drugs on the weekends, he'd basically kept the habit in check. His life had become unhinged when he'd seriously injured his foot, which had basically been crushed by a two-ton air conditioning unit that fell off its bracket while on a job. His life had gone rapidly downhill as his addiction to the Oxycontin pain pills had spiraled out of control.

This night would be the first "job" they pulled together, and Dennis didn't place much trust in Weezer. Instead of being just the lookout, Dennis decided to become the second gunman and enter the drugstore with Weezer. Inside their stolen Chevy Impala, they donned their black ski masks and removed the guns they had hidden behind the vehicle's dashboard. They rushed into the near-empty business, guns in hand, like two kids playing cowboy in their mom's kitchen. While Dennis ran down the aisles, he realized he should probably have test-fired the old revolver he only recently purchased for fifty bucks on the streets. He hobbled to the rear pharmacy area as fast as he could with his bum foot, and spotted Weezer dragging the young pimple-faced manager down the aisle. A new employee working the front counter, who was not familiar with Weezer's robbery theory, reached under the counter and activated the silent alarm.

Angelo was in the middle of a traffic stop and was hot under the collar. The punk had ran a red light and was mouthing off about the ticket Angelo had just given him, when the call came in—Beachside P.D. Zone One officers were dispatched to the robbery-in-progress call. Angelo was only a few blocks away; instead of pulling the punk out of his car and pounding him, he responded as a backup unit.

Stan Faber, a ten-year Beachside P.D. veteran who looked like a mix between a math teacher and a vacuum cleaner salesman, arrived on scene with his female trainee. He told Angelo to secure the front while he and his female partner went inside. The trainee, who hadn't practiced enough with her duty weapon, was having trouble removing her .40 Caliber SIG Sauer handgun from her brand new Safariland Level III leather retention holster. Angelo decided he might have some fun and blow off some steam this night, got back in his car and drove round toward the back of the business. Faber saw Angelo pulling away, and shouted to his partner, "Goddammit, I just told him to watch the front."

Angelo pulled up to the rear loading dock area and looked for the back door. Once he located it, he exited his car and leaned against the front quarter panel of his vehicle and waited. Approximately a minute later, a disturbingly obese masked subject exploded out the back door and ran right towards Angelo. With his baton in hand and doing his best Babe Ruth impression, Angelo hit the supersized subject square on both knees. The large man crashed to the ground, making a loud *whumping* sound as the air was expelled from his lungs. Angelo followed up with his patented heel stomp to the head and knocked the hulking robber unconscious.

The second subject, ran through the half-open door at a full sprint, tripped over his large, downed accomplice. He quickly regained his balance and continued to flee, running with a significant limp. As Angelo started his foot pursuit, he looked over his shoulder and saw Faber and his partner emerge from the door. Faber and his trainee pointed their weapons at the grounded subject and issued loud verbal commands, despite the fact that he was unconscious. Angelo could have easily caught Del Rosario, but he allowed him to run for a few blocks. When Del Rosario entered the deserted dark alley of a closed bagel shop, Angelo decided this was the perfect spot. He easily foot-tripped the exhausted Del Rosario, who sprawled face forward onto the ground. Angelo used his newly issued metal flashlight as a weapon of opportunity, and clubbed Dennis several times on the head until he was unconscious. He took a quick glance around and rifled through Dennis's pockets for his first on-the-job bonus.

Ten minutes later, Sgt. Burke arrived on scene and went over to Angelo, who had Del Rosario lying on his stomach and handcuffed inside his patrol car. He looked at the still-unconscious subject and then at Angelo, and stated, "Good job, rookie. Just do me a favor and call for Fire Rescue to take a look at him. It makes the administration happy when we provide full service to the suspects, and your boy has got quite a nice knot on his melon."

Just as he was about to ask Angelo what happened, an angry Faber flagged him down, then asked, "Sarge, can I talk to you a second?"

Walking towards Faber, Burke asked, "What's up, Stan?"

"You need to talk to officer Tony Soprano."

"Regarding?" Burke asked, casually.

"Not only am I the senior Officer on scene, I was also the primary on this call and I told Mr. Jersey Shore to watch the front, and he disobeyed."

"Looks to me like he made the right decision."

"That's not the only thing. We're missing a little over two thousand dollars. The manager said the subjects grabbed approximately eight thousand. We only recovered about fifty-eight hundred so far."

"So you think the new guy might have taken it?"

"Certainly looks fishy."

"Do a thorough canvass of the area where the subject ran. If you don't find it, let me know and I'll speak to him," Burke said, without much enthusiasm.

At thirty-two-years old, Zack Rosenfeld couldn't catch a break. Every time he started to make some money by day trading, the market would take a crap. He once worked for the top brokerage office in Miami but lost his job when *that fucking Colombian bitch wife* of his had him arrested for domestic violence. Rosenfeld's temper was always pretty bad, but when he was in the middle of his bodybuilding low-calorie diets, it got much worse. Tonight's argument started when his wife complained he wasn't spending enough time with their five-year-old son. *Doesn't she fucking understand that right now I need to concentrate on work, and money doesn't grow on trees?* When his son broke Zack's thousand-dollar laptop that night, while looking for apple juice in the refrigerator, it was the last straw.

At 0330 hours, Angelo got dispatched as the back-up unit on the domestic violence call in the Intracoastal Apartments. The dispatcher also provided the information that the apartments had a history of 911 hang-ups, and that the department had made two previous arrests for domestic violence at that location. They further provided that the subject had a past record of resisting officers with violence.

Upon his arrival downstairs at the valet area, Angelo saw Faber, Faber's trainee, and another female officer walking into the lobby. He parked his cruiser and quickly downed a welcome shot of Cuban coffee.

Angelo entered the well-furnished, spotlessly clean apartment, and saw that all parties were already inside the living room. Angelo observed a short but very muscular male in his boxer shorts yelling and flailing his arms. Hanging above a crème-colored leather couch was a large painting of the same guy in a muscle-flexing pose, wearing a small Speedo-type bathing suit. What a fuckin' jerkoff, he thought.

Faber and the two female officers were standing directly in front of the subject trying to get his attention. Sitting on the couch was a pretty, middle-aged Latin woman dressed in a bathrobe. She was crying and cradling a small boy in her arms.

Faber using his best negotiating voice, "Sir, you need to comply. I need you to turn around and place your hands behind your back."

Rosenfeld, always the victim, answered, "I didn't do nothing, she's lying, I never touched her."

The female cop, in a louder and more authoritative voice now, said, "*Sir, put your hands behind your back, now!*"

Rosenfeld was now fixated only on his wife, who he blamed for all his problems. He was also seething at the fact that these officers were in his house and had no right to interfere in his personal life. *These low pay security guards never understand my side of the story.* He continued to show his disdain to the officers by refusing to even acknowledge them.

He pointed at his wife with an accusatory, stubby finger and yelled, "You want me to fucking lose everything, you stupid bitch, this is all your fault!"

As Rosenfeld continued to hurl insults at his wife, she sat helplessly trying to calm the small, crying boy who cowered in fear on her lap. Faber continued to issue commands to Rosenfeld, but to no avail. Faber then grabbed his arm but Rosenfeld just stiffened up and continued berating his wife, refusing to budge. The child lifted his head from his mother's arms, and Angelo saw swelling and a huge purple welt developing on the child's face.

Flashes in the deep synapses of Angelo's brain occurred so fast he never processed what they meant. His reaction was as immediate as a reflex, and his body was once again on violent autopilot. Blinding rage distorted his vision, making the room appear as if filtered through a violet and red light. His auditory senses were also altered, rendering all sounds as if everything were underwater.

Angelo's stiffened body flew across the room and he snatched up Rosenfeld by the throat, with his right hand. His strength and momentum drove Rosenfeld off his feet and sent him crashing over a glass end-table. Rosenfeld's head was the first body part to make contact with the wall. Angelo landed on top of Rosenfeld and his fist pumped like a piston into Rosenfeld's shocked face.

Fortunately for Rosenfeld, the first punch knocked him into a state of semi-consciousness, while the rest proceeded to distort his prized features. His nose was the first to break and then his teeth. His lips and mouth were lacerated against the now-fractured shards of teeth. While Angelo continued in his frenzied rage, he didn't even notice Faber and the females yelling and trying to pull him off. The beating wouldn't end until Angelo said so, and Rosenfeld still had a long road to go. After the facial rearrangement, Angelo moved next into rag-dolling the limp-bodied abuser into several pieces of expensive furniture. Most of the furniture shattered under the dead weight of Rosenfeld's almost lifeless body.

As Angelo slowly emerged from his trance, the first of his senses to return was his hearing. The room exploded into the chaotic screams of the officers and the wailing child. The only calm person in the room was the mother, who had a serene, detached look on her face. He remembered that exact look on his own mother's face. His mind returned him to that unforgettable moment in his living room. With perfect clarity, he remembered the feeling of the baseball bat as it made contact with his father's head. The wet thwacking sound it made, as if he were hitting a ripe melon. But the most intense memory of that evening was the unbelievable satisfaction of finally having power over his father.

Dade County Fire Rescue Engine number 18 had their paramedics on scene treating Rosenfeld. They advised Sgt. Burke that the prisoner would need to be transported on a backboard with a neck brace, in case of a spinal cord injury. Jimmie Burke watched as they carefully loaded the suspect into an ambulance. When he arrived, the suspect was in a semiconscious state and wasn't coherent enough to answer any questions. He also observed numerous lacerations and a large amount of swelling on the subject's face. He walked over to Angelo, who was in the process of cleaning his hands at the trunk of his vehicle. Trying his best not to smile, he asked, "Okay, Angelo, what happened?"

"Well, Sarge, not for nothin', but I saw the subject resisting the officers, so I attempted to assist. The subject took a combative stance and resisted me with violence. In order to protect myself, I utilized equal to—how do you say—necessary force, and then I redirected him to the ground and placed him into custody," Angelo stated, in a matter-of-fact tone.

"Really?" Burke was utterly amazed that Tedeschi could put that many words together in a cognizant sentence. *You know, I think I'm starting to like this squirrely bastard.* He looked Angelo in the eyes, thinking that as long as the other officer's stories matched, then they were all golden, and he wouldn't need to stay after his shift to talk to the Lieutenant in the morning.

Faber and the female officer waited purposely away from *that lunatic Tedeschi* for Burke to arrive. Faber told the trainee to wait in the car, because he knew this was a not situation for a trainee to overhear. This was a case of an out-of-control officer, and Stan Faber would put a stop to it immediately, he told himself. He watched as Burke interviewed the mother, who now appeared a lot calmer and stronger then she had in the apartment. After several minutes, Burke walked towards him, crossed his arms and asked, "Okay, Stan, what happened?"

Very animated, Faber pointed accusingly towards Angelo, and said, "That guy is mentally unfit for duty. We had the situation completely handled and under control until he went nuts."

The female officer quickly chimed in, "Sarge, I don't ever want to work with him, you should go to I.A. first thing in the morning."

Burke lifted his hand in a just-wait gesture and said, "I just spoke to the wife and kid and by the way the Fire Rescue Lieutenant informed me that the little boy has a broken orbital bone and they're taking him to Joe DiMaggio Children's Hospital. The wife said her husband has been beating on her for years, and that you two were afraid of him."

Faber sputtered in disbelief, "That's not true I was in the proce . . ."

Burke cut him off in mid-sentence, finishing with, "I'm not done. The wife said she will sign a sworn affidavit that her husband was out of control, and would have killed the both of you if it wasn't for Tedeschi. Now listen to me very carefully, because the next time I hear you two fail to do your job, I will write you both up for dereliction of duty. Matter of fact, I'm writing Tedeschi a commendation for his work tonight, from the drug store and here. You are both dismissed."

Before getting back in his patrol car, Burke passed Angelo and said, "Tedeschi, good job, meet me at the station and I'll help you write up your Use Of Force report the correct way."

As Burke drove away from the scene, he looked at Faber and called him a "pussy" under his breath. He remembered the unfortunate day the department hired him. Before he was a cop, Faber had worked as a manager in the cruise line industry. He had no people skills, no athletic ability, and the only reason he wanted to be a cop was for the power. He initially had no chance of getting hired as a cop at Beachside, until he approached Lieutenant Hagen. When Hagen found out Faber worked for one of the biggest cruise lines and still had a lot of pull there, he hired him immediately. Burke shook his head at the memory and thought if he only had a couple more Angelos, maybe he'd be filling out less officer injury on the job reports.

The next several weeks, Angelo went through the gambit of calls for service that a road patrolman routinely handled. The calls ranged from the tedious to the hilarious to the tragic. For the tedious, there were the hours of paperwork for documenting incidents like identity theft and arresting juveniles. There was a mountain of checklists an officer had to perform before each shift, like check his emails, check his phone messages, check and sign off on the new policies and procedures in the computer, check his vehicle for maintenance, and on and on.

One of the funniest moments Angelo had was going on a call of an elderly female who was having trouble breathing. Beachside P.D.'s policy was always to dispatch officers to critically sick or injured persons, along with Fire Rescue units. His partner on that call was a veteran officer named Jerry Stann. Jerry was known throughout the law enforcement community as one of the funniest guys ever to do the job. Even the usually serious Angelo couldn't help himself when Jerry was on a roll. As they arrived on scene, Jerry was already in rare form and had the building doormen in stitches. Fire Rescue was still a few minutes away, and it was up to Angelo and Jerry to try to stabilize the victim until they arrived.

Upstairs at the apartment, an elderly female answered the door and explained that her friend had passed out and was on the floor in the other room. Angelo was carrying his department issued AED, and he and Jerry hurriedly entered the small bedroom. The elderly woman, who appeared to be around eighty-years-old, was lying supine and looking very pale. As Angelo opened the AED and started to prepare the equipment, Jerry checked her vitals. The elderly friend entered the room and watched them work, deep concern on her face.

Angelo tried his hardest not to look at Jerry, because he knew Jerry would do his best to try to make him laugh. Jerry put on his cheesiest soap opera deep voice and mimicked a doctor hamming it up, as he called out her vital signs. Angelo gritted his teeth and continued to remove items from his First Aid kit, like the disposable electric pads that might be needed if her heart failed. Not getting a response from Angelo, Jerry joined him in removing the medical items. Jerry first snapped on the rubber gloves with the comedic genius of Jim Carrey. Angelo felt the laugh start to build in his chest, but he fought it off and shot Jerry the dirtiest look he could come up with. Jerry then picked up the disposable razor that was used in cases where the male victim's chest is too hairy for the pads to make contact. Jerry looked at Angelo with the razor blade in his gloved hand and said, "Hey bud, do you want me to shave her?"

That was it. Angelo lost it right there, laughing uproariously. Jerry was so amused about getting the stone-faced New Yorker to react that he also started laughing out loud. The victim was slowly regaining consciousness, and looked up with unfocused eyes at the two laughing idiots standing above her. Then, for some unknown reason, the elderly friend also started to laugh out loud and the three of them stood in the room, laughing hysterically in an unbelievably surreal moment. At that moment, Fire Rescue arrived and

entered with all their equipment. The firemen were completely shocked by the outlandish behavior of the three cackling
onlookers. Angelo and Jerry rushed out of the room to allow
them to work and most of all, try to regain their composure.

Within minutes, Fire Rescue had the woman on their
gurney, in order to have her transported to the hospital for
further care. As they wheeled the victim out of the apartment,
she was clearly wearing a big smile under the oxygen mask
and actually looked better. Without missing a beat, Jerry
turned to Angelo, and said, "See bud, laughter is the best
medicine."

Cops like Jerry were worth their weight in gold, as they
helped their colleagues to forget all the negativity and the bad
calls they were dispatched to on a daily basis. Calls for service
like suicides, child abuse, and fatalities were among the worst.
Angelo's first fatality came over the radio as a driver on a
scooter who'd hit a tree. It was 2:00 am, and Angelo was the
first officer on scene. It was obvious the driver, a young Latin
female approximately twenty-years of age, had lost control of
her scooter and struck a palm tree in the center median. She
was lying in the street unconscious, bleeding heavily from her
head. Angelo quickly made sure she had a pulse and requested that Fire Rescue run lights and sirens. All the other Beachside units were unavailable, due to being tied up handling a
small condominium fire.

Angelo tried to remember everything he was taught as a
first responder, and made sure he didn't try to move the girl
in case of spinal cord damage. Even though she was bleeding
heavily, she had a strong pulse and her breathing was normal.
All Angelo could do was monitor her vitals and wait for rescue
to arrive. Within two minutes of their arrival, however, the
girl's breathing was starting to become more labored. Angelo
stepped back and allowed the paramedics to do their work.
The four rescue responders were quick and professional,
tending to her injuries, but within thirty seconds they stopped
working on her. When Angelo saw this, he walked back over

and asked, "Why the fuck are youse stopping? She's still breathing!"

The Fire Rescue Lieutenant replied, "That's just agonal breathing. She's gone." Angelo looked hard at the Lieutenant, who continued, "She wasn't wearing a helmet and her skull is almost completely crushed. That's not just blood on the floor, it's also brain matter. There's nothing anyone can do for her now."

Angelo dropped back down to his knee and grabbed the girl's hand. Within ten seconds, the horrible agonal breathing had stopped. Several minutes later, Jimmie Burke arrived and called out the T.H.I. officer (traffic homicide investigator). That night was the first time Angelo started thinking this job wasn't as easy as he'd initially thought. After several months of police work, it quickly dawned on him that a cop's job was a roller coaster of highs and lows and he'd better remember to strap in and hold on tight every time he got on that ride.

Chapter 17

A ngelo had built up a little vacation time and decided to take Lorenzo's advice about going down to the Florida Keys for bartenders week. Bartenders week was a raucous five-day event that took place at the Tiki bar on Islamorada Key. Employees from Florida's nightclubs, bars, and restaurants would flock there for a hedonistic vacation retreat. Angelo drove down with a couple of Lorenzo's best-looking waitresses and dancers. These were girls that he'd already hooked up with over the last few months, and knew they would be up for a good time. He reserved the best suite at the hotel at $700 a night, and even that was a bargain.

The first night they arrived, Angelo took the girls to the main outdoor bar. The place was packed and even he was shocked with how wild it was. Beautiful topless and tanned women were at the bar downing shots of Tequila, while numerous couples were openly having sex on the beach just fifty yards away. Once at the bar, he started downing shots of vodka, Kahlua, and tonic—better known as Mind Erasers— with Lorenzo's top earner, a knockout Colombian girl named Tanya. Even in a resort full of beautiful women, Tanya turned a lot of heads with the men, and even more with the women. A short Brazilian girl, wearing only a thong bikini and half-cut tee shirt covering her outrageous curves, approached Tanya and Angelo. She was obviously attracted to Tanya and the two were quickly getting acquainted. Angelo's mouth was actually starting to water at the thought of taking the two knockouts back to his suite.

While the girls made conversation, he looked across the bar and was hit with a jolt of electricity. His first thought was that he couldn't believe his eyes. His second thought, strangely enough, was of an old memory of him and his dad.

The memory was from a time when he was eight-years-old, and his dad was watching television in their little kitchen. The television was a small orange Panasonic with two big rabbit-ear antennas covered in tinfoil. Rosario thought the tinfoil helped with reception and, when that didn't work, he hit it a few times with his big meaty hand. It was late at night, way past Angelo's bedtime, but he couldn't sleep so he approached his dad in the kitchen. It was one of the rare times his dad actually welcomed his presence. Rosario pulled out an extra bowl from the cupboard and shared some of the Italian Ices he was already eating. He pointed to the TV and told him that the movie he was watching was a classic called *Casablanca*, starring Humphrey Bogart. Angelo loved the old black-and-white movie with its gangsters and wild nightclub life. He remembered how his dad sneered at the TV every time a German soldier appeared. Angelo's favorite scene in the movie was when Bogart was sitting at the bar and delivered the coolest line he'd ever heard, about Ingrid Bergman, "Of all the gin joints in all the towns in all the world, she walks into mine."

Back at the Tiki bar, Angelo stared across the bar at the only woman he'd ever loved: Mia Lavalle. As he gazed at her, his mind kept trying to compute the odds of seeing her here. Here he was, over thirteen hundred miles away from Brooklyn, on a tiny island in the Florida Keys, yet fate had somehow put her there. She looked amazing, with a dark tan and a short, white sundress. She was standing with a tall blonde pretty boy and they were laughing and drinking as if they were very familiar. She hadn't seen him yet and he shielded himself behind some of the crowd. His date Tanya was getting comfortable with her little Brazilian friend and they grabbed Angelo and told him they wanted to go some place quieter.

Angelo was still in a fog when he allowed the girls to lead him away from the bar. As the music from the bar started to fade, he reflected on his life. The idea that he somehow always came up a bit short buzzed through his mind. He watched the friends he grew up with eventually evolve from their days of partying to become husbands and fathers. Maybe not the most faithful husbands or the most responsible fathers, but at least they tried. Here he was in his forties, with no family, having still not made that big money score, with nothing to hang his hat on to say he'd accomplished something. "Fuck this shit," Angelo said out loud, startling the giggling girls who were already affectionately all over each other. He turned on his heel and headed back to the bar with a sense of purpose. His plan? Well, he didn't have one . . . besides throwing the pretty blonde boy into the ocean.

Although no more than ten minutes had passed, he couldn't find Mia. He was furious with himself for not immediately going over to her when he'd had the chance, and at least saying something. *Did she leave the resort? Did she go back to her room with pretty boy? Did I really see her? Yeah I saw her, and yeah I screwed up again and missed an opportunity. Opportunity for what? Was I going to bang her, were we going to have a few drinks and talk about old times?* He wasn't sure what he was going to do but he at least would have wanted to talk to her, hear her voice again, and possibly her laugh. *Yeah, that would have been nice after all these years.*

He threw the bartender at the main bar a fifty-dollar bill, and grabbed a bottle of Absolut vodka. He headed to the beach to clear his mind and, most of all, to be alone. In the dark, he almost tripped over several couples who were rolling in the sand. He finally found a quiet, deserted spot on the far side of the resort. He dragged a lounge chair just to the edge of the surf and started drinking.

As the alcohol worked its way through his body and he started to relax, he realized it was actually a beautiful night.

The sound of the rhythmic waves, along with the shimmering light reflected from the bar onto the ocean, helped ease his foul mood. Lost in thought, he wondered why he never took the time to slow down and enjoy the simple things in life.

Looking at the stars reminded him of another night with a beautiful sky — the night he watched his good friend John Pomorico die. His mind started to replay that night in the endless video loop he'd already watched too many times. As he slipped deeper into his remembrance, he heard a very distant but recognizable voice say, "Hi, stranger."

He brought himself out of his reverie, looked up and there, miraculously, was Mia. She was standing in the moonlight looking like an angel, with her amazing smile and spar-kling green eyes. For the first time in his life, he was caught completely off guard and struggled to think of something to say. She folded her arms in mock anger and tapped her foot, waiting for a reply. When his senses finally returned, he stood up and delivered the following line flawlessly, "Outta all the beaches in all the towns in the world, you gotta walk into mine!"

She laughed, threw her arms open, and hugged him with all the intensity of their yearning. She joined him on the lounge and they talked about their lost years. As she updated him on her life, he kept thinking *this has to be destiny, she has to really be the one and this time I ain't letting her go.* As far as the pretty boy blonde she was with, he was actually a gay co-worker who'd taken the trip with her as a friendly companion.

That night, she stayed with Angelo in his suite, and for both of them, it was so much better than they could have imagined. The next morning, Angelo called Jimmy Burke and was able to get a few extra days off work. He and Mia drove south to Key West and jumped onto a private cruise on a 44-foot Morgan sailboat that included the captain and a crew member. For Angelo, every day became more relaxing and enjoyable than the next. They swam in the clear blue ocean, walked on the most picturesque beaches, and ate the freshest seafood. They cruised around the Bahamas and even did a little gambling at the resort's casino. It was one of the rare times Angelo actually won at the craps table, and he was already feeling like a winner before he ever touched the dice.

On their last night on the cruise, Mia told him the truth about their predestined meeting at the Tiki bar. It wasn't so much about the power of destiny, but more about the power of Lorenzo. Tired of hearing a year's worth of Angelo's drunken ramblings about the best girl in the world that he lost, Lorenzo decided to do something about it. He located Mia in New York and gave her a call. It turned out she was just as nostalgic as Angelo about their lost relationship, and Lorenzo decided to set up a meeting. With Angelo, he knew you couldn't tell or suggest to him anything; you had to let him figure it out for himself. So, two weeks prior to the event, he devised a plan and set up the whole Tiki bar "accidental" meeting.

When Angelo heard the story, he first thought of killing Lorenzo for interfering with his life, but he quickly realized, *shit, he gave me back the best thing I ever had, and now I owe him big time.* Two days later at the Miami International Airport, they said their goodbyes, although she made immediate plans to return in two weeks to spend more time with him.

Chapter 18

At his home in Davie, Florida, Detective Michael Frakes walked into his bedroom closet and started to get dressed for work. His equipment was laid out in perfect order, with each piece in its precise designated spot. He built special cubbyholes, shelves, and hooks to keep everything organized. That's one thing he always appreciated about his time in the Marine Corps: it taught a man to be disciplined. He tried to instill those qualities into his daughter, but she was very resistant to conformity. With his wife's passing, he imagined their bond would naturally grow stronger, but the police psychologist warned him the opposite could occur, and unfortunately the doc was right.

Seventeen-year-old Amanda Frakes took after her free-spirited mother. Her immediate plan was to leave home as soon as she turned eighteen, and then backpack around the world and experience other cultures. She remembered with great admiration all her mom's colorful stories she told about traveling and working for the Peace Corps. Despite Michael's objections Amanda took an after school job to start saving for her trip. She also started hanging out with some new friends that had Michael very worried.

After re checking his department issued Glock .45 caliber handgun for the last time, he slid it into his concealed paddle holster that was belted to his hip. The last item he put on was his badge and that always reminded him of his sworn oath, to protect persons and uphold the law. Once fully dressed he walked into the kitchen to talk to Amanda. She was making one of her non-fat all natural vegan shakes that he had trouble believing she actually drank. He said, in his most cheerful tone, "I may be stuck late on this surveillance, I left you money to order in food for later. Also, no friends at the house 'cause I want you finishing your homework."

Amanda shut her eyes and clenched her teeth as the sound of his voice disgusted her. She couldn't wait for the day she could get away from her dad. She mumbled under her breath, "Fuck you."

"What did you say?" Michael asked in shock, although he'd clearly heard her.

"Nothing," answered Amanda, a disdainful look on her face. At seventeen, she didn't really understand her anger for her father; she just knew that everything he said and did annoyed her. Michael tried to keep his temper in check and told her in a much sterner tone, "Don't start this now. Your attitude lately has been getting worse and I'm telling you not to push it. I have been working my ass off so you can have everything you need, like your cell phone, your clothes, your laptop. You need to start helping me a little."

"Yeah, whatever."

It was amazing to Michael how much his daughter looked and sounded like Susan. Her striking resemblance rekindled the pain inside him that he knew wouldn't end until his last breath.

"Baby, you know I love you and I'm sorry I'm working this much, but I'm doing my best. It's just me and you now, so we need to stick together."

"It's just not fucking fair!"

"I know, baby, I know."

He instinctively went to hug her but she pushed him away and ran out of the room. This incident had been repeating itself more often than Michael could believe and unfortunately it appeared to be getting worse.

Chapter 19

Inside the Beachside Police Department, fifty-nine-year-old Captain Mark McPherson sat at his desk working on his latest investigation. He came to Beachside PD after retiring from the City of Miami Police Department as a Sergeant. Most people at the department considered him a little strange and an outsider, which actually suited McPherson just fine. He didn't go there to make friends; he only wanted to do the job as professionally as he could. He knew friendships could be difficult and affect your judgment, a point even more pertinent when you were in charge of the Internal Affairs unit. With only three more years to go at Beachside to become vested in the city's pension, he became even more withdrawn and guarded.

Michael entered the police station with that same feeling he always had: *what could possibly go wrong today?* After grabbing his mail and documents from his wooden inbox, he headed down the hall towards his office and ran into McPherson. Although they were never the best of friends, he respected Mark for his work ethic and honesty. For a period of two years he worked with Mark side by side in the Internal Affairs unit. Due to his aloofness, Mark was a difficult guy to get to know, but that was just fine with Michael. His only flaw as Michael saw it was his refusal to back down on issues that really didn't need pursuing.

Early on in his career, a mentor taught Michael the phrase, "is the juice worth the squeeze?" He adopted the saying as a guide to help him make the right decisions. Mark approached Michael and gave him his usual firm, dry handshake, and asked, "Hey Michael do you have a minute?"

Michael smiled to himself because he hadn't seen Mark in months and, as usual, the man got straight to business.

"Sure Captain what do you need?"

"Let's go into my office."

Mark sat down behind his neatly organized desk and put on his reading glasses.

"Michael, why don't you shut the door. First, how's Amanda?"

"It's still been rough on her. We seem to be banging heads and she refuses to talk to a shrink."

"Give her some time, it's only been a year-and-a-half since Susan passed."

"I know, I know. I'm just worried 'cause she's been hanging out with some questionable people."

"Well, we're cops and everyone is questionable to us."

Mark would quickly tire of useless small talk in conversations, believing it to be an inefficient waste of time. He was smart enough to realize its necessity, however, in today's world of social etiquette, and he quickly transitioned to saying, "Speaking of questionable people did you see the new officer Hagen hired?"

"The obnoxious New Yorker, yeah. I also hear he's not the cleanest cop around."

Happy to hear Michael was in full agreement, Mark nodded, and added, "I'm hearing the same. You know, if I go to the Chief, Hagen will jump in and squash it like he did for that alcoholic buddy of his, Mickens. This new guy is assigned to Jimmie Burke and so far Burke hasn't brought me anything, which isn't surprising considering Burke's reputation. I'll only have one shot at this and I'm hoping to finally bag Hagen, so I need your help."

"You know me, Cap, I can't stand dirty cops, and Hagen definitely ain't no choirboy, but now that I'm out of I.A., how could I help?"

"I already spoke to Lt. Travis. He will do me the favor and have Hagen's boy transferred into your unit. I need you to help me build a case against him so air tight that we can charge him federally, and then offer him a deal and get him to flip on Hagen. All you got to do is give him enough rope and he will hang himself."

As Michael heard Mark's speech pattern pick up its pace and rise an octave higher, he recognized Mark was starting to work himself up. Mark's excitement reminded him of his old Mastiff, Matt. When Michael prepared his food, that dog would work himself into such a frenzy it looked like he was having a seizure. Michael decided to try to slow Mark down before he blew a gasket, and said, "Hold on a second, Mark. If this guy's as bad as I hear, he can do a lot of damage in my unit. I'm sorry, but it's too risky and I can't jeopardize my guys' safety on this. I'm going to have to say no."

Almost frothing at the mouth Mark leaned out of his seat towards Michael and exclaimed, "Too late. He's already being transferred, and don't you realize this is a huge opportunity for us to finally finish Hagen?"

For the first time in their relationship, Michael let a comment slip that he wish he could have held back. But the fact that McPherson once again was taking things way too far, way too fast caused the untimely outburst. He exclaimed loudly, "This freaking vendetta of yours is going to get a lot of people hurt . . . Mark my words . . . Mark!"

Mark sat back in his chair and his whole demeanor abruptly changed. His excited high-pitched tone of voice switched to a slow, over-pronounced, demeaning drone and he said with finality, "Well, Detective Frakes, you don't have to like it, but you will do it, and that is an order. Now, please shut the door as you leave, because I have other important matters I need to attend to."

As Michael stormed out of the office, he thought about buying McPherson a book by the author Herman Melville.

The book was a story about another Captain who lost his perspective as he pursued his old nemesis in a bloodthirsty quest for revenge.

Inside his office, Michael was sitting at his desk glancing continuously at his watch. He picked up the phone in frustration and dialed the extension for Lisa, the front office secretary. It rang several times, then went to her voice mail. He stalked angrily down the hall towards her office, muttering about having another crappy day. Entering her office, he saw the new guy he'd been waiting on. The big bastard was standing over her, and they seemed to be flirting with each other. After he cleared his throat to get her attention, she finally looked up and said, "Oh sorry, Michael, I was about to send him in."

Recognizing his new boss, Angelo put on his best face and stuck out his hand.

"How's it going, Sarge? Angelo Tedeschi."

Ignoring Angelo's outstretched hand, Michael answered, "Officer Tedeschi, you were supposed to be in my office twenty minutes ago. Let me first explain to you . . ."

As Michael talked, a brief impulse to knock *the little jerkoff out* flashed across Angelo's mind. Not shaking a man's hand was a very disrespectful thing to do. Although Angelo could stop his temper boiling over, he couldn't disguise his obvious contempt for his new boss.

He cut Michael off in midsentence and said, "Hey pal give me a second, and let me finish up with this beautiful young lady."

Angelo turned his attention back to Lisa. "So, what were we just talking about?"

Michael's face became bright red and his blood pressure escalated to a dangerous level. He was instantly furious over Angelo's unbelievable insubordination. No, worse than insubordination. This was an outright lack of respect for his position. *That freaking McPherson had to do me the favor of sticking me with this piece of garbage.* As the anger rolled over him, the "what the hell else could go wrong today" voice screamed louder in his head. He turned his back on them, exhaled deeply, and left the office, shaking his head.

After downing a handful of antacid stomach tablets, Michael finally calmed himself down by using the breathing exercises he'd learned in his stress awareness classes. As Angelo walked toward his new boss's office, he heard the all-too-familiar voice of Eddie repeating in his head, warning, *don't fuck this up, Ange.* Despite the door to Michael's office being open, Angelo knocked on it anyway, now trying to show a little respect. After making his point by taking his time getting there, he figured that would be the right thing to do. Also trying to step back from his anger, Michael waved Angelo in, with a calm look on his face.

In his most friendly manner, Angelo said, "Hey boss, you ain't already bangin' that chick are you? 'cause I can back off."

Never a big fan of New Yorkers with their big attitudes, Michael actually grimaced in pain, and said, "No, Officer Tedeschi, I'm not banging her, and from now on, you will address me as Sarge or Sergeant. The next thing you will do is . . ."

See what happens when you try to be nice? Angelo thought to himself.

"Listen boss, drop the fucking tough guy shit, 'cause I didn't ask to be in this unit and I just tried being a gentleman to you. If it's a personal problem, then let's handle this outside like men. Otherwise, save your bullshit for the ass kissers that already work for you."

"Get out of my office!"

Michael was so furious his hands were shaking. After Angelo had coolly walked out, he picked up his phone and dialed McPherson's extension. As soon as McPherson picked up, he didn't even give him a chance to say hello and instead just screamed.

"Mark there's no freaking way I can do this! That son of a bitch

was already insubordinate to me. I can't handle this crap right now!"

Michael ground his teeth as he listened to McPherson, who once again took his time to inform him he had no choice.

"I understand that, Mark, but . . . I know . . . but . . ."

Out of frustration he slammed the phone down, and yelled, "Goddammit . . . I can't take this crap right now!"

Chapter 20

Lorenzo and Angelo drove down to South Beach in Lorenzo's convertible white Mercedes. Their first stop was lunch at the world-famous Joe's Stone Crab off of Washington Avenue. Angelo loved seafood and in all of Florida, Joe's was top of his list. After finishing off several key lime pies, they headed to Nikki Beach Club on 1st and Ocean Drive to lay out, catch some rays, and enjoy the views.

Lifting his sunglasses, Lorenzo said, "I don't understand why you're so upset about being transferred. It seems like you can get a lot more stuff done for Eddie as an undercover."

"Yeah, but I was just beginning to make some real money working mids with this guy Burke. I started taking action with Hagen's degenerate gambling buddies. He hooked me up with them and I was throwing him a few bucks every now and then. These motherfuckers not only got a lot of money, but they just hand it over. Maybe it's the uniform, but I haven't had to crack one yet. I also started a few other scams with the local businesses and the money's startin' to come in. With Burke, as long as I back him and the other officers up, he doesn't give a shit what I do. At the end of my first week, he tells me to do what I got to do, but just don't be stupid enough to get caught, that's all. You gotta love a guy like that."

Lorenzo nodded in agreement and added, "No doubt, he sounds like a good guy. How's things with you and Mia?"

"Couldn't be better. She's coming down every other weekend now, and I'm starting to warm up to the idea of her moving down here permanently."

"You got to be shitting me — the lone wolf, the last of the Mohicans, Mr. Ladies Man is thinking of settling down! Now I've seen it all."

Angelo leaned out of his chair and, despite Lorenzo's excellent job of covering up, was able to land several hard punches to Lorenzo's chest and shoulders. Grinning, Angelo said, "Well, I'm starting to slow down with these young broads, and it's nice having a good woman around who understands me, and where I come from."

Lorenzo lifted his beer and Angelo followed suit, and they clicked bottles, Lorenzo adding, "Amen to that, cuz, amen to that."

Inside the Beachside P.D. crime suppression team's office, Michael, Bobby, Angelo, and several of the other UC detectives were in the room, making small talk. Finishing some paperwork, Michael stood and said, "Alright, listen up, guys. This is the new guy, Angelo Tedeschi. He's real green so I would appreciate if everyone helped him out. He mostly will be riding with me, till I feel he's safe enough to cut loose. Bobby, I know you have some new info for us, so go ahead."

Bobby, who repeatedly had to lift his pants because he was so thin, stood up and addressed the guys, "I just got back from my monthly meeting with the Feds. They are asking for our assistance in helping track down who the new movers and shakers are with the high powered weapons.

Apparently, some new group is starting to take over and knock out all the smaller operations. They think it's possibly the Russians, since they're the new hungry kids on the block. We really need to start pumping our C.I.s for info. The other thing I'm hearing is the gym on 207th Street has become real active with the dopers, so we need to keep an eye on them. Well, that's all I got."

Michael patted Bobby on the shoulder, and wrapped it up with the guys.

"Alright, guys, give me twenty minutes and let's make it the spot at 178th Street. I need some Cuban coffee, bad. Angelo, stay here, I want to talk to you."

Michael gave a signal to Bobby to close the door and stay put. Michael then turned to Angelo, and said, "Angelo, why don't we have ourselves a little talk? I spoke to Jimmie Burke about you and he gave you high praise. I worked with Jimmie for over ten years and I like him, but I've told him to his face what I'm about to tell you. Jimmie is a cowboy, and cowboys are dangerous. Do they get results? Yeah, sometimes, but they can also get people hurt. I'm telling you now, if you do anything stupid, I will personally make sure you get what's coming to you."

Looking down at the floor, Angelo almost whispered, "You threatening me, Mike?"

Knowing this already wasn't going well, Bobby shook his head and was about to intercede in order to keep the peace when Michael shot back, "No, it's a promise. And what did I say about freaking calling me . . .?"

The part of Angelo's brain that usually helped him remain calm must have been taking a lunch break, because without hesitation he jumped out of his chair, grabbed Michael by the shirt and slammed him up against the wall, knocking down a large map of the city. Bobby jumped onto Angelo's back and tried to get an arm around his neck for a chokehold. Angelo ignored Bobby and put his face up close to Michael's. Michael, who hadn't been manhandled like this since he was a kid in junior high school, was frozen in disbelief.

As Angelo looked into Michael's eyes with rage, he started hearing Eddie's voice once again. It brought him back from the brink of his madness and he let go of Michael, who slid down the two inches he'd been hoisted. Through gritted teeth, he told Michael, "Remember, I didn't ask to be in your fuckin' unit. I'd much rather work for Burke. At least he ain't a fuckin' little pussy."

Now recovered from the initial shock of Angelo's boldness, Michael felt his mind go blank. After all the trials and tribulations he'd put up with this last year, he'd reached his breaking point. Walls of discipline that had taken half a lifetime to build crumbled in that split second, like a house of cards. Michael reached down to his hip and pulled his gun from the holster. Before raising the weapon up toward Angelo's face, reason started to flow back into his brain. As he was able to regain control, he stopped his arm rising any higher. His emotions were still raw, and instead of biting, he barked, "Motherfucker, if you ever put your hands on me again, I will fucking kill you."

Bobby jumped in between them and tried to calm his boss. In the six years he'd known him, he'd never heard Michael utter a curse word, or even lose his temper.

"No, no, Mike! Relax. Relax bro, it's not worth it."

Angelo's anger dissipated instantly and left him, at the ridiculousness of the moment. He laughed out loud. *The balls of this little fuck, pulling a piece on me.* With a big smile, he said, "You gotta be kidding me with that. But I'm glad we're finally starting to understand each other."

Deciding it was best to remove himself from the situation before doing anything else stupid, Angelo left the room. Carefully, Bobby watched Angelo leave, turned to Michael when he was sure it wasn't a trick, and said, "Mike, are you fucking crazy? Bro, that shitbird ain't worth it. He's playing you 'cause he wants out of the unit. Why don't you just kick him out or suspend his crazy ass?

"I can't," Michael said, still shaking with rage. "It's a long story, but I can't talk about it right now."

"Then let him fuck up and get himself jammed up on his own. It's only a matter of time for a guy like that."

"I know. I just don't want to see any of us get hurt until he does."

"Mike, you got to keep it together. If you want to go to McPherson's office right now, you know I got your back. I'll testify to the fact of Tedeschi putting his hands on you."

As calm replaced his rage, Michael felt a deep regret at what had just happened.

"No, I shouldn't have pulled out my gun, I seriously messed up."

Still trying to back his friend, Bobby added, "What gun? I didn't see anything."

"Bobby, I practice what I preach, even when it comes to a dirtbag like that. I won't bend the rules and make up stuff, it's just not my way. Now let me go outside and try to talk to that animal."

Bobby shook his head in disbelief and said, "Mike, you're a better man than me."

Chapter 21

Three days later, Angelo was sitting in the passenger seat of Michael's undercover car. Michael pulled the vehicle into an empty parking space that faced an alley. The alley was directly behind a mixed martial arts gym. The neighborhood they were in was considered by law enforcement to be a high crime area. Almost every fifteen minutes, they observed a male exit the back of the gym and conduct a hand-to-hand drug transaction with either a person in a vehicle or a pedestrian.

Michael turned to Angelo and explained, "These guys certainly are doing some good business. We'll grab the next buyer and flip him so you can see how we work our way up the chain to get to the big boys."

Angelo gave Michael a serious look and said, "I got a better idea. Let's get ourselves inside their gym and then we can see if they're sellin' more than just drugs."

"Really? And based on all your years of undercover police work, how do you propose we get into a tight knit group like these guys" retorted Michael.

Angelo smiled, and said, "I got a plan, but I don't think you got the balls for it."

Michael wasn't going to let this New York asshole get the better of him. A lifetime in the Marine Corps, and close to twenty as a cop, gave him plenty of balls.

Michael answered with, "I'll tell you what, here's your one and only chance to try it your way. If you screw this up, from now on you do everything I say. Is that a deal?

Angelo shook Michael's hand, "Deal."

The next day, Angelo and Michael walked into the gym carry-ing gym bags and wearing workout attire. The interior was a lot smaller then they'd anticipated and much dirtier then they could have imagined. There was a young, heavily tattooed, muscular male working the front desk. Angelo approached the guy, put his gym bag on the counter, and asked, "Hey boss, how ya doing?"

Twenty-four-year-old Shaun McCullen smiled to himself. *Since the popularity of the Ultimate Fighting Championship, every Joe Blow out there wants to be a cage fighter. Here we go again, two old dudes having a midlife crisis who now want to be badasses.* Under his breath, he looked at the shorter, stiffer-looking man and said, "You got to be fucking kidding me."

Angelo ignored the comment and started up again, "Me and my brother-in-law are looking to get in shape. How much to join?"

Shaun shook his head and said, sarcastically, "Hey Pops, this ain't no country for old men. I suggest you guys try yoga or some other shit."

Angelo smiled because it was a good one, and said, "Very funny, wiseass. How much?"

"Money ain't the problem. Nah, the problem is, I can't have two guys trying to recapture their youth come into my gym and get hurt, and then try to sue us."

Angelo offered, "Listen kid, we'll be fine. My brother-in-law here happens to be a black belt in Karate."

Shaun took a good look at Michael and laughed, "Yeah, right. If you guys want in, then you got to prove you can hang with the other guys."

"Then bring it on," Angelo simply answered.

Angelo gave Michael a big grin and they followed Shaun into the middle of the gym. There was a modified cage with a dirty, bloodstained floor. Shaun pointed in the direction of a bunch of fighters working on heavy bags and asked Angelo, "Which one of you wants to go first with Conan?"

Michael believed this was his opportunity to show Angelo what he was made of. He turned to him, and said, "I got this. I was number one in the academy in defensive tactics."

"Go get 'em, killer," Angelo said, shaking his head.

Angelo helped Michael put on his boxing gloves and handed him his mouthpiece. Michael walked into the middle of the floor and proceeded to engage in some type of strange warm-up exercises. Angelo wasn't really sure if he was warming up or having an epileptic fit. His opponent, a two-hundred-and-thirty pound, heavily-muscled Brazilian named Conan, walked into the cage. Michael couldn't believe the size of the guy, and started thinking that maybe he'd bitten off a little more than he could chew.

They met in the center of the cage and touched gloves in a sign of respect. They circled each other for several seconds and, to Angelo's surprise, Michael moved pretty well for such a tightass. As the combatants moved forward to engage, Conan jumped into the air using his right hand in a superman punch like a piston, and connected flush on Michael's jaw. Michael wobbled as his knees buckled, looking like a drunken man stepping into potholes. Conan actually stepped back instead of finishing him, giving Michael a chance to either recover or quit.

When the punch connected, Michael saw bright white flashes, and heard a buzzing sound somewhere deep inside his head. He also tasted a strange, coppery taste in the back of his mouth. He could have taken a knee and quit, but an old jarhead never quits—he improvises, adapts and overcomes. As his vision started to clear, he decided to go for broke, and threw his hardest looping overhand right. Conan saw the punch easily, took a half-step back, and executed a check hook with his left hand, clipping Michael squarely on the chin. This perfect compact punch turned off Michael's lights and he dropped like a stone, knocked out cold. Angelo ran into the ring and attended to his unconscious boss.

Looking down on Michael's limp body, Angelo knew he had to give it to the little guy — he may not have been much of a fighter, but he sure had heart. Angelo knew too many wannabe tough guys who wouldn't have had the balls to even try to throw hands with Conan. Within a few seconds, Michael started to recover and Angelo eventually helped him stand up. He walked him into the bathroom, where Michael proceeded to vomit up his lunch and part of his breakfast.

Ten minutes later, Angelo wrapped his hands with boxing gauze and started his warm up. Shaun McCullen approached Angelo, and shook his head in disappointment. "You boys should quit before you really get hurt," he said in a tone laced with sarcastic regret.

Angelo smiled and answered, "You fuckin' kiddin' me? That looked way too fun for me not to have my turn."

"Sorry, but I can't let you get into the cage. Even though you look like you used to throw some hands back in your day. Pops, your buddy almost got his head knocked off. I can't allow you to fight, there's just no way."

Angelo had a Danny Phillips-like thought and answered, "Five hundred bucks says I can make it three minutes with your boy."

Shaun without hesitation answered, "You're on, grandpa."

Propped up on a nearby stool, Michael gave Angelo a stern look, then shrugged his shoulders and told him, "It's your money."

Shaun walked over to Conan wearing a big smile, and the two had a short conversation. Conan strutted into the cage with an abundance of confidence. This time, there was no respectful touching of gloves. Upon hearing the electronic buzzer, both fighters started towards each other. As Conan stalked around the cage, he immediately recognized Angelo knew what he was doing. The way Angelo bladed his body, giving much less of a target, and the way he tucked his chin to his chest, let Conan know this guy was going to be a little tougher than his little buddy. Conan started by throwing several feeling-out punch combinations. Angelo took them well, rolling with them. He tried answering with a few jabs to Conan's face, but his timing was still off.

Angelo's background was boxing, and for him, these new mixed martial arts guys threw punches at weird angles. Conan was getting tired of playing and decided to put some real pop behind his punches, so he could get this over with. He connected with several shots, but the old bastard did not appear in the least bit fazed by them. Angelo felt Conan's power and knew the guy could hit. *If I can stay up long enough to get this guy's timing down, I might be able to get some respect.*

Conan started getting cocky and threw a lazy jab with his left hand. Angelo timed it perfectly, stepping into him with a straight right hand over the top that caught Conan clean on the chin, buckling his knees. The on-looking fighters were shocked, because no one had ever buckled Conan before. Conan quickly recovered, realizing he had a fight on his hands. Although Conan landed his hardest punches cleanly, over and over, his stubborn opponent would not go down.

Conan's youth and strength that originally seemed to create a mismatch was now being nullified by Angelo's pure technique and experience. After a three-minute war in which both fighters traded heavy punches, Angelo was still on his feet. As the timer alerted them to the end of the round, all the fighters, including Conan himself, approached and congratulated Angelo. They understood he was one of them, and welcomed him into their warrior world.

As Michael watched them spar, he also realized Angelo was the real deal, and was glad he didn't do anything as stupid as challenge him the other day. Michael had never seen a guy able to absorb punishment like Angelo just had. In the punching exchanges, Angelo would take five hits just to give one back. *Well, however unconventional that New York meathead's plan was, he did get us in.* Shaun put his arm on both of their shoulders and said, "You guys need a lot of work, but you both got heart. Welcome to the Hammer House." Shaun reached into his front pocket and removed a giant wad of cash, held together by a rubber band. He peeled off five one-hundred dollar bills and handed them to Angelo as if it were petty change. Michael and Angelo didn't need to say anything to each other to know Shaun was probably doing more than selling gym memberships.

Chapter 22

Leaving the Hammer House, Michael drove back towards the station so Angelo could pick up his personal car and go home. They were heading northbound on I-95, and even though it was way after rush hour, the traffic was backed up as usual. They were barely going two miles an hour, and Michael's head was still buzzing with pain. Angelo commented, "This fucking traffic is worse than New York!"

Michael's headache had put him in a foul mood, and he leaned into Angelo snarling, "You know what, Angelo? What is it with you New Yorkers? It pisses me off with your attitudes, your swagger, and your freaking New York Jets. Why do you guys think you're so much better than us in Florida?"

Angelo was not offended by the question. "It's not that we're better, it's more like we're just proud of our city," Angelo replied with a straight answer.

Now here was a topic Angelo could get into. He could talk for hours about his beloved New York. He took a sip of his protein drink and dove passionately into his speech, "Here's the thing, Mike. New York is a city built on a foundation of solid bedrock. On top of the bedrock is concrete, it's a virtual city of stone. Now, Miami was built on swamplands, marshes, and beaches. It's soft, like a city of sand. When you stand on the stone in New York, it supports you, like our neighborhoods do. Our neighborhoods go back many generations of families, and most New Yorkers will never leave their beloved city. They, in turn, will pass on their history and moral character to their next generations, which filters back into the neighborhoods. That means your word and reputation is everything.

"When you stand on sand, it doesn't really support you, it avoids you, it slinks to the side in order to escape taking on the responsibility and the weight of a man. It's like the people here, transients. They come in and out with the tide, just like the sand at the beach. It's the city where they say 'fake it till you make it' and other bullshit lines. A guy can come down here and lease a Ferrari and penthouse and then tell everyone he's a big shot millionaire. 'Cause nobody knows him, there's no neighborhood for him to betray. The only difference between Miami and a city like Las Vegas is at least the people in Vegas know it's all an illusion."

Thinking about what Angelo had said, Michael couldn't think of a single reply.

Angelo took another sip of his protein drink and continued, "The one thing I will give you about this place is, like the sand at the beach, even when you leave, some of it stays with you."

Michael glanced over at the big goon in his passenger seat. *Maybe this guy isn't as stupid as he looks.*

Thirty minutes later, exhausted, sore, and with the worst headache he could ever remember, Michael drove up to the front of his house. As he approached the door, he heard music blaring from inside the house. He put his gym bag down in the hallway, and marched into the living room, where Amanda was hanging out with several of her friends. Michael didn't recognize two of the guys sitting on his couch who looked like weightlifters, but he did know they seemed a little too old to be hanging out with his daughter.

Trying to control his temper, he turned off the stereo and said, "Amanda, it's time for everybody to leave. Please get these people out of my house."

Embarrassed, she said, "It's my house too. Why do you always have to be like that?"

Michael turned to the crowd, waving his arms, "Lets' go, everybody out, the party's over."

Amanda grabbed her purse and exited the house with her friends. Michael followed her outside and grabbed her arm and said, "You're not going anywhere."

Rage behind her eyes, she answered, "You can't keep me locked up forever. I'm not one of your prisoners. If Mom were here, you wouldn't be treating me like this."

Michael's headache went from aching to piercing.

"Well, until you turn eighteen you're my responsibility, and I don't want you hanging out with dirtbags!"

Crying, she ran back into the house and slammed the front door. Michael saw it as the perfect ending to another crappy day. First getting beaten up at work, then abused at home by his own daughter.

Chapter 23

Angelo walked into Hagen's office and immediately knew there was a problem. Hagen was sitting at his desk with a thousand-yard stare on his face. Angelo walked up to him, shook his hand and said, "Jimmy, what's going on? You look like shit."

Shaking his head, Hagen answered in a weak voice, "Have a seat, Ange, my boy. We have a problem . . A real clusterfuck problem."

Angelo took a seat, then a deep breath, "Okay, Jimmy, what did you do?"

"Me? Nothing." Hagen pushed a manila folder across his desk and said, "*Sorry, paisan,* unfortunately it's your ass in the sling this time."

Angelo opened up the folder and saw numerous surveillance photos of him meeting up with one of his pigeons, a term Angelo called his customers who used him as their bookie. The gambler in the picture was a friend of one of the guys Hagen had introduced him to. When Hagen had given Angelo a couple of names of guys he knew who were looking for a local bookie, he'd warned him to stay away from their friends. Wanting to expand his operation, Angelo had taken a few risks and added a few customers Hagen hadn't vouched for.

"Ange, I tried to warn you about going outside my contacts. That guy in the pictures with you is really a Metro Dade undercover named Bryan Alvarez."

Angelo tried to get his brain to work and figure out how he could have been fooled.

"Bottom line is, you walked into an undercover operation targeting organized crime that's been going on for the last six months. Their main objective is the Russian mafia. Ange, they got you not only on video surveillance but they also have audio on you."

Angelo was really starting to sweat now, not because he was worried about getting arrested and losing his job, but the fact that he would be letting Eddie down because he'd once again fucked up.

"What are we going to do, boss?" Angelo asked in an almost desperate voice.

Hagen shook his head like a father who was disappointed at his son for the first time. It was also the first time Angelo had ever called him boss. Hagen ran his fingers through his thinning grey hair, and said, "Alright, for now I need you to do absolutely nothing. Ange, until I can figure out how deep your ass is in this thing, I don't want you calling New York or trying to have your cousin reach out to someone to fix it, because that would only make it a thousand times worse. Give me a day or two for me to try to work something out. I need you at work to be business as usual, I don't want you acting weird, because then they would know you were tipped off. If Alvarez tries to contact you, just tell him you'll get back to him. Ange, honestly, I don't think I can fix this, but I will give it my best shot, 'cause you have been real loyal to me and I do appreciate the little gifts you've been giving me every other week."

Angelo's head was spinning like a top, but just like in a fight, he always knew he had a puncher's chance, which meant he wasn't out of it *until the fat lady sang, or some shit like that.*

The following day, Angelo got the call to meet Hagen after work at the Red Room Pub. Angelo found Hagen sitting in the back and quickly joined him. Hagen was amazed at how cool and collected Angelo was, because he thought if he'd heard that same news yesterday, he would have been a mess. Angelo ordered an Absolut on the rocks and then got down to business.

"Okay, boss, what have you got?"

Hagen finished his beer and said, "Alright Ange, I reached out real deep on this one. Real deep. I got a hold of an old friend I used to work with in Metro. He in turn will reach out on my behalf to the undercover cop's boss. We are going to go with the story that we have also been working a long-term undercover operation, and I was the one who fucked up and didn't do my D-9 check. Are you familiar with what a D-9 check is?

"No, not really."

"It's an operational plan that must be submitted by supervisors to Florida Department of Law Enforcement before the start of all long-term undercover operations. Its purpose is to prevent separate agencies from overlapping or stepping on each other's investigations. So here's the deal—and I'm doing something I said I would never do, which is putting all my eggs in one basket, and that basket is you. Now I have to fraudulently doctor up all the paperwork of our alleged long-term operation and hope the Chief or that fuck McPherson never catches wind of it. McPherson, especially, would make sure I did some serious prison time, and I'm too old to be rotting away my last years."

After Angelo walked out, Hagen couldn't stop himself from smiling. *This old dog still has a few tricks up his sleeve.* When his latest string of losses at the racetrack started to pinch his wallet, he could have cut out some of the finer things in life. Instead, he came up with a much better idea. *Tedeschi is making good money,* he thought; *with all his scams, he should be giving me more.* He knew he couldn't strong arm Tedeschi, but he could trick him. Hagen put the wheels in motion and used an ex cop who now worked as a private eye to follow Angelo for a few days and get him those pictures. There was no officer Bryan Alvarez. The guy in the photos was really who he said he was, Richie Lefkowitz, a retired bus driver.

The only part of the plan Hagen worried about was what if that lunatic Tedeschi tried to whack the guy. That's why Hagen told Angelo the following day that he had a plan. He wanted Angelo to stew a little but not long enough that he would do something stupid. He also figured that by carrying out this little ruse, he was doing Angelo a big favor. The favor being, that he was waking his ass up to the fact he was getting sloppy. If Angelo wasn't sharp enough to spot that old washed-up private eye tailing him, he could be in trouble in a real investigation. Hopefully, this would teach him a lesson and keep him on his toes. When he told Angelo a week later that they were all in the clear, Angelo did exactly as Hagen predicted, and his little financial tribute to his Lieutenant was now doubled.

Chapter 24

Inside the undercover car after a long day of surveillance, Michael headed to the police station — another day with little to show for it.

"Drop me off at the Hammer House. I'm going to train tonight and try to work that kid Shaun," Angelo said.

"Alright, but let me know immediately if he's going to work with you. You're not ready to start setting up deals, and we have certain procedures for everything."

By this time, Angelo knew what a stickler Michael was about procedure and therefore kept his mouth shut and nodded his head in acknowledgement.

"Before I drop you off, I got to do a quick surveillance and check on a subject."

Michael parked the UC car down the block from an outdoor restaurant. Twenty minutes went by and Angelo started getting restless because the Hammer House would be closing in two hours. Michael watched as his daughter exited the business and took off her waitress apron. Although half a block away, Amanda easily spotted him. She stopped walking, turned, gave him a one-finger salute, and jumped into the passenger side of her girlfriend's car, and they drove away.

Trying not to laugh, Angelo said, "I think we were made, who is she?"

"My daughter Amanda, and don't ask."

"Don't worry, I don't get into other people's business, but

not for nothin', spying on your daughter? I don't think that's a good idea."

"This is coming from a guy who raised how many kids?"

"I'm just saying that doesn't seem the way to build trust, that's all," Angelo said.

"Now I've seen everything—the guy who bangs every filthy stripper that walks is giving me advice on how to raise my daughter. Unbelievable!"

Angelo shrugged his shoulders, "Not for nuttin', I'm just saying."

Angelo was inside the musty locker room of the Hammer House gym. He was slouched on a corroded metal folding chair, totally exhausted and sweaty from his workout. As he slowly unraveled his hand wraps, Shaun walked in and sat down on the bench next to him.

"Good job today, you seem to be getting your timing down. You just got to watch out for those leg kicks."

Angelo waited for his breathing to return to normal before he replied, "Yeah, it's all starting to come back to me, but the problem is, it's taking too long to recover from my workouts. And everything in my body fuckin' hurts."

Shaun's eyebrows raised and he asked, "Maybe you need to take some vitamins?"

"Oh yeah, what kind of vitamins you got in mind?"

Shaun took a quick look over his shoulder and then turned back to Angelo, "I'm talking about vitamin S, a little juice. You know about that?"

"I did a cycle with some Dbol years ago, but I heard the stuff is hard to get nowadays."

"I'll take care of you, no worries, why don't you start with a little testosterone and HGH?"

"HGH?" Angelo asked, skeptically.

"Yeah human growth hormone. It's the fountain of youth."

"How much?"

"Give me four grand for an eight-week cycle."

"What, are you kidding me? Try again. How about three grand and throw in some Vicodins for my back?"

"Vikes are a little harder to get, make it thirty-five hundred and I will throw in a dozen Vikes."

Angelo reached his hand out and they shook on the deal.

"Done. And that includes needles?"

"Yeah I'll throw them in, the small ones diabetics use."

Angelo stood up and stretched his aching back.

"I'll tell you what, if it's good stuff, I will get you some orders from my other old guy buddies who need a little help."

"Cool," answered Shaun.

Inside the Sushi Siam restaurant, Mark McPherson was meeting with Michael. They were sitting at the well-concealed police table in the back, where the cops sat throughout their shifts. Far too often, members of the public liked to approach the cops when they were eating, and ask questions like, "My cousin's wife's friend knew a guy that got a ticket for . . . blah, blah, blah." This way, they could mostly avoid that kind of distraction.

Mark finished his plate of spicy tuna rolls and turned to Michael.

"So, what have you got for me so far?"

Michael pulled out a small notepad.

"Well, in his first two months, I have at least several excessive use of force complaints, I documented three separate cases of insubordination, and one case of a preventable car accident where he damaged thousands of dollars of city equipment."

After wiping his mouth with his napkin, Mark took his time then said, disdainfully, "Really, Michael, are you serious? Because you better get me more than that. I've been telling A.S.A. Waxman that we got a real bad apple on our hands, and I would be bringing him hard evidence."

Michael shook his head.

"That's not going to be as easy as you think. This guy is pretty sharp, in a street-smart type of way. On two separate occasions, I left money and jewelry in spots where I thought he would take them, and he hasn't yet. You got to be patient with a guy like this. I know dirty cops and this guy will eventually screw up, and I mean screw up big time."

Chapter 25

Angelo, Lorenzo, and Joey Salerno were seated inside the VIP room in Lorenzo's strip club. The exclusive room with brown leather couches was not only used for upscale clientele, but also doubled as an office for his less official meetings. The room was on the second floor, and with its giant one-way reflective mirror, it overlooked the entire club. There was a phone in the room that went straight to the floor manager's phone so the big rollers could choose their women and order their drinks. The waitresses wouldn't enter the room unless they were given permission. A small mechanical dumb waiter sent drinks up to the room straight from the main bar. Angelo was drinking his usual Absolut, while Joey and Lorenzo drank Jack and cokes.

Angelo leaned into Joey and said over the music, "Why didn't you tell me you were coming down? I would have taken off for a few days, and we could have hit the casinos in the Bahamas."

"Nah, I just found out at the last minute about a business deal. I'm only here for two days," Joey answered.

"That sucks. You need somethin'?"

Joey wiped his mouth.

"I'm having my first meeting with a mid-level Russian guy down here, named Sacha. My dad wants me to iron out a few things and feel him out. Apparently, Sacha has been stepping on some toes of friends of ours, and I'm down here to play peacekeeper. Louie and Steve are also flying in, and they'll make sure nothing gets too froggy in the meeting. I'll need some handguns like .45s, and I need you to find out if any of your guys are in the area. I have been photographed by the Feds more than enough times in the last few weeks."

Angelo thought about what Joey just said, a small knot formed in his stomach—he downed his drink in one gulp . . .

"The guns are no problem. I got clean, untraceable ones right out of the factory. About the counter-surveillance, I got to speak to Hagen, 'cause he still has much more clearance then me."

"Good, take care of that. The last thing is, my father wants the most current list of all the undercover guys you work with. Try to also give us physical descriptions and addresses."

Angelo felt the knot in his stomach get a little tighter, because he knew that wouldn't be so easy.

"Yeah, Joe, he's got to give me a little time to work on that. I'm just starting to get a feel for these guys. I've also been starting to earn a little bit down here. Here's something for your dad." Angelo handed Joey an envelope swollen with a wad of one-hundred dollar bills.

"Okay, I'll let him know you're on it, and thanks for the tribute. Now, which one of these skanks have you already fucked here, 'cause I don't want my dick going into anything after you?"

Spotting several guys with young girls walking into the club, Angelo thought something seemed a little off about the group. Making his way to the bathroom about ten minutes later, he spotted the group sitting at a table. He immediately recognized one of the heavily made-up young girls as Michael's daughter, Amanda. He went back upstairs, finished his drink, and turned to Joe and Lorenzo—who were now getting lap dances by several strippers.

"Fellas, I gotta go. I'll call you later, Joe."

He went over to Amanda's table and grabbed her arm, lifting her out of her seat with ease. The guys she was with started to protest, but Angelo gave them a hard look and they immediately quieted down. He grabbed the hand of one of the guys still standing and shook it with an extremely tight grip. As the guy winced, Angelo introduced himself.

"How ya doing? I'm her uncle Angelo; everyone calls me 'the mouthraper.' I got that nickname in prison. Youse guys got a problem with me taking my niece here home?"

The guy whose hand Angelo had grabbed didn't say a word, and neither did anyone else in the group. Angelo pulled Amanda off to the side to talk to her. Amanda first thought that Angelo worked for the club as a manager or bouncer and that he must have known that her I.D. was fake. She decided to try to play it tough and said, "I don't know you, get off me!"

Angelo quickly snapped back, "Yeah, but I know you — I work with your dad."

Amanda knew the jig was up. "Ah shit . . ."

Joey looked up from between the dancer's Double-D implants and saw Angelo downstairs. He moved the girl off his lap and turned to Lorenzo, "That broad looks a little young even for Angelo."

Lorenzo moved his girl to the side to take a look.

"He ain't banging that, she looks like she's sixteen, tops. She shouldn't even be in the club. Fucking doorman, I got to fire his ass. Don't worry about Ange, he's been doing real good down here. You know he's back with his ex, Mia, right?

Joey was taken aback for a moment, then he said, "No, he didn't say anything to me about it."

Joey thought about Mia, and was immediately furious. *I was the one who first spotted her working in the restaurant all those years ago. Every night, I'm dropping her big tips of fifties and hundreds, but she was just too good to go on a date with me. Always giving me the bullshit about having some make-believe boyfriend. To make matters worse, every time Angelo comes in she's always jocking him. Yeah, I remember telling Ange to go ahead and try hitting on her, but I thought he would have no chance, 'cause she's a stuck-up bitch. When I heard he was taking her out, I figured he would do the right thing and just bang her two or three times and then dump her. No, not this guy, not my boy Ange, next thing I hear they're living together. What kind of friend does that? 'Cause now, he's just rubbing it in my face. Then, to make matters worse, every fucking holiday he's gotta bring her to my dad's house, making me look like a fuckin' finocchio.*

One New Years Eve at Eddie's house, Joey got really drunk by downing a whole bottle of Sambuca. In his inebriated state, he believed Mia was looking at him all night with lust in her eyes. He waited till she went to use the upstairs bathroom and followed her up to make his move. As she walked out of the bathroom, he gave her a playful shove and forced her back inside and shut the door. Mia played it cool, knowing this could start a big problem and tried to joke her way out of the situation. When Joey didn't take the hint and started putting his hands on her, without hesitation she hit him in the face with the ceramic soap dish. Joey's first thought was to snap her neck, but decided that she wasn't worth ruining a holiday over, and let her go. Not wanting Angelo to catch any wind of the incident, Mia grabbed her coat and ran outside to smoke several cigarettes. At the table, Eddie asked Joey what happened to his red, swollen face. Joey laughed and said he drunkenly walked into the bathroom door just as Mia exited. All eyes turned to Mia, and she confirmed the story, prompting a big laugh from everyone, including the clueless Angelo.

Inside his strip club, Lorenzo added, "Yeah, she's practically living with him now, and she flies down almost every other weekend. Your old man would be proud of him, he's starting to really settle down and keep his head together. Matter of fact, I can't even remember when was the last time he lost his temper."

"Listen, my old man's always proud of Angelo," he paused to wipe his mouth. "Me, all he does is give me grief. If I pulled half the shit Angelo has pulled, my father would have disowned me, but not Ange — Ange is his boy."

Lorenzo was getting a little uncomfortable with the direction of the conversation and tried to redirect it by saying, "You're kidding me! Your dad busts Angelo's balls all the time."

Joey continued, "Ah, you're just saying that 'cause he's your cousin. You must have heard that he put his hands on Carmine's cousin, Nicky. You know how much heat my dad had to deal with to straighten that one out. Do you have any idea how much aggravation and stress that caused him? If that was me beatin' Nicky, I don't think I would have gotten a pass as easy as Ange."

Lorenzo was surprised by Joey's comments, but he kept it to himself.

"Joe, you're the next in line after your dad retires. He rides you hard 'cause you will soon be making all the tough decisions. I love Ange, but you know he will always be a worker — because of his bloodline, he could never be a made guy."

Wanting to avoid any dissention with Angelo or Lorenzo, Joey changed gears like his dad had taught him.

"Don't get me wrong, Lorenzo. I love Angelo like he's my brother. Shit, me and him have been through so much crazy shit in the last twenty years, forget about it. I just get a little worked up, that's all. You know me: when I swing, I swing for the fuckin' fences."

Chapter 26

Inside Angelo's Escalade, Amanda sat silently with her arms folded for ten straight minutes. Finally, she turned to him and asked in an accusing tone, "So, now you're taking me to my dad?"

"Do I look like a rat or a probation officer? I'm taking you to the diner cause I'm hungry, and I want a cheeseburger. Also, you shouldn't be in a club like that."

"Oh yeah, what were you doing there?" Amanda snapped back.

"I like those type of women—shallow, nasty, with hearts as dark as mine."

"You sure don't seem like a cop."

Angelo, smiling, "I get that all the time."

Angelo pulled into the Flashback Diner just off Hallandale Beach Boulevard. For a New Yorker, diners were essential for survival. It's where they ate breakfast, lunch, and sometimes even dinner, but always after a night of drinking, the diner was the place to go and debrief with friends on the night's adventures. If Angelo had a dollar for every 4:00 a.m. cheeseburger with French fries smothered in turkey gravy he ever ate, he would have been a millionaire.

Once at the diner, Angelo picked a booth in the rear, avoiding all overhead vents, and sat down with Amanda. A waitress approached for their order. Angelo ordered a Cheeseburger Deluxe and a Coke.

Amanda picked up the menu, skimmed through it, put it down, her decision made—French Fries and a diet Coke.

The waitress took the menus and left. They sat quietly looking at each other. Finally Angelo asked, "So what's your beef with your old man?"

"What's it your business?" Amanda asked.

"Humor me."

"He doesn't trust me, and is always on my ass for every little thing. You know what it's like having a cop for a father?"

"Can't say I would."

The waitress brought their food and drinks. Angelo was hungry and started on his Burger, Amanda poured some ketchup on her plate and used a fry to make designs on her plate.

"It sucks, he thinks everything's a conspiracy and all my friends are no good. I'm not about all that negative energy. My Kabbalah teacher thinks he's a burden to my karmic force. And then he won't buy me an iPhone—I just have this crappy little flip phone. It's seriously embarrassing!"

Angelo shook his head and tried not to laugh. He pointed to a four-inch scar on his scalp.

"You know what my father gave me? See this? He busted my head open when I was around eleven and gave me twenty stitches. He broke my hand once for talking back to him. He was a nasty alcoholic who beat on me and my mom so many times I can't even remember. So I don't know, not for nuttin', but maybe your dad ain't so bad."

"That's messed up."

"Look kid, I'll give you a lift home after we eat. If you want to go in or leave, that's your business but trust me, your dad ain't that bad."

"You know, for a cop you're okay, Angelo."

With his best comedic Brooklyn attitude, Angelo said, "Thanks kid, now eat your fuckin' fries, 'cause fuhgedaboutit, I'm paying for them."

Chapter 27

Now that he'd established himself in South Florida, Viktor Matyushenko was finally beginning to make some real money. He started off by building a small burglary ring. He trained his thieves to target vehicles in shopping center parking lots, gas stations, and gym parking lots. He used only young illegals who needed quick cash, and who had at least some level of intelligence. He broke the ring into three separate teams, mostly comprised of South Americans.

Team One would conduct surveillance on tourists and people buying electronic devices. Their most successful tactic would be to follow customers who'd just purchased high-end laptops from electronic stores. If the people placed the items in their trunks or back seats and walked away to shop elsewhere, the team would immediately hit on the vehicle. They would make entry either through the window, using a piece of a spark plug to silently shatter the safety glass, or via the driver's door, using a screwdriver to jimmy the lock. Viktor had several connections in South America, where he would ship and resell the items for just under the original retail price in the States.

Team Two would work all the gas stations in Dade and Broward County. They would set up somewhere inside or close to the station and wait for a female to start pumping gas. Most women would only take their credit cards to the pump, leaving their purses on the passenger seats with the car doors unlocked. The thieves would either drive up to the vehicle, or covertly sneak over on foot and snatch the unattended purse. Many times, the women were either on the phone or not paying attention, and had no idea their purse had just been stolen.

Working the gym parking lots, Team Three knew that most people visiting gyms would leave their valuables inside their car. Once they'd seen someone pull in and park, they knew they had at least an hour before the person returned . . . only to discover their vehicle had been broken into.

When his guys stole wallets or purses containing credit cards, they were instructed to go immediately to the nearest electronic store and purchase high-end electronics. On rare occasions when the local police caught some of the teams, the arrestees didn't know enough about how the operation worked to give up any info on Viktor. After the arrests, they would usually be held in a detention center until they could be deported.

After purchasing his first warehouse through a dummy corporation, Viktor started dealing weapons locally. Impressed by his professionalism toward his electronic operations, his South American contacts also started purchasing the weapons. After six months, Viktor no longer dealt in anything but high-powered weapons, and had already accumulated over five million dollars in cash and properties. One night, while driving his leased white Bentley from Miami's famous Star Island, he was pulled over by a Miami Beach police officer for weaving in and out of lanes. Viktor had only been arrested twice in New York and had purposely flown under the radar in Miami, working hard to stay out of trouble. Seeing the unbelievable potential Miami offered, he wanted to accumulate as much money as quickly as he could.

When he failed the road side sobriety test, he wasn't worried in the least because he now knew he had enough money to buy himself out of most criminal charges, especially something as minor as a D.U.I. After blowing a .16, which was double the legal limit, Viktor was transported to Dade County

Jail for processing. Dade County Jail, one of the oldest such buildings still operating in the country, was known to most as a filthy hellhole. For Viktor, however, it was a country club that included a delicious peanut butter and jelly sandwich.

In the next several weeks, Viktor's confidence was soon shattered. After making numerous donations to many law enforcement funds and judges' campaigns, he was furious when his lawyer told him the case was still open. Despite several more attempts at bribing government officials, Viktor was nowhere closer to squashing his arrest. It was what the Russian old timers in New York had tried to teach him — that it would either take years of bribery or some type of deal with the Italian mafia to get the political connections that really mattered in this country.

Viktor's other main problem was his infatuation with his much younger new Cuban girlfriend, Lucinda Castro. Women were always his Achilles Heel and his latest girlfriend had him under her spell. He first saw her when he was living in his first apartment in Miami Beach. She lived down the hall from him and for the first six months, she wouldn't give him the time of day. Lucinda was working as a supporting actress on a Spanish soap opera at the time. Although she acquired a degree of fame from her TV work, most people didn't realize that the non-union Spanish soap stars really didn't make a whole lot of money.

Viktor was finally able to get her attention when he promised to financially back a local independent filmmaker. Viktor's only request was that she be the lead in their next project. Lucinda got the role and Viktor got himself a new outrageously beautiful young girlfriend. Unfortunately, Lucinda didn't come alone or cheap; she had a younger brother Jorge, who always seemed to be in trouble.

At only twenty-five years old, Jorge drove a Porsche despite the fact he couldn't hold onto a job and basically lived off his sister. He walked around with a huge chip on his shoulder because, being one of those types who felt he was entitled to the finer things in life. Often referred to as the famous Lucinda's little brother made him feel even more slighted. Jorge spent much of his time during the day at Vortex, an exclusive South Beach outdoor pool café. It was located on the roof of the most expensive hotel on Ocean Drive.

Half the time he spent picking up women, the other half collecting some extra cash by selling "Drank" and cocaine. "Drank" was Promethazine Codeine syrup—basically, liquid Vicodin/Hydrocodone mixed with Sprite. It was the latest in designer drugs and definitely a high-ticket item that Jorge could make a quick buck on. Jorge's good friend Emilio Periso provided him with as much product as he could sell. Only a few months into his new lucrative business, a drug task force arrested Emilio. The arrest didn't discourage Jorge at all, because this was the easiest money he'd ever made. Hastily, he found another supplier at a gym he used to train at, called the Hammer House.

Lucinda decided her new boyfriend Viktor would be the perfect person to straighten out her troubled brother. She was aware of Jorge's drug dealing and was constantly begging him to quit, in fear of him getting hurt. Jorge told her the only way he would quit is if he managed to find a quicker or more profitable way to make money. Always trying to appease her requests, Viktor helped Jorge find many different types of legitimate jobs that all paid well. Somehow, Jorge managed not only to lose the job due to his attitude, but also damage Viktor's reputation with those contacts.

With few other options left, Viktor decided to put Jorge to work at his warehouse, and try to teach him the business. For his part, Jorge was very eager to learn how Viktor had obtained all his wealth in such a short period of time. Within the first month of working at the warehouse, Jorge was already scheming about how to supplant Viktor and take over the entire business. Viktor's relationship with Jorge was constantly being pushed to the brink, and several times he even contemplated tossing Jorge off a roof, but his weakness for Lucinda always overruled any ideas of helping Jorge learn how to fly.

Chapter 28

Michael and Angelo were in the UC car, parked in the middle of a large shopping center. They were watching a jewelry store that had been robbed several times in the last few weeks. Michael was rummaging through his last bag of cashew nuts that were doing nothing to alleviate his hunger.

He looked at Angelo, who was watching the store through binoculars and asked, "So what part of Italy is your family from?"

Angelo was caught off guard by the question. Where he was from, he wasn't used to people asking personal information. He had friends for years whose last names he didn't know. *Shit, there were guys in the neighborhood I knew since I was a kid, and I only knew their nicknames.* He turned to Mike and snapped a little harder then he should have.

"Sorry, Mike, but that ain't none of your fuckin' business!"

Michael didn't say anything for a little while, but more to himself, he sighed.

"So that's how it is, okay, okay."

After an uncomfortable silence between them, Angelo realized that since Mike wasn't from Brooklyn, he didn't know the rules. The one thing Angelo didn't tolerate was disrespect, and in this instance he was the one who was wrong. He turned to Mike and said in an almost apologetic tone, "Naples."

"Huh?" Mike asked.

"You asked where my family was from, and I'm telling

you. My dad was from Naples."

Michael perked up as if he already knew it and said, "I figured as much. I knew you were from either Naples, Rome, or Piedmont."

Angelo was caught off guard again.

"How could you possibly have guessed that?"

"My grandfather was a soldier in World War II and he was attached to the 36th Infantry division and they were in Italy from 1943 to 1944."

"No shit," remarked Angelo.

"Yeah, he used to tell us that it was the most amazing and beautiful country. I always had an interest in Italian history, so I did a little research on the word Tedeschi. Obviously, you know Tedeschi or Tedesco in Italian means German, and you also might have some Jewish blood in your family tree."

"Man, you really do your homework, and I'm impressed, but you got it all wrong."

"How do you figure? It's all clearly documented," Mike said, a bit confused.

"'Cause very few people know this, and I'm only tellin' you 'cause a minute ago I was disrespectful to you—and for that I apologize—my family's real last name was Moretti, and . . ."

Michael's cell phone started to ring and he answered it after looking at the screen and seeing it was a private number. Angelo was glad for the reprieve and hoped that Mike would forget about the subject of his family's past.

"Detective Frakes," Michael said into the phone.

Amanda was on the line, crying and slurring her words.

"Dad . . . they won't let me go . . . and they must have put something in my drink."

Angelo saw Michael's face change and instantly knew something was seriously wrong.

"Where are you? He shouted.

Over the phone, Michael heard a struggle and heard his daughter scream before the line went dead. He tried calling his daughter's cell phone back and it went straight to voice mail. Not even looking at Angelo, he put the car in gear and ripped out of the parking spot, smoking the tires. He screamed, "Fuck! We got to get to the station, I have an emergency!"

Knowing Michael rarely swore, Angelo asked, "What's up?"

"That was Amanda, and she sounded drugged up. All she said was they wouldn't let her go. I got to get a hold of the team and have them start using the triggerfish to track her cell phone."

Accelerating through the parking lot, he barely missed hitting several cars.

"I got to get to the station."

"Mike, hold on a second."

"No, we gotta fucking . . ."

He cut Michael off and grabbed him by the shirt, trying to get him to snap out of it.

"Mike, Mike! Relax! If you lose your fuckin' cool, you're gonna make mistakes, and time is the biggest factor. Get on the phone, get a hold of Jimmie Burke, and let the team start to work the triggerfish. Let me call my cousin and see if he can help us track down where she's at."

At first, Mike didn't even acknowledge Angelo, but eventually his words hit home and he pulled the car over. After taking several deep breaths, he asked Angelo to repeat what he'd just said. Nodding slowly, Michael agreed to follow Angelo's advice, and they got on their phones and started making calls.

Several minutes later, Angelo turned to Michael.

"Alright, one of the shitheads your daughter hangs out with works at The Sport Clinic Gym as a trainer, and he should be working there now."

"What if he won't talk?"

Unable to stop his smile, Angelo answered him.

"Let me handle that."

The Sport Clinic Gym was just ten minutes away, on the north side of town. It was a smaller gym that catered to mostly high-end clientele. Angelo and Mike entered and showed their badges to a front desk employee wearing a nametag of Pete Jr. As they walked through the gym, Michael pointed to a muscular trainer and said, "That's him. He knows my daughter, I've seen him at the house."

Angelo approached the guy, who was in the middle of training a client.

"Hey pal, I need to talk to you," barked Angelo.

The trainer didn't even look at Angelo, and said smugly, "Can't you see, bro, I'm working with my client? Come back in an hour."

Well, I gave him his chance. Angelo shrugged his shoulders at Michael, grabbed the trainer by the back of the neck and shoved him forcibly across the gym floor. He opened the men's locker room door and gave the trainer one last shove inside. Everyone in the gym stopped what they were doing and converged on the locker to see what was going on. Michael posted himself outside the door and, in his most authoritative voice, announced: "Police business. Everything's okay, go back to your workouts."

Inside the locker room, Angelo stood face-to-face — or rather, chest-to-face — with the short trainer.

"I need you to answer some questions."

"I don't talk to the fucking cops without my lawyer."

Angelo had to laugh at that one, because this kid was making it way too fun for him, and said,

"That's okay, 'cause I'm not a real cop."

Angelo reached into his sock and pulled out several small Ziploc baggies of cocaine. The trainer was mesmerized with Angelo's actions, and couldn't believe what this guy was doing. Angelo grabbed the waistband of the trainer's sweat pants and underwear and dropped the bags inside. The reality of what was about to happen started to hit the trainer, but it was a little too late.

"What the hell are you . . . ?" he stammered.

Still smiling, Angelo started pummeling the trainer with his fists, knees, and feet. Outside, the crowd overheard the commotion and again began to walk towards Michael.

"Folks, it's okay. Everything's fine, just regular police business."

At the precise moment Michael said the word "business," the trainer's bloody head smashed through the thin door. *Ahhh, fuck it!* Michael said to himself, as he looked around uncomfortably. Angelo dragged the trainer out of the locker room and slammed him to the floor of the main room. He then forced the trainer's hands behind his back and 'cuffed him. Slightly out of breath, in a voice loud enough for the crowd to hear, he spoke to Michael.

"I think he's hidden the drugs in his underwear."

Michael reached into the stunned trainer's underwear, and pulled out the small Ziploc baggies, displaying them for the crowd to see.

Michael knelt down and asked the trainer, "You want to talk now and work off these charges?"

The trainer who was only now starting to recuperate from his beating, the trainer told Michael in a trembling voice, "I'll talk, I'll talk, whatever you need to know!"

Inside the UC car, the trainer—whose name turned out to be Chad—rode in the backseat with Angelo. They took him with them to verify they were going to the right house, and to make sure he wasn't bullshitting them. The house was all the way out west in Broward County, not far from the Everglades National Park. As they pulled up to a quiet, unassuming block, they saw a house on the corner, loaded with cars and motorcycles.

"That's it," said Chad.

Angelo shoved the bewildered Chad out the rear door and told him, "Get the fuck outta here! And jerkoff, next time I say I want to talk, you better tell me everything I wanna know."

They watched Chad walk the opposite way as fast as he could, looking back every few steps as if worried they would change their minds and snatch him up again.

"Jimmie and the guys won't be here for at least ten more minutes. We got no backup, but I don't give a damn—it's my daughter, I'm going in."

"That's my man," Angelo said as he patted Michael's shoulder. "But don't worry, backup just arrived."

Michael hadn't noticed the black Chevy Suburban that slipped in behind them as they traveled west on Highway 595. Now, it pulled up and parked behind their car, and Lorenzo and a very large, bald guy got out. Earlier, as they left the gym and once Angelo had known they were heading west, he'd told Lorenzo to wait for him on the service road of 595. Angelo gave Lorenzo a quick hug, shook hands with the big guy, and walked with them to the back of the truck.

"Mike, you already know my cousin, and this is our buddy, Frankie The Fixer." Michael shook hands with both of them. Lorenzo removed a large duffel bag from the back of the truck. As he opened it, Michael saw that it contained numerous bats, pipes and what appeared to be an axe. He handed a wooden baseball bat to Frankie, which looked small in his giant hands, and then took one for himself and asked, "Ange, wood or aluminum?"

"Let me try the aluminum, I hear it improves your swing. Mike, let's keep it simple—you go to the front door and distract them, and we'll go through the backyard."

"Okay, let's just hurry," Michael said frantically.

Angelo, Frankie, and Lorenzo went around the back of the house and located an unlocked gate that opened to the backyard. The demeanor of all three men was professional, as if they were factory workers clocking in for their normal day's shift. Once in the backyard, they didn't encounter anyone, but heard loud music pumping from inside the house. They made entrance into the house through a sliding glass door that led into a large living room. The hulking Frankie went in first, followed by Angelo, who was holding his gun in one hand and the bat in the other. Lorenzo secured the rear and stayed just outside the sliding glass doors.

As Frankie stepped into the living room, he saw about nine people standing, drinking, and lounging on couches. Several of the men at the party were heavily tattooed and muscular. The women all looked pretty good to Frankie, and he hoped after the job was over he could try to get a phone number or two. There was some cocaine residue scattered on a glass coffee table, and the entire room was filled with a heavy fog of marijuana smoke.

A man about twenty-five years old launched himself off the couch at Frankie, and shouted, "What the fuck are you doing in my house?"

Frankie didn't even use his bat, but picked the guy up by the throat with one hand, spun him around and choke-slammed him into a small bar. Two of the other large guys in the room rushed Angelo. One-handed, he swung the bat, connecting with a clean shot to the first guy's jaw, shattering it along with several teeth. After watching his buddy go down, the second guy hesitated, and seeing no other threats, Angelo tucked his gun into his rear waistband.

While this was going on, Michael was banging on the front door. Realizing he probably couldn't be heard over the loud music, he opened the unlocked front door and walked into a hallway. A large, bearded biker-looking guy with a beer in hand, immediately confronted him. The bearded giant looked to be in his late 40s. *You pathetic old fuck, partying with a bunch of kids.* Michael started frantically telling the guy he had an emergency and needed to use the phone. The biker lifted his beefy arm like a tollgate, and told him to fuck off and get out before he got hurt. Michael heard the loud commotion coming from further inside the house, and knew Angelo and the guys must be already doing damage. Michael whipped his gun out, pointed it in the biker's face and shouted, "Shitbird! I will give you one chance to tell me where my daughter is."

The biker put his hands up, dropped his beer, and coolly answered, "Take it easy, man."

"Where's my fucking daughter Amanda?"

"I don't know any Amanda, I just came here to drop off some weed."

Michael grabbed the bloated biker and shoved him towards a flight of stairs and handcuffed him to the metal railing.

He sprinted into the house with his gun in the low ready position, and his badge hanging outside his shirt. Reaching the living room, he saw several males lying around the room in weird positions, bleeding heavily and apparently unconscious. Angelo was in the process of choking and slapping a guy on the floor. In between chokes and slaps, he would ask, "Where the fuck is Amanda?"

The other people in the room were now cowering in a corner, where Frankie was holding them at bay with his bloody bat. A skinny young guy bolted past Frankie and ran out through the sliding glass doors into the backyard. Even from inside and over the music, they all heard the loud thump of Lorenzo's aluminum bat, knowing the young man was probably now asleep. The guy Angelo was interrogating wisely spat out, "They're in the back bedroom." Angelo hit the guy with his hammer-like fist and knocked him out. He and Michael dashed down the hallway kicking in doors, looking for the bedroom.

Angelo kicked at a solid oak door and it barely budged. He took a running start and used his shoulder and all his weight to batter it open. The door exploded off its hinges and landed a few feet inside the room. Angelo saw a young guy on a bed trying to rip Amanda's clothes off as she weakly fought him off. Her exaggerated and slow, sloppy movements made her appear highly intoxicated or drugged, or both.

The shirtless male with a face full of acne scars turned towards Angelo. He glanced briefly towards the nightstand, where a small Walther P22 handgun was resting. The would-be rapist realized he couldn't get to it in time, and decided to charge at Angelo head-down, like a football player. Angelo clubbed him viciously on the back of his head and shoulders with the bat, completely stopping his forward momentum. The guy crashed to the floor, face-planted into the cheap carpet, and moaning in pain.

Michael ran into the room and saw his daughter on the bed. Although her face was partially concealed under a sheet, he saw she was crying hysterically and appeared to be hurt. After seeing his daughter in that horrific state, he immediately turned to the downed dirtbag and, without hesitation, started kicking and stomping on the man's head and neck, *you mother-fucking rapist I'll kill you!*

While Michael worked out his frustrations, Angelo went over to Amanda to try to console her and assess her condition. Sitting beside her on the bed, he saw how bad her face had been worked over—her nose definitely looked broken and she was missing several teeth. Angelo didn't say a word, but stood up and calmly walked over to where Michael was still kicking the guy. He pushed Michael out of the way and, without any signs of emotion or thought, pulled his gun from his waistband, and shot the would-be rapist twice in the body and twice in the head.

When the shots rang out, Frankie ran into the bedroom with his bloody bat cocked for the next customer. Dazed, Michael stood frozen in place, staring at the now-dead subject. He wasn't angry with himself for allowing the cold-blooded murder of an unarmed man; it was the fact he was robbed of the pleasure of killing the animal himself. Angelo went over to the subject's nightstand and picked up the Walther. He kneeled next to the body, away from the pooling blood, and placed the gun in the dead subject's hand. He wrapped both of his hands around the subject's and fired the weapon with the dead man's finger. He shot straight up into the ceiling once, and then a few shots into the wall next to the door. Leaving the gun in the dead man's hands, he grabbed Frankie.

"Get her out of here, and have Lorenzo take her to his doctor friend in Hialeah. Pay him in cash and we'll be there in a few hours after we clean up this mess. Our undercover guys, along with the local P.D., will be here any moment."

The big man scooped up Amanda and started to carry her out the door. Michael blocked his path. Angelo walked over to him and placed his arm on his shoulder.

"She's in good hands, Mike. We need to get her out of here now, before our other guys get here."

Michael nodded his head in acknowledgement, and kissed his daughter. Frankie hurried out of the room with the weeping Amanda in his arms.

"You alright?" Angelo asked Michael. Despite still being in a daze he answered, "Yeah, yeah, I'm fine."

Having been in tougher situations many times, Angelo looked Michael in the eyes.

"Alright, here's the deal. We were doing surveillance of this drug house and we heard shots fired. Due to the exigent circumstances of saving lives, we had to make immediate entry. We observed a gang fight, with several subjects wielding bats. The bat-wielding subjects got away, and I had to pop this shithead cause he fired on us. Mike, it's going to be fine. Just relax and let me handle it."

Still in a stupor, Michael walked out of the room while Angelo pulled out the police radio that was clipped on his hip under his shirt. He keyed up the microphone, and said, "India four six three, priority. We have shots fired at a drug house located at 6901 Orange Drive, Davie. Myself and India four hundred are making entry, hold the air . . ."

Angelo walked around the room and started looking through the drawers and closets. In a shoebox, he found a large amount of cash that he impounded in his pocket for safekeeping. He also found another Walther PPK handgun concealed in a high-top sneaker and shoved it in his sock. He then got back on the radio and said, "India four six three, start Fire Rescue lights and sirens. I have one subject down from gunshots, and several suffering from broken bones and impact injuries. I'm starting CPR."

As he exited the room, Angelo saw Jimmie Burke and several of the undercover officers running into the house. Once inside the living room, they handcuffed the rest of the partiers.

Chapter 29

Several hours later, Angelo and Michael arrived at the front of the small doctor's office. The predominantly Cuban neighborhood had numerous small businesses on the streets, including medical offices and pain clinics. They entered the office and were immediately met by the owner of the business, Dr. Alonso. Michael shook the doctor's hand.

"Doc, how's she doing?"

Dr. Alonso answered in a heavy Cuban accent, "Well we had to pump her stomach and she's now on IVs. It looks like she ingested a large amount of G.H.B. Are you familiar with that?"

"Gamma-hydroxybutyrate, the date rape drug. Yeah, it was the big thing a few years ago, but we haven't seen it much lately. "

"If she wasn't brought here in time, she could have easily slipped into a coma and her lungs could have shut down. It probably would have killed her."

"Thanks for everything, doc. When can she go home?" Michael asked, shaking the doctor's hand again.

"I already called in my nurse to stay here with her tonight. I'd rather monitor her vitals all night, just to be sure, but she should be good to go home tomorrow."

"What do I owe you?"

"It's all been taken care of and, of course, there will be no record of this."

Michael shook the doctor's hand one more time and entered

the little examining room. Amanda was lying on a hospital bed with an IV in her arm. Her color was very pale and her eyes were half closed. When she saw her father walk into the room, she perked up out of fear and embarrassment. Michael sat on the edge of the bed and gently took her hand.

"How are you, baby?"

Amanda began crying again, "I'm so sorry, Dad, I'm so sorry."

"It's alright baby, just rest, you're going to be fine."

"You told me to stay away from them and I didn't listen. I'm sorry, I'm sorry."

"Baby, forget all that. I'm just happy you called me when you did, and that you're okay."

"I love you so much, Dad. I'm sorry I've been so shitty to you."

"Baby, I know that, and I miss your mom just as much as you do. If I lost you, I would have nothing to live for. You are my life."

In the other room, Angelo was sitting down with Dr. Alonso, drinking shots of Cuban coffee. They were finishing the last of their negotiations with another doctor who shared office space there. That doctor was ready to retire and he wanted to sell his prescription pads that would also be pre signed. Angelo already had a buyer lined up who would pay big bucks for the pads. Angelo was starting to feel like he was back in the groove and was beginning to make some real good money. Later that night, he was meeting up with a guy who said he had over 100 credit card and ATM account numbers, including the victims' social security numbers and PINs. *A few more weeks of big scores and I'm going to need my old friend Danny Phillips to help me figure out how to hide all this money.*

While wrapping up his business with the doctor, his cell phone rang. It was Joey Salerno and he sounded real pissed. Angelo left the office so he could talk.

"What happened, Joe?"

"The meeting went bad, and Steve took one in the stomach."

Normally, Angelo would have told Joey to drive him to Dr. Alonso's immediately, but with Frakes here, that wasn't going to work.

"Okay, put him in the car and start driving towards Hialeah, and I will arrange a place for him to get taken care of. I'll call you back with the exact address."

Angelo went back inside and spoke to the suddenly popular Dr. Alonso, explaining the new problem. Alonso told him he had a place he could take care of his friend, but this one would cost a lot more money than a drug overdose. Angelo called Joey back, and gave him the address — that of a small veterinarian hospital already closed for the day. Alonso knew he could pay the owner for use of the place and equipment for around three thousand dollars, with no questions asked. At least, that was what he'd been charged last time he'd needed it, for a drug dealer who'd been shot several times.

Twenty minutes later, Joey pulled into the rear of the business. Steve was lying in the back seat, wrapped in numerous bed sheets and in a lot of pain. Joey and Louie carried him in, and Alonso waved them towards a cleaned up table. As soon as they laid him down, Alonso started to assess his new patient. After talking to Angelo, he called another doctor friend of his, along with a nurse and an anesthesiologist. They would be there within the hour, and the price tag for the entire team would be $20,000 . . . a price that would stay the same whether the patient lived or died.

Joey and Angelo left the doctor to do his work, and headed to a small coffee shop down the street to talk. Joey was still upset.

"Fuck, Ange, this ain't good."

"What the fuck happened?" Angelo asked.

"These fuckin' Russians are animals; they have no respect whatsoever. I walked in there just trying to play it cool, and this guy starts right off insulting me and the family."

Angelo now knew where this conversation was going. He'd known Joey way too long to know the story wouldn't end well, and that killing the Russians wasn't the problem with it. The problem for Joey would be explaining to his father how he'd blown another business opportunity. Joey had been sent down here to calm relations with the growing Russian syndicate, not inflame them. Angelo cut to the chase.

"So, they're gone, right? You did them?

Happy he didn't need to retell the entire story Joey said, "Yeah. Sasha and his brother, we took them to that spot in the Everglades. I'm just sorry Stevie took one in the stomach, and I didn't have a chance to kill them slow."

Steve was successfully operated on using equipment usually reserved for animals. Alonso was very proficient in removing the bullet and stabilizing his patient. After a week on heavy antibiotics, he would be good to travel and head back to New York. Louie would take him back to the hotel and watch over him. Alonso would visit the hotel the next day to check up on his patient. Meanwhile Joey, would return to New York that same night so he could fill his father in as fast as possible.

When Viktor heard the news the arrogant and foolish Sasha and his brother had been killed, he was ecstatic. *Those two fools didn't know how to talk to people, and I knew someone would put them in their place.* He heard it was the Italian mafia, but no one was exactly sure at the moment. *That idiot brought way too much attention to our business in South Florida with his amateur strong-arm tactics. With him gone, it clears the way for me to take over all the territory in Sunny Villas and after that, I want all of Florida.*

Chapter 30

Angelo was meeting up with Shaun in the back alley of the Hammer House gym. This was the meeting place for all gym members and customers looking to make some discreet purchases. Although everybody inside the gym knew what was going on, outside customers still liked to be careful and keep their business to themselves.

"How ya feeling?" asked Shaun.

"I'm starting to feel stronger and the Vikes are really starting to help my back."

Shaun removed a knapsack off his shoulder and opened it up and turned to Angelo "Okay, I wasn't able to get the silencers, but these 40s are H and Ks. That's the best I can do . . . and I threw in an extra fifty Vikes."

"Nice, very fucking nice. What did your guy say about getting' some long guns? Like SAWs or Barrett .50 cals?"

"Negative, right now. The only guys moving that type of stuff are the Russians, and they're such a close knit group that unless they know you're with some heavy hitters, they won't even talk to you, no matter how much you offer. If you give me a little time, I might be able to get something going, because I just started working with a guy whose sister is dating one of the biggest Russians down here."

"Alright, let me know, 'cause I have some real serious friends in New York who would be very interested, and that could mean big money for you, if you set somethin' up."

Angelo pulled a plain envelope containing a large amount

of cash out of his back pocket, and handed it to Shaun. Shaun flicked briefly through it, and handed him the knapsack.

Jimmie Burke was hosting a barbecue at his house. Michael, Angelo, Bobby, and several of the other undercover cops, along with their wives, girlfriends, and children, were there. Angelo decided to take Mia with him and this would be the first time she would get to meet his coworkers. The mood was upbeat in the backyard, with people drinking beers and tropical drinks. Jimmie had a little playground with swings and a slide set up for the kids. Most of the guys at work had children and they brought them along to play and have a good time.

Bobby—who at work was beyond hyper with his non-stop motion—was a lot more subdued this afternoon. He was wearing an oversized Depeche Mode tee-shirt, cargo shorts, and flip-flops. He handed Angelo and Mia two mugs filled with ice-cold beer. Bobby introduced Mia to his wife, who took her inside for a tour of the house, and to meet the other girlfriends and wives.

"Nice girl, Ange, and she's a beauty. I hear you're doing great work with Mike's gym operation," Bobby said.

"Thanks, Bobby, but we'll see. I haven't gotten anything big yet."

Bobby stepped back, becoming more animated.

"Are you fucking kidding me, bro? You just got ten stolen guns off the street. Angelo, any one of those guns could have been used to shoot a cop or, God forbid, used on one of our kids."

Angelo, in deep thought, quickly re-did the math, and realized Bobby was right. He'd forgotten for a moment how many guns he'd actually turned in to the P.D.'s property room, and how many he'd sold or given to his associates. As they were talking, Bobby's five-year-old son Lucas toddled over to them. Bobby picked him up and kissed him.

"Hola, Popi. How's my favorite little man?" He then turned his boy to face Angelo, "Say hi to Uncle Angelo."

Although Angelo smiled and played around with the kid, shaking the child's tiny hand, it was obvious he was uncomfortable. He wasn't uncomfortable to be around the kids, he loved them *it's just that these guys are cops and they were supposed to be the enemy and it wasn't good to start thinking of them as anything else. Mixing business with friendship will only fuck you up. It certainly was true in John Pomorico's case.* Once again, Angelo saw that night replaying in his head. Bobby was looking Angelo straight in the eye.

"You alright, Ange? You faded out on me for a second or two."

"Sorry, just got caught up in my mind for a second. You know how it is with old boxers and getting hit in the head too much. Look, I got to take a leak, I'll be right back."

Angelo walked away to the side of the house and stopped to observe the cops and their families. For some unknown reason, lately, he'd been having vivid flashbacks from his childhood. Too many times, he'd been hearing his father's voice in his head, yelling, "You're a real piece of shit, I wish I had a real fucking son, now get outta my house!"

Michael came up to Angelo and startled him from his daydreaming.

"Angelo, you got a second to take a walk?"

Angelo tried to get his bearings back, "Yeah sure, Mike."

They walked to the far end of the fenced-in yard, to an area with a couple of beach chairs set up for people to drink and smoke away from the kids. Michael in his usual serious manner—the only demeanor Angelo ever saw him with—turned to him and said, "Before we talk about what happened with my daughter, I wanted to let you know you have the potential to be a great cop."

"Potential huh?"

"I've been doing this job for twenty years and you have the best raw instinct as a cop I've ever seen. What I'm trying to say is, I don't know much about your background, except to say I'm sure before you got here you had a colorful life, and if you could only control your temper and some of your other nonsense, then the sky's the limit for you. If that's what you truly want, of course."

Angelo figured Michael was just blowing smoke up his ass, but let it pass.

"Thanks Mike, I'm just trying to get by and make a living, that's all."

"Here's something I'm sure you didn't know about when I came to Beachside PD all those years ago. I worked for one of the best Sergeants a guy could work for. This guy was an unbelievable cop and he could do no wrong. Before he became Sergeant, he had won more Officer of the Year awards than any other man in this department. Then, things started to go downhill for him. He left his wife for a younger woman and then got re-married. Within a year, the new young wife left him high and dry, and that's when he started to do all those stupid things you hear about with guys having midlife crises. You know, the Corvettes, expensive clothes, big money vacations. Then, when the money started getting even tighter, he began taking shortcuts at work, and you know what I'm talking about. The shortcuts brought him easy money and with that, he developed a bad gambling problem."

Angelo, under his breath, said, "*Hagen.*"

"Bingo. That's the guy . . . and he even saved my life once on a sting operation that went bad. All I'm saying is, I've seen a lot of good guys fall down. That's what this job does to you, with all that temptation. Angelo, I'm telling you this from my heart—every guy I've seen over the years who took shortcuts is now living in a world of shit, and you can take that to the bank."

Michael let Angelo digest that for a minute.

"Now, about my daughter . . ." Michael began to add.

"Nothing to talk about," Angelo quickly cut him off. "What's done is done, and you don't owe me any favors, 'cause it's always favors that will get you killed."

Michael thought about that for a little while and then

continued, "Fine, fair enough, but just let me say this: I owe you at least the truth. You were brought into my unit for only one reason—so I could get dirt on you, and pass it on to McPherson. He's got it in for you, and for his old nemesis James Hagen, so watch your back." After another long pause, Michael said, "When we started working together, you were just a suspect to me, now I hope to say you're not only a cop, but also my friend."

Mike reached out and they shook hands. As Angelo shook his hand, he knew nothing good could come of this. He wasn't down here to make friends, he was here to earn as much as he could, and serve the family's wishes until either he got caught or they said it was time to go home. *Family. What a strange word. It's something I know nothin' about.* The only people he could count on were himself, Danny, Jay and Mia. Although it didn't occur to him at the time, it was odd he didn't include Eddie "Mambo" or Joey on that list. Angelo came back from his thoughts and turned to Michael.

"Alright, as your new friend, when was the last time you went out on the town and actually had some fun?"

"A long time, a real long time. And I'm still not ready yet, but thanks for the offer."

"Sorry Mike, but as they say, this is an offer you can't refuse."

Angelo and Michael returned to the barbecue, and Angelo spotted Mia in the middle of a large group. She was working the crowd and had everyone in the palm of her hand, as usual. Angelo wasn't sure how he'd gotten so lucky with Mia. She was definitely head and shoulders above the rest. She saw him standing off to the side, excused herself from the crowd and walked over to him. She stood on her toes and gave him a kiss.

"Want to take a walk?"

"This is my second walk tonight," Angelo said with a smile. "And I'm starting to feel like a dog!"

He grabbed her hand and they headed for the same area

he'd just been talking with Michael. He found a fence, leaned back on it and pulled Mia closer to him.

"So, what's going on, young lady?"

She leaned into his chest.

"Your friends are really cool, and I know I have said this before, but I'm so proud of how you've completely changed your life. There were so many times in Brooklyn when I wasn't sure about us, but I always knew that somewhere deep inside you, there was this good side you hid from everyone. I always prayed for the day you would get out of that crazy life, but I never believed in my wildest dreams that you'd become a cop."

Angelo had never told Mia the exact reason he'd come down to Florida to be a cop. He did, however, feel he'd told her the truth when he said he wanted to change as a person, and that he was trying.

He looked at her and wondered why she had this effect on him.

"I would never have believed it, either, but the opportunity opened up, and I went for it."

Mia got real serious, looked Angelo straight in the eye, and said, "Well, besides being my hero, you are also going to be a father."

Mia hadn't been sure how Angelo would handle the news, because this was something they'd never talked about. To her relief, a big smile grew on his face, and he grabbed her in his excitement, lifting her in the air and exclaimed, "Are you fuckin' serious? I'm going to be a dad?"

For the next half hour, they discussed their future together, now they were going to be a family. Angelo insisted they get married before she had the child, and Mia was now on cloud nine.

Angelo had a sudden thought. "I want us to get married on Bora Bora."

Mia had never heard of Bora Bora, or of Angelo's childhood dreams, and wasn't even sure whether he was making it up, but she said with complete conviction,

"Anywhere you want us to get married is fine with me."

And that's why I love this woman so much. She's always got my back and she makes my life so much fuckin' better.

Angelo was in his U.C. car, eating a sandwich while on surveillance. His throwaway hidden cell phone started to ring with a private number. He answered it.

"Yeah?"

"Ange, it's Joey"

"What's up Joe? How ya doing?"

"Good, good. The big guy wants to know about the grocery list you were supposed to get him?"

"Yeah I'm still workin' on that. You know that type of produce can take a little time to gather."

"Not for nothin', but this is the second time he's asked for it. Is there a problem, Angelo?"

"No, Joe, I'm on it. It's just taking a little bit longer to gather than I thought it would."

"Here's a piece of advice, cuz—make sure it gets done sooner than later."

"Yeah, just . . ."

The line went dead.

Shit, last thing I need is Joey and Eddie upset with me.

On top of this, Angelo was also a little troubled about hearing no news from either Eddie or Joey about the Russians who'd gotten wacked. *Is there going to be a war? Do they expect some type of retaliation? How the fuck do they expect me to keep an eye on Eddie and the family's interests if they don't keep me in the loop?*

Chapter 31

The 60-foot Palmer Johnson sport yacht was heading north towards Fort Lauderdale from Miami's beautiful Biscayne Bay. Lorenzo's attorney Jaime Kalem had purchased the boat a month ago, and wanted to take it for a test run. Jaime wasn't known as the most ethical of attorneys, which was why Lorenzo used him. He had numerous high-level government contacts, which helped him in squashing cases. Jaime's father was a big time real estate guy who made his money purchasing malls and golf courses. Jaime's Achilles Heel was trashy women, and that's why he kept so close to Lorenzo.

On the boat that day were Angelo, Michael, Lorenzo, Frankie the Fixer, Jimmie, Bobby, and two other friends of Jaime's. Also along for the ride were a bunch of the girls from Lorenzo's club. As soon as they cast off, Jaime started popping bottles of champagne for the girls and the party was on. Angelo and Bobby had tricked Michael into coming along by telling him they'd set up a big drug deal where they were posing as buyers. By the time Michael realized he'd been set up, it was too late, and they refused to turn back and drop him off at the dock. After forcing him to drink several shots of vodka, Angelo saw Michael drop the tight ass routine for the first time, and actually smile.

The yacht traveled north up the Intracoastal and pulled up to the Shooters bar and grill. The place was packed on this beautiful Sunday afternoon. With the assistance of the dock employees, the boat captain docked the boat next to another yacht. To get into the bar, they would have to walk across the back decks of three other yachts. In the yacht next to theirs was a bunch of preppie-looking college guys also partying and getting sloppy drunk with some girls.

Angelo challenged Michael into a shot-drinking contest, and with Michael refusing to back down from a challenge, they matched each other shot for shot, for a while. After Michael's first drink, he decided to let it all go and get completely hammered. On the preppie yacht, the girls had grown bored with their present company and decided to join the party on Jaime's. This pissed the preppie guys off who'd been sure they were getting laid at some point, and *now these old fucks docked next to them had their women.* Jake Worthington, whose dad owned the boat, was the first to start the war of words, yelling at the girls, "You're a bunch of stupid whores! If we'd known you wanted to party with a group of old men, we would have dropped you off at the Irish pub."

Angelo shook his head and growled, "Jerkoff, watch your mouth."

Now slamming down his sixth beer, Michael sloppily grabbed Angelo's arm.

"Angelo, buddy, it's not worth it, they're just punk kids, let it go."

Angelo shrugged Michael's hand off him, and continued to stare at the yelling yuppie. Even drunk, Michael had the wits to stumble inside the cabin and tell Lorenzo what just happened, "Before Angelo loses it, why don't we go back to South Beach, 'cause you know if we stay here, there's going to be a big problem."

Lorenzo walked out of the cabin and looked over at the preppie boat. He saw they were starting to eyeball Angelo in a bad way. He turned back to Michael and said, "I'm with you, I want to fuck, not fight!"

Lorenzo filled Jaime in on what was going on. Unfortunately, Jaime loved the commotion as he'd never been involved in a real fight, and wanted to stay to see what would happen. Lorenzo finally convinced Jaime to listen, and Jaime reluctantly told the Captain to prepare the yacht to leave. By this time, the preppie guys were even more upset, realizing the girls would now be leaving with these new guys. As the Captain pulled the yacht away, the preppies started yelling and cursing up a storm. When Jaime's yacht was about 20 yards away, Jake Worthington held up a rope that belonged to Jaime's boat, and yelled, "Hey assholes, you forgot your rope!"

Angelo looked at Lorenzo, and they both nodded in unison. Lorenzo went back to the Captain and told him to turn around. Thinking to himself these guys were all nuts, he looked to Jaime for instructions. Jaime, all pumped up on beer muscles, excitedly told the Captain to go back. Initially finding the whole thing comical, Michael couldn't quite believe they were now going back, and he turned to Lorenzo and Angelo.

"You guys can't be serious — it's just a cheap rope!"

As the yacht got closer, Jake and his buddies were starting to realize taunting these guys might not have been such a good idea. Angelo readied himself to be the first to jump into their boat. He never got the chance, because at the last second, he was elbowed out of the way by a pumped-up Bobby Dee. Bobby launched himself onto their back deck and started throwing flurries of punches at any hapless target near him. Angelo was next on board, followed by Lorenzo, Jimmie, and Frankie The Fixer. Michael couldn't believe his own highly trained, highly disciplined guys were fighting alongside Angelo's maniacs over a dirty old rope. He tried calling Jimmie and Bobby back, but it would have been easier breaking up a bunch of pit bulls in a dog fight. Maybe it was the alcohol, maybe it was his breaking point, but Michael finally gave in to the wild scene, with an *ahhh fuck it, I'm going to get me some*! He leaped onto the boat, landing on the back of some tattooed teenager with tweezed eyebrows and an Ed Hardy tee-shirt. As Michael pounded the metrosexual frat boy's head into the side of the boat, he looked around and surveyed the carnage.

What he saw was sheer chaos combined with complete absurdity, that caused him to double over in hysterical laughter.

Angelo looked up from choking a guy and saw all his guys, including Michael, beating the crap out of what he thought of as a bunch of spoiled douchebags. Like a skilled field general assessing the battlefield, Angelo made a quick decision. He turned to Lorenzo and the Fixer and told them to grab the douchebags' two big ice coolers filled with beer and sandwiches. Bobby gave Lorenzo a hand carrying the big cooler back to their boat. Angelo had to call out several times to Jimmie Burke, who was very focused on hanging a guy off the side of the boat and dunking his head in and out of the water. With that order from their impromptu General, the triumphant marauders made their drunken departure, with their ill-gotten booty, back to the getaway boat.

On the way back to the dock a half hour later, Angelo was sitting in the yacht's kitchen with a bag of frozen peas on his swollen right eye. Somehow, he'd been sucker-punched by somebody, and his primary suspect was Bobby Dee with all those wild punches he'd been throwing. Lorenzo, whose $300 Armani shirt was ripped, sat down next to Angelo.

"You alright, buddy? Maybe next time we can take on some ninth graders instead."

Angelo laughed and Lorenzo continued.

"Listen Ange, I got a weird vibe from Joe the other night."

"No shit. You know Joe's outta his fuckin' mind."

"I'm being serious, Ange. Watch your back with him, that's all I'm saying."

"Gimme a fuckin' break. Me and Joe are like brothers. You didn't grow up with us. He's always saying this and that, but by the next day he either forgets or changes his mind. That's just Joe."

"Yeah, you know him better than me, cuz, but I don't know, I'd still watch my back. Remember you said a while back you'd tell me the real story with what happened with

Nicky Ferrozo? Well, how about now?"

Angelo took the bag of peas off his eye.

"I had no choice. He was banging Joey's girl, and Joey would have gone nuts and whacked him without permission."

"Joe owes you then, what did he say?"

"You fuckin' kidding me? He don't know and hopefully he doesn't ever find out. I knew it would be bad for me to crack Nicky, but I owe Eddie so much I had to protect his son."

Lorenzo was flexing his right hand. It was just starting to swell.

"Well, you're a better man than me, 'cause I would have just let Joe do his thing."

The yacht finally got back to the dock at 4:00 a.m., and Angelo wanted to hit South Beach and keep drinking, but everybody bailed on him. With Mia not coming back till next weekend, he wanted to enjoy a night out with the boys. The other guys, including Michael, were hooked up with the girls they'd met and all decided to stay on the boat. Angelo could have banged this one little redhead college girl but decided not to, because she couldn't compare to his Mia.

Walking into his empty apartment and without turning on any lights, Angelo crashed down on his couch. He thought about the conversation he'd had with Lorenzo earlier, and something about it made him think of his father and their past. While watching a half hour infomercial for a headlight lens cleaner, he polished off a bottle of whiskey, before slipping into a deep, dreamless sleep.

Chapter 32

Inside Hagen's Office at 9:00 am Monday morning, were Angelo, Michael, Bobby, and Jimmie. The mood was solemn because all parties, including Hagen himself, were nursing hangovers. Hagen was drinking his usual French vanilla coffee while rubbing his temples, hoping for just an ounce of relief. His eyes were throbbing with bloodshot veins and capillaries that looked like a tourist map full of crisscrossing lines. He'd just returned from a three-day trip to the Bahamas with his latest girlfriend, a twenty-four-year-old bartender named Carmen. His recent taste in women was skewing younger and younger, along with their ability to "*comprende ingles*." He'd also managed to lose the $2,000 Angelo had just given him.

As Angelo started making more money, he would always throw a little piece to Hagen, and then send a bigger piece to Eddie, via Joey. Hagen, who obviously wasn't in the best of moods, looked Michael in the eye and pointed at the other guys in the room.

"I expect this type of behavior from these lunatics, but you, Mike? Really?"

Michael winced at the sound of Hagen's voice, because anything above a whisper caused shards of electrified broken glass to dig into his brain. He took a few seconds to regain his composure and collect his thoughts.

"I can explain, Lieutenant. We were attempting to retrieve some stolen property from some hostile suspects when . . ."

His headache pounding like a drum, Hagen shook his head

in disgust.

"Cut the bullshit! You animals know the victims and the Coast Guard want to press charges against you all for piracy . . . fucking piracy! You idiots are lucky I'm in real tight and play golf with some of the bosses over there, or this would never have gotten squashed. Now, let's make sure this sort of thing never happens again. Get the fuck out of my office!"

They left the office with smirks on their faces, even the ever-serious Michael. Once they were all gone, and his door was closed, Hagen allowed some of his anger to dissipate. Then, the thought of the sheer ridiculousness of the incident caused a small smile to grow on his face. *Pirates, ha! I got freaking pirates working for me. Next time those bastards better invite me.*

Chapter 33

Eddie and Joey Salerno were meeting with two mobbed up associates in the backroom of Connie's restaurant in Brooklyn. The associates, who were brothers, just finished a weapons deal that Eddie was one of the investors on.

The older brother Rob Conte did most of the talking, and was placating Eddie, "Sorry it couldn't be more, but we lost half our load after our guys cleared the ports."

Eddie knew the risks of the deal, but still wanted to know what had happened.

"Were they Feds?"

"No, they were local plainclothes detectives," answered Rob.

Eddie shot a disparaging look at Joey, and told the brothers, "Fellas, give me a second."

The two associates got up from the booth, and Joey moved closer to his dad. Taking his time finishing his linguini with white clam sauce, Eddie finally asked Joey, "I thought Angelo told you he knew of no UCs working anywhere near the ports."

Joey shook his head, "Not only that, but I told him to call me immediately if he wasn't sure, or if plans changed."

Eddie's irritation was starting to show. As his anger rose, he started rubbing his eyes, as if he could relieve the pressure building behind them.

"I still didn't get the list from him, and I also got a report he's been earning down there and he's yet to send me my tribute. This Angelo, what the fuck is he doing? I told him not to screw around, 'cause this whole project is costing me a lot of money and favors."

Joey tried to look neutral and said, "I don't know what's going through his head, I really don't."

"Well, I'm sure he has a reason, 'cause I can't believe he would just blow me off, not my Ange. When you go down this week, I want you to find out what's going on with him."

Joey was about to talk back to his father, but instead decided not to push it. *When I screwed up with the Russians, he goes fuckin' nuts and doesn't speak to me for a week. When his golden boy Ange fucks up, absolutely nothin'.*

After the killings of the Russians, Eddie only calmed down when he found out that Sasha and his brother were actually outcasts of the Russian community. Once he was assured of their hated status, he knew there wouldn't be any retaliation. Glad he was able to control his temper, unlike Angelo, he followed up with, "Okay, I'll take care of it, but I'm sure it's like you say — he must have a reason. I got to run an errand. I'll catch you later."

Joey drove straight from the restaurant to Charlie Gallo's Apollo Trucking Company in Linden, New Jersey. Charlie's son Carmine ran the day-to-day operations, and was out on the dock checking the manifests of the day with his drivers. Joey, who'd worked there one summer when he was in his teens, met with Carmine.

"Carmine, thanks for meeting with me."

Carmine put down his paperwork on a pallet of electronics, and shook Joey's hand.

"No problem, Joe. How's your father doing?"

"He's good, very good. And he appreciates the fact your family was able to squash that beef. How's your cousin Nicky doing?" Joey asked.

"He's alright. It took a lot for him not to make a beef, but he understands the loyalty to the family."

"Well, that's the thing I wanted to talk to you about in person. I want to talk to Nicky to find out what really happened, and I was hoping you could approach him and ask for the sit-down."

Carmine thought for a few seconds and said, "Joey . . . it's already squashed. There's no point for you to bring it up again, 'cause Nicky really had to swallow his pride once, already. He keeps telling people he don't want to talk about it, 'cause it's in the past."

"I would really like to talk to him," Joey pushed forward. "Anyways. I heard some things, and I just wanted clarification."

Carmine was shaking his head. *Shit, don't get me in between you two freaking lunatics. I don't need this in my life right now!*

Out loud, he said, "Joe, you and Ange are like brothers. Why don't you leave it as it is?"

Even more curious, Joey was now positive Carmine wasn't telling him something.

"What the fuck, Carmine? Don't bullshit me, something's up."

Carmine had known Joey long enough to know he wasn't going to drop the subject. He sighed.

"I was the first to get to the hospital immediately after the throw down, and I spoke to Nicky. He said this all started 'cause he caught Angelo messing around with your girl. Nicky told Angelo something to the effect that you and him are made guys and Angelo isn't, and he violated the rules. That's when Angelo lost it, and they went at it."

"You sure about that?"

"That's what he said that night, but he wouldn't talk about it later when the bosses asked him about the beef."

"Okay, that's all I needed to know."

Looking sorry, Carmine said, "Joe, I know how tight you and Ange are. That's why I stayed out of it."

Joey didn't answer him, but left the dock deep in thought.

Chapter 34

Inside Angelo's apartment, Mia was cooking him his favorite dish of seafood pasta. The apartment was just starting to feel like home and she was getting used to the brutal South Florida humidity. It had been a little over a month since she quit her job in New York and made the move south. Angelo still had his weird peculiarities she remembered from when they'd lived together over eight years ago. Quirks like not allowing her to use the ceiling fans in the house, or having the air conditioning vents face their bed. Before going to sleep, he still took his sleeping pills each night before he went to sleep, although it seemed like he might have upped the dosage.

His sleep patterns were one of the first big things she noticed. He used to sleep pretty soundly, and barely rolled over during the night, but that had drastically changed. It was on her fourth night there that she saw how bad it had become. He would start by talking in his sleep, and then he would start moving and rolling around. She knew sometimes it was nightmares of his dad, because he would shriek, "Stop it, you're killing her!" or "No, pops, no!" Other times, he would quietly mumble words like, "sorry John, sorry, I didn't know." Whether he liked it or not, the ghosts of Angelo's past were starting to catch up with him.

She did notice he had changed for the better in other areas of his life. Three days earlier, they were driving to her doctor's office to get a sonogram of the baby. Angelo found a parking spot that was about to become available close to the building, and patiently waited while the elderly driver pulled out. Just before he could pull in, two young guys driving a little Honda stole the spot. Angelo gripped the steering wheel until his knuckles turned white, and then he did the most amazing thing. He let out a deep breath, unclenched his hands, and drove away to look for another spot. Whether it was age, the police job, or just acquired wisdom, Angelo had for the first time shown some discipline and restraint. What Mia didn't know was that Angelo had memorized the license plate and would be looking for these guys next time he was out without his pregnant fiancée.

Over the last several weeks, Angelo had reassured Mia many times he would be happy whether it was a girl or boy. That day at the doctor's office, however, he showed his true colors when they learned it was a boy, and celebrated wildly, almost crushing the doctor in a massive bear hug.

Chapter 35

The UC office inside the Beachside PD was packed. All Michael's guys were there, along with a group of federal agents. As Michael stood up, everyone quieted down.

"Guys, as you know, three City of Miami officers were killed today in a botched bank robbery. The suspects had the tactical advantage with their fully automatic long guns. A joint task force is now being set up with ATF, FBI, and ICE agents. The ATF has now designated Miami as the number one hub for all weapon-smuggling operations in the country. If we don't start disrupting this flow, a lot more of our guys won't be going home to their families."

For the next hour, the group talked about gaining intelligence and working together. Once everyone cleared out, Angelo approached Michael.

"I might have made a connection through the Hammer House that will get us closer to one of the biggest weapons dealers down here."

"I like the way that sounds. Fill me in."

"Shaun introduced me to this kid Jorge that just happens to work for Viktor Matyushenko."

"I've heard of Viktor. He's supposed to be one of the bigger guys down here."

"He is, and I requested a meeting with him for this week."

Angelo didn't add that he'd had to use Eddie Salerno's name as a reference. Right after he'd met with Jorge, Angelo had called Eddie in order to fill him in. Since Joey's disaster, Eddie had also wanted another way to get in with the Russians, and was relieved when Angelo told him he'd made a connection.

Viktor refused Angelo's initial request for the meeting, even after Eddie had vouched for him. Viktor stated he would only meet with the top guy, which was Eddie. Eddie Salerno didn't take meetings with anyone outside of his circle, and he made it clear to Viktor's people that that wasn't going to happen. Viktor reminded all parties involved that he wasn't the one seeking the meeting, and that the last meeting between the two syndicates hadn't gone too well for his people. An arrangement was finally reached whereby Viktor agreed to have a face-to-face with Joey. His stipulations were that it would have to be on his turf in South Florida, and that Joey must come alone.

Viktor was checking the crates that were being unloaded into his warehouse. Joey had arrived ten minutes earlier, and was watching Viktor run his operation. He was very impressed with how organized and efficient everything ran.

If I could only get my lazy fuckin' guys to work this hard, Joey thought. Fuhgedaboutit.

Speaking to one of the workers in Russian, Viktor said, "Tell your boss that he can now send me as much as he can get his hands on. I need my supply to catch up with the demand."

He then turned and spoke to Joey in his heavily accented English, "You were saying?"

"My father agrees with you that a war serves none of our purposes. After all, we are businessmen. We are also looking into the matter of what happened to your two compatriots. If anyone from our organization was responsible, I assure you they will be dealt with. Now, we were hoping that you would reconsider our new proposal," said Joey.

"The money was a fair gesture, but my backers have more than enough. We need access to your political connections and unions more than the financing," "The big bosses in our

families don't move that fast when cutting deals with outsid-
ers. That's why we're suggesting we start working together
on a few smaller projects, and then we can start talking about
political support."

Viktor took his time thinking of another angle.

"As a gesture of good faith, or as you say here, to sweeten
the pot, what could you offer me besides the money?"

"Let me speak with my father and get back to you. I might
have something besides money that could be of value to
you."

Chapter 36

Angelo and Joey were sitting at an outdoor café eating lunch on Miami's famous Ocean Drive. Between bites of his cheeseburger, Angelo said, "Joe, it's not that I have a problem giving up the list, it's just not that easy to get all the files. I'm working a lot of things right now, and I've been making some good scores."

Angelo covertly slipped an envelope to Joe.

"That's another four Gs for Eddie."

Joey took the envelope and placed it in his shorts pocket.

"Yeah, he thanks you for all the money you've been giving me, but you need to get on the ball. I hope you're not starting to think you're a real cop now."

Angelo shook his head.

"Come on Joe, quit bustin' my balls. You know I'm only doing this cop shit for your dad."

Joey wiped his mouth and, in a serious tone, asked, "What was the real story between you and Nicky? And don't tell me the bullshit he-got-mouthy-with-you answer."

Angelo gave Joey his best are you fucking serious not this shit again look and said, "Joe, I told you a thousand times already. You know my fuckin' temper. He got loud and I only meant to crack him once, but you know how it goes."

I got you, Angie-boy, lying to my face, and if I really push you might change your story. Then again, I also know if I force you into a corner you might do something real stupid, like flip over the table and take a swing at me. I don't fear you, my brother, and if we lock horns we're both going to get real hurt.

Instead he did what his father taught him to do in lose-lose situations and switched gears by saying, "Okay, okay, I believe you. I thought of something you could do for us to redeem yourself with the family. That fuckin' Russian is playing hardball, he wants all types of shit from us, but he offers nothing in return. So here's the plan: I'm going to try to talk to his number two guy about putting something together. Obviously, I can't whack this fuckin' Viktor, so if you and your cop buddies can take him down and make it stick so he never sees the light of day, then we all win."

Angelo wasn't too happy with the way Joey emphasized "cop buddies." *What's he trying to say? That I'm more loyal to the police department than to him and Eddie?*

"My guys have been actually trying for the last six months to get a deal with him or one of his subordinates, but they won't bite, and he already turned me down personally."

Joey was proud of himself that he was able to follow his dad's advice about dealing with the Russians. He was also very pleased with his ability to fool even Angelo with his performance, and manipulate him into doing what he needed. He put his arm around Angelo.

"That's 'cause you didn't have your big brother with you to help, now let me take care of the details of setting up a meeting."

It was Sunday afternoon, and Angelo didn't want to sit on this new info until he saw Michael on Monday morning, so he called him at home. Instead of meeting at a restaurant, the way Angelo felt most comfortable, Michael invited him over to the house. Michael fired up the barbecue and put a couple of steaks on the grill. Amanda was out of the house and Michael didn't mind having some company. When Angelo got there, Michael had a cold beer waiting for him and Angelo took a seat on a lawn chair. After making small talk, Angelo got down to business.

"My guy set up the deal, we're going to be buying a crate of Barrett .50 cals for a hundred and fifty thou."

Michael opened up his second beer and said, "That's gonna be tough, 'cause you won't let me certify or talk to your connection. That means no paperwork on him in the system and the most the Chief has let us use in the past was one hundred grand."

"I know, that's why I say let's use the Feds. They have the money and resources to make it happen fast."

Michael thought about Angelo's proposal for a few minutes while sipping his beer.

"Angelo, when I speak to the Chief, I will be sticking my neck out for you on this one. If this goes bad, shoot, I don't even have to say what will happen to us, but the payoff to get in with the Russians is too good to pass up. If this does work, we will be the first agency in South Florida to get inside a major Russian syndicate. I'll make phone calls and will try to get the ball rolling without the Feds."

That night, Angelo drove to Joey's hotel in South Beach. Joey welcomed him with his usual big hug, "Here's the deal, Ange. The meeting is all set — you, me, and only two of your guys are going to meet with Viktor. First thing in the morning, I will call you and tell you where we're meeting him. At that time, have your moneyman do a drive-by, and then he'll direct us to the location where the deal will go down."

Angelo tried to picture it in his mind and asked, "How many guys will he have with him?"

"He's supposed to have the same as us: four. Here's the thing. These guys are experts in counter surveillance. Viktor always picks locations in the middle of nowhere, with no concealment, so I'm telling you if your guys are anywhere in a three mile radius, they will be spotted and things will get real ugly."

Angelo was uncomfortable, "Joe, that puts us in a real bad spot. What if he decides to just whack us and take the money?

That's what we would do if the situation was reversed."

"Very true, but money is nothing to them. Shit, we offered him double that for access to just one of their Afghanistan weapons dealers and they turned us down. Viktor won't rip us off, because he needs to start building a relationship with our families. The Russians have all the money in the world, but they don't have our political contacts over here. Shit, those contacts took us over fifty years of bribery, threats, and blackmailing to build."

Angelo thought about it for a moment.

"Okay, that makes sense to you and me, but my supervisors don't know that, so we still have to make it as safe as possible for my guys and the money. The only way to do it then, is to have a spotter plane in the air and put a trackin' device on the money. We will have guys on the ground, but they will stay back and keep at least a two-mile perimeter from the final location. After the deal, my guys can take down the bad guys and recover the money as they're leavin' the area."

"I'm with you. I would also like a little more backup, 'cause who the fuck knows what these crazy Russians might do, but that's the best deal I could make. Remember, like I said before, Ange, that's why you were sent down here to make things like this happen for us. It's a win-win situation. We get rid of the competition, you get a commendation or promotion. Forget about it. It's a win-win."

Driving back to his home, Angelo went over in his mind the conversation he'd just had with Joey. Something Joey had said set off an alarm for him, but he couldn't pinpoint it. He tried again to focus on Joey's words and suddenly, it brought back a vivid memory. It was the night John Pomorico was killed in upstate New York.

After Joey shot him, he and Angelo drove another hour deeper into the country to an abandoned farm. The entire area was pitch black and when Angelo got out of the car, he was amazed at how clear the sky was, and how he could see all the stars. As a city kid with all the lights at night you can barely see any stars, but there in upstate New York it was remarkable. At the farm, Angelo recognized two other neighborhood guys who Joey trusted. They were busy digging a deep hole in an empty field. *I guess John never had a chance. They were already digging his grave.*

Joey hadn't said a word to Angelo the whole drive except, "Clean the blood off the window and help me put him in the trunk, 'cause we got a long drive and I don't wanna get pinched."

Once the two neighborhood guys had finished shoveling, they walked over to the car and Joey opened the trunk. As they lifted John's lifeless body, one of the guys lost his grip and John fell to the floor with a thump. The guys started laughing, and Angelo finally lost his temper. He growled and pushed them away.

"Get your hands off him, and then get the fuck outta' here. I'll take care of it."

When the two walked away, Angelo gently lifted John off the floor and dragged him into his final resting place. For the next twenty minutes, standing in complete silence, Angelo shoveled dirt onto his old friend. Joey didn't say a word to him the whole ride back, and they never spoke again about that night. With a chill, Angelo now remembered how earlier in the diner Joey had deceived John with that bullshit win-win speech.

Chapter 37

Michael was alone in his office trying to catch up on some paperwork, when his phone rang; he answered it with his usual, "Frakes."

Mark McPherson was on the line and after a few pleasantries said in an impatient tone, "Just so we have this clear, you are still telling me that you haven't obtained anything of value."

For the last two weeks, every time McPherson saw Michael in the hallways, he would hound him about Angelo. Since he never wanted to be any part of this project from the beginning, Michael expressed his utter frustration.

"Mark, you were wrong about this guy. Yeah he's a cowboy who's a little heavy-handed, and yeah he does break almost every department policy, but that's all I got. What do you want me to do? Make up some shit or plant something on him? I'm telling you I got nothing."

"I'm very disappointed in you, Michael, but I guess people change. Maybe I should have been looking closer at you all this time."

That was all Michael needed to hear to finally push him over the edge. Years of intense dislike exploded from him.

"Fuck you, you cocksucking piece of shit! You want to look at me after all my years here? Go ahead and take your best shot!"

With that, Michael ripped the phone off his desk and hurled it into the wall like one of his old college-day fastballs. When he did finally calm down, he realized that he'd just made himself a powerful new enemy, and that everything he did from now on would be evaluated via McPherson's microscope.

Michael entered the Beachside P.D. SWAT locker room, where he had a meeting set up with the team's head, Jason Youngblood. At twenty-eight years old, Jason was the youngest S.W.A.T. team leader in the entire County. A highly thought-of football player out of high school, Jason instead decided to follow his first dream and become a cop. He led the department in arrests his first four years running, and was one of the most tactical officers Michael had the privilege to work with.

His first specialized unit was as a K-9 officer. From there, he worked with Michael on undercover work leading to his present job on the S.W.A.T. team. After telling him once he'd be happy to have a son like Jason, Michael had a running joke whereby he would call Jason "son" in public, which would cause confusion among the civilians due to Michael's stuffy white guy image and the contrast with Jason's smooth, laid back demeanor (he was of mixed race, Jamaican and white).

Seeing Jason always brought back the memory of a call they responded to, involving one of the local Beachside P.D. residents. Troy Rollins was a Gulf War veteran who had been suffering from post-traumatic stress and other mental issues. Troy, who had already been Baker Acted by Michael a few years back, called the police department and told them he wanted to kill himself. Based on Troy's past history of mental illness, his training with weapons, along with his physical size of 6 feet 5 inches, 250 pounds, the call was given the highest of priorities.

After uniform officers responded to his apartment, they learned from his wife he wasn't home. Throughout the day, Troy would call the department, but he refused to give out his location. Finally, an off-duty Beachside officer working at a shopping center, spotted Troy walking into a shoe store. Riding together in their UC car, Michael and Jason were already inside the shopping center when the officer called it in. Jason had his AR-15 long rifle in hand, while Michael un-holstered his Glock .45 caliber firearm. They sprinted into the business with their weapons out, and the customers panicked. Some shoppers fled for the doors, while others ducked to the ground in fear.

As Michael and Jason rounded the cash registers, they spotted Troy heading towards the back. Troy had his back to them and was wearing a fanny pack around his waist. He had his right hand tucked into the fanny pack and seemed to be holding an object. Michael brought up his weapon and looked through his sights and got a good picture on Troy's back torso. As he removed his finger from along the slide railing and put it on the trigger, he focused on controlling his breathing. He knew if he called out Troy's name, he would probably spin around and get the first shot off at either him or Jason. He wasn't comfortable, however, with the idea of shooting Troy in the back, especially since he couldn't be sure whether Troy had a weapon.

These were the split-second decisions cops make throughout their careers. Michael knew people who'd never done one day of police work in their lives would probably Monday morning quarterback his millisecond decision under a microscope.

Troy was now approximately ten yards ahead of them, and appeared to be walking with a sense of purpose. At the moment a decision needed to be made, fate stepped in. For no apparent reason, Troy turned abruptly to his left to walk down an aisle. In a blur of speed, Jason accelerated into a full run and, having the angle on the target, exploded fully into Troy's chest with his shoulder. Worthy of an NFL highlight reel, the impact was so violent that all of Troy's 250 pounds flew through the air and crashed into the metal shelving at least five feet away. The impact caused the shelves to bend under the tremendous weight and force.

Michael, who was three steps behind Jason, jumped onto

Troy's back, digging his knee into his neck. He and Jason pinned the stunned man's hands behind his back and hand-cuffed him. When they removed his open fanny pack, they found a large eight-inch Bowie knife ready for action. It was one of the bravest things Michael had ever witnessed an officer do in what he believed to be a critical situation.

If they had shot Troy, there was the chance the bullets could have hit innocent civilians. If they'd chosen not to shoot him, he could have killed numerous shoppers in a grim reen-actment of the unfortunately recent phenomenon of active shooters. As had Michael, Jason had also believed Troy was holding a gun, yet Jason still attempted the more dangerous tactic without regard for his own safety.

As Michael replayed the incident, he watched Jason finish cleaning his duty weapon. Jason looked up at Michael and with his friendly smile, gave him his usual greeting, "Father."

Michael smiled and answered, "Son."

Michael briefed him on Angelo's deal and the take down, but Jason shook his head.

"I don't like it. We don't have the chopper available for a quick reaction force. If things go bad, it will take us at least eight minutes to get to you in the S.W.A.T. van."

"I don't freaking like it either, but it's the best chance we have to get those weapons off the street," said Michael.

Jason, however, had known Michael long enough to know something else was wrong.

"You alright, Mike?"

"Yeah, J, everything's fine. I just got a lot of crap on my plate right now. Alright, let's just try to get the best tactical plan together with what we got."

With that, Jason dropped the subject and went to work planning the logistics.

Back in his office, Michael was looking through a cabinet for a file. It wasn't there. After searching in vain throughout his office, he came to the conclusion McPherson must have taken it. The file contained the earlier documentation he'd kept on Angelo. It had some violations McPherson could use, but it also had personal notes Michael had written to himself about leads to follow up on. McPherson could use that file against Michael, claiming he'd failed as a supervisor to discipline his employee and was therefore an ineffectual leader, and derelict in his duty. Michael grabbed the phone and called Bobby's cell phone.

"Bobby, I need you to get into McPherson's office tonight after he leaves, and locate a file. It contains info on Angelo, and I want it immediately destroyed. That's right, you heard me, I don't care if you have to rip that place apart. Just do it."

Chapter 38

Michael, Angelo, and Joey were driving in a rental car Angelo had picked up the night before. Angelo was taking no chances using his assigned UC car. The meeting point was a gas station located in an isolated rural area, way out West in South Miami. Angelo had introduced Joey to Michael at Joey's hotel room earlier, and both men were immediately distrustful of each other. As professionals in their respective fields, however, both men kept their feelings in check in order to conduct the more important business of the day.

Angelo's GPS brought them to the isolated gas station at exactly the designated time. About ten minutes later, Viktor and two of his bodyguards pulled into the gas station and headed for the car wash located in the rear of the business.

Angelo and Joey exited the car and were immediately hit with a thick wall of South Florida humidity. Under his breath, Joey began cursing in Italian about the outdoor sauna they'd just entered. In that short walk, both men were drenched in a layer of sweat. Joey introduced Angelo to Viktor and both men sized each other up in seconds. Angelo broke the ice and asked Viktor, "Okay, where do you want to do this?"

"What do you have for me?" replied Viktor.

Immediately, Angelo gave Michael the signal. Already on the phone, Michael said a few words then nodded in acknowledgement. An older model Chevy driven by Bobby pulled into the gas station, and then drove slowly by Angelo and Viktor. As he cruised by, he opened up a gym bag on the passenger seat, lifted it up and showed Viktor the large sum of money it contained. Bobby never actually stopped the vehicle, but kept it rolling in case of a rip off. He then drove off the property as a safety measure, and awaited his next instructions. Satisfied, Viktor turned to Angelo.

"Go ten miles south on U.S. Highway 1 and make a right on Old Cutler Road. You will then see an old airport about three miles in."

Angelo and Joey got back in the car with Michael and headed towards the airport. Joey immediately turned up the car's A/C and angled all the vents in his direction. Michael radioed in the location of the meeting area to the backup officers in the area. He also requested they find the blueprints of the interior structures of the airport. As they drove south, Angelo appreciated how perfect a location Viktor had picked to do the deal — so good that Michael had even debated calling off the whole operation due to safety concerns. The problem was the stakes were just too high, and Michael knew unless someone made some headway and started breaking up the weapons smuggling, more cops would die.

The rural area they drove through still showed the effects of Hurricane Andrew that had devastated the area in August of 1992. There were still some remnants of flattened businesses, but otherwise it looked like a scene from a post-apocalyptic science fiction movie. There were black forests of dead, twisted trees as far as the eye could see. Lost in his thoughts, Michael didn't say anything as they drove. The charred, darkened landscape only enhanced the morose feelings that were growing inside him. After two tours in Iraq and all his years in law enforcement, he couldn't shake this feeling of foreboding and inevitability. A distant melody began to play inside his head. It was the song whose title he always had trouble recalling. The one he listened to as a boy on the couch with his dad that day, so long ago. The chorus went:

"Bye, bye, Miss American Pie
Drove my Chevy to the levee but the levee was dry

Them good ol' boys were drink-
ing whiskey and rye, singin . . .
This'll be the day that I die
This'll be the day that I die."

At last, Angelo saw some standing structures in a large field
and he recognized them as an abandoned airport. Angelo and
Michael now knew there would be no backup, because there
was no way any officer would be able to get closer than three
miles without being seen. As Angelo pulled into the deserted
airport, he saw a Russian man in a crumpled suit standing
in front of a chain link fence. The man waved them in and
checked the vehicle's interior and trunk for hidden passengers. He pointed to the inside of the warehouse, and told them
to park inside, where Viktor was already waiting for them.

Inside the hangar, Viktor was once again going over the
plan with Lucinda's brother Jorge. Viktor didn't want to
include Jorge in this meeting, but figured since he'd set it up
he should see how to properly close a deal. He also contemplated darkly that if any one of his guys was going to catch an
unfortunate bullet, Jorge would be best qualified for the job.
Viktor reiterated again and again to Jorge not to make a move
until he gave the signal. The other two Cubans were professionals and tried their best to distance themselves from the
cocky amateur.

As Angelo parked the rental vehicle inside the hangar, he
looked at Michael and Joey and said, "Well, just like the guy
yelled as he was falling off a roof: so far, so good!"

All three men exited the vehicle and walked towards
Viktor.

"Let's see what you got?" Angelo calmly asked Viktor
while wiping the sweat off his face with the back of his hand.

Viktor motioned to his guys with a wave of his hand.

"Bring it out."

Two of the muscular Cuban men walked over to a white
van parked inside the hangar. They opened the rear doors
and carried out a large wooden crate with U.S. military mark-

ings stenciled on the side. They heaved the heavy crate onto a rusty metal table and it groaned under the weight. One of the men pulled open the lid and Angelo walked up and observed two fifty-caliber Barrett sniper rifles packed neatly inside.

"Where's the rest?" asked Angelo as he turned towards Viktor.

Viktor tilted his head to the side and said, "Call your money man and I'll show you."

Angelo motioned to Michael.

"Go ahead and tell him to come in."

Bobby entered the hangar carrying the bag of money and placed it on top of a large crate. Angelo opened it up and showed the money to Viktor once more. Viktor looked at the money. The plan was for him to knock it off the table. It was a distraction technique so his guys could get the advantage in the ensuing firefight.

Having been in several firefights, Viktor knew they were quick and vicious, and the winner was always the party that started shooting first. Before he could walk over to the table, he saw out of the corner of his eye that *imbecile Jorge* starting to reach under his shirt. Viktor didn't even make it to the table before Jorge had prematurely pulled out his weapon and started firing. If he'd had the time, Viktor would have shot Jorge himself, but instead dove immediately for cover. Realizing the plan had just gone out the window, the other two Cubans pulled out their weapons and started blasting away. A few seconds before the shooting started, Joey had managed to maneuver himself inconspicuously to the far side of the hangar.

Joey recalled the meeting he'd had with Viktor inside this same airplane hangar, four days earlier. They were alone that time, and the temperature was at least 10° cooler.

Joey had told Viktor, "In response to what we talked about in the last meeting, here's what I can offer you. I can give you three undercover cops who I'm sure with the right persuasion will tell you everything, from their partners to their other operations. I'll set up a bogus deal for one-hundred-and-fifty thou. We split the money, and you keep the cops."

Viktor had shaken his head and replied, "They will first write up an operational plan and my name will be in bold letters on the top of the report. They will also have back up. How would we get away?"

"Easy. First I'll tell them that you got cold feet and that I got in touch with your biggest competitor Alexi and he has even a bigger surplus and really wants the deal. Then I'll tell them the truth that Alexi's counter surveillance is excellent and they should just have a spotter hidden in the area, to pick up your vehicle. They would then have their marked police vehicles make the traffic stop takedown after the deal. I'll further explain to them that all the other cops will need to hang back a mile or two because of Alexi's extreme paranoia. All we have to do is jump in their car, and have one of your guys as a decoy driver take your car out of the hangar, hauling ass and driving like a maniac. By the time they figure out what happened, we will be long gone."

Viktor pondered the idea for a little while, "You're a dangerous man . . . and that's why I like you. Okay, set it up."

Back inside the hangar, the shootout had just begun, and the previously-silent interior erupted into the deafening, repetitive, hammering sound of high caliber weapons being fired. Michael was the first officer to be hit and go down. He was struck by one of the initial rounds fired from Jorge's gun. The 9mm bullet creased the side of his head, cutting a large gash just above his ear and down the side of his head. It knocked him to the ground, rendering him unconscious. A few centimeters over and the bullet would have gone directly into his brain.

Joey dropped to a knee and turned his gun on his primary target, Angelo Tedeschi. Angelo was already on the move, seeking cover, a half second before Viktor's other two thugs pulled their guns. He had known to move when he spotted the youngest Latin thug adjust his feet slightly, and blade his body into a shooter's stance. That slight shift had given him the split-second warning to start moving. He dove to the ground and was able to get out of Joey's line of fire.

As Angelo looked towards Joey and the two made eye contact for the briefest of moments, he immediately knew that all the years of Joey's jealousy, insecurity, and paranoia had finally caught up with him. He had been betrayed by his so-called brother. But he couldn't concern himself with anger now; survival was paramount. He continued cranking off rounds at targets, and moving as fast as he could.

Another of Viktor's thugs, who had concealed himself in the SUV, started to make his move. He was waiting for the shooting to start and when it did, he rolled nimbly out of the rear passenger side door and scanned the scene. Joey was having trouble getting another clear shot at Angelo, and waved the new shooter in towards him. He hadn't known about Viktor's extra shooter, but was glad to have more firepower on their side. The shooter sprinted deftly toward where Joey was peering around a cement wall he was using for cover.

The shooter carried a large semi-automatic in hand as he crouch-ran towards Joey. A few feet before he reached Joey's location, he lifted the gun without even breaking stride, and pointed the weapon straight at Joey's shocked face. A crimson cloud of blood sprayed out the back of Joey's head as he was shot point-blank in the face. Even before Joey's lifeless body could hit the floor, the shooter shoved it out of the way and ducked behind the same wall Joey had been using. The shooter's original plan had been to first take out the cops and then Joey, but since Joey had waved him in he took advantage of the opportunity.

The shooter's name was Sergei Valuev, an ex Russian special forces mercenary Viktor had requested for this task. Sergei was flown in from New York as a loan from some of his earlier associates. Viktor had outlined the plan earlier.

"When the shooting starts, I want you to take out all but one of the American cops. I want one alive, so we can take him with us for questioning. This man . . ." Viktor pointed to a surveillance photo of Joey, "is the man responsible for killing Sacha and his brother. He's an Italian Mafioso, and they think they're fucking running the show down here. His people's days are over; it's our time now. After the cops are neutralized, I want him dead."

While reloading, Angelo got hit in the shoulder by a ricochet and jumped behind a wooden crate that offered concealment but not adequate cover. Lying on his back, Michael regained consciousness and opened his eyes. He looked up at the steel reinforced ceiling, *that's strange, they also use steel rebar to build their structures in heaven.* Hearing the distant gunfire brought him back from the brink of death, although his immediate thought was that he was back in Iraq, fighting the battle for Fallujah. As his senses returned and he recognized that he was still in the hangar, he knew he had to get back in the fight. Although his brain was sluggish, his body reverted to its years of training. His gun was still next to him on the concrete floor, and he deftly snatched it up. He rolled onto his stomach in a prone shooters position, relaxed his breathing, and concentrated on putting his gun's sights on targets.

His first gunshots were at the young punk who'd just shot him. When the shooting started, Jorge was the only person who failed to move towards cover. He also didn't have any fire discipline and wasted all his rounds in the first few seconds of the fight. Standing in the middle of the hangar, fumbling with another magazine while trying to reload, he was hit clean in the chest by every single one of Michael's rounds. One of the Cuban pros, who'd also thought Michael had been killed in the initial volley, was Michael's next victim.

Bobby was shooting at the moving targets when he was hit in the back by what he thought was a sledgehammer. The Russian guard had run into the hangar and started to spray rounds at the backs of the undercover cops with his AR-15 rifle. After absorbing that first round in his upper back, Bobby was able to spin around and get off two rounds of his own, before he fell to the ground. His first shot hit the guard in his lower abdomen while the second shot tore into the side of the guard's neck, severing his carotid artery, and killing him within seconds as the blood spewed in a red frothy fountain.

The Cuban shooter assigned as the decoy driver jumped into the SUV and drove out of the hangar at a high rate of speed. Seeing the decoy take off, Viktor hoped some of the backup officers would take the bait and follow. Sergei and Viktor were the last shooters still standing. Sergei had the angle and fired on Michael, who was now in a kneeling position, reloading his gun. Michael was hit cleanly on the right side of his ribcage, twice. Sergei now turned his aim towards Angelo, who was heading for better cover behind a cement wall. Viktor signaled to Sergei to wait. The chaotic hangar that had just been filled with ear-pounding gunfire became suddenly, eerily silent.

In a grassy field approximately a mile-and-a-half away, a SWAT team sniper worked his way on foot towards the hangar. He was lying prone in the grass and using his binoculars, when he spotted the SUV pull out. He radioed the direction of the fleeing vehicle to his supervisor and the other units in the area. The SWAT supervisor, Lt. Glenn Kapitinokis, gave the signal for all SWAT officers to move in on the hangar. The ten undercover officers in unmarked vehicles would stay back and maintain the outside perimeter points.

Viktor and Sergei carefully approached Angelo's position from opposite sides, gaining the tactical advantage. Viktor called out to Angelo.

"You don't have to die here, you were set up by your Mafioso friend. I'd rather not kill you, it's bad business, why not come work for me?"

Angelo was busy exchanging bullet magazines.

"Alright, let's talk. Drop your guns and slide them over here, and we will work somethin' out."

Using hand signals, Viktor motioned for Sergei to start flanking Angelo.

As they got closer, Viktor added, "Nice counter-proposal. How about you drop your gun and when we're done talking, you leave with half the money your guy brought. Blame it on us, say we took it all."

Angelo decided not to wait for them to out flank him, and bolted in a suicide rush from behind the wall. He ran straight towards the nearest person, who happened to be Sergei. The surprise tactic caused Sergei's first shot to go high, while Angelo's three rounds were tightly grouped and caved in Sergei's chest cavity. Viktor's shot didn't miss, though, and it hit Angelo in the middle of his left thigh. The bullet's velocity caused him to twist in the air, and he landed hard on his back with a heavy thud. The impact of the ground caused Angelo's gun to fly out of his hand.

Viktor approached Angelo, keeping his gun pointed and said, "Last chance. Live or . . ."

Michael's vest had absorbed the kinetic energy of the two earlier rounds. The immense impact to his torso had knocked the breath out of him and shattered two of his ribs. As he tried to get his breath back, his ribcage sent burning waves of excruciating spasms through his upper body. He rolled agonizingly onto his side, almost losing consciousness with the pain, and unloaded his last bullets into Viktor's shoulder and head.

Chapter 39

Jason Youngblood and his SWAT operators were the first on scene to observe the carnage. They turned quickly from lethal weapons experts to First Aid responders. Several SWAT team members carried satchels of First Aid gear, including blood coagulates, field dressings, and tourniquets. Angelo was the first recipient of a tourniquet, and it was applied high up on his left thigh. Two other SWAT team members were engaged in CPR on Bobby, who was unresponsive. Angelo was rushed via rescue helicopter to Ryder Trauma Center due to the fact that the bullet had ruptured his femoral artery, and he was losing too much blood. Michael, who was also taken to Ryder via ambulance, was later given over twenty stitches for his head wound, and a tight corset for his ribs. Once the perimeter was secure, Fire Rescue paramedics moved in onto the scene, and pronounced Bobby KIA.

Of the Cubans who were shot, only one actually lived, although he would be a paraplegic for the rest of his life after taking a bullet directly into his spine. The Cuban who'd fled in the SUV was eventually caught after a lengthy car chase from one end of the county, to the other. Michael would be released from the hospital only two days after his arrival, while Angelo would need at least four more days to recover. After hearing the news directly from Jimmie Burke at her apartment, Mia raced to the hospital and spent every night and day at Angelo's side. Hagen was also a frequent visitor; he was worried his cash cow might be in serious jeopardy. Lorenzo made several attempts to see Angelo, but was denied by uniformed patrolmen guarding Angelo's room.

Lorenzo was experiencing some problems of his own. He had just received the news his tax accountants, Suarez and Frido, were in trouble with the IRS. The accountants, who handled almost every large liquor license establishment in South Florida, were giving fraudulent advice to their clients. Lorenzo's strip club, along with several others, was notified it would be audited for the last five years. Lorenzo knew that any investigation could bankrupt him at the very least, and at the worst he could be convicted of tax evasion.

Angelo tried to protest as to why Lorenzo was not being allowed to see him, but was denied because the orders came directly from McPherson. Although he'd never had any real interactions with McPherson, Angelo knew something was wrong when he saw the Captain roaming the hallway, just outside his room. McPherson was livid because someone had stolen back the Angelo Tedeschi file from his office. When he'd taken it from Michael's office, that hadn't been theft, since all documentation belonged to the department. He further believed he was acting in the department's interest, and that it needed to be "liberated" due to Michael's lack of cooperation.

As soon as Angelo was discharged from the hospital, McPherson would be ready with a lot of questions for Hagen's *golden boy*, and he sure wasn't going to allow Angelo to hide behind some peon PBA union rep for protection.

Before Michael was discharged, he and Amanda went down the hall to Angelo's room. Amanda gave Angelo a big hug and kiss, and left the room with Mia so the two could talk in private. Michael talked briefly about the mountains of paperwork and hours of routine I.A. interviews stemming from the incident, that were awaiting them. Michael's next words caught Angelo completely off guard.

"As soon as we finish with all that paperwork, I'm handing in my resignation."

Thinking Michael was joking, Angelo smiled, but Michael

didn't smile back.

"You kiddin' me, Mike? You love police work and in all our time together you never said nothin' about quitting. C'mon, you're just fuckin' with me."

"No Ange, I'm serious. Here's the thing, the only thing I love more than police work and being with the guys, is my daughter. Ange, inside that hangar, things got as bad as they could get, and it's a miracle we both made it out of there. If it wasn't for Bobby—God rest his soul—taking out that rear gunmen we wouldn't be here having this conversation. If something happened to me, she'd be all alone, and I can't be that selfish."

Angelo nodded his head in acknowledgement, thinking about his own responsibilities, now that he was becoming a father. The idea had come to Michael on the ambulance ride to the hospital, when he was informed Bobby hadn't made it. All he could think of was, if something happened to him, Amanda would be left alone and he couldn't risk that any longer. He also figured that, after all his years in the military and twenty-one years in law enforcement, it was time to quit pressing his luck and hang it up. Finally, he explained to Angelo that he already had a job lined up through an old friend. He would work as a technical advisor on a new police television show that was going to be filmed in South Florida.

Before he left, he asked Angelo one last question, "You never finished telling me the story of your family's past. You mind telling me now?"

Angelo had hoped Mike would never bring the subject up again, but he also knew that he'd earned the right to know, and with resignation in his voice, said, "Sure, Mike, if you really want to know, here's the story. During World War II, a young German soldier took a liking to my grandmother in her village. Some said she sacrificed herself so her family would receive better treatment, while others said she was a *meretrice*, a prostitute.

"Back in those days, even though she was only fifteen and

probably didn't have a choice, everyone—including her own family—looked at her with disgust. Who really knows what the soldier promised or threatened her with, so she would be with him? He was known by the townspeople for his brutality, as he routinely shot and beat on anyone he believed was against the Third Reich. My grandmother was moved into his house, which he took over from one of the wealthiest farmers in the area.

"That was where my father was born. When the allies finally landed and the German soldiers fled Southern Italy, the town took out all their hatred for the Nazis on her and her half-German son. My father was beaten over and over and called a *Tedesco*, which of course is the Italian word for German. By the time he was fourteen, fearing for his life, my Grandmother saved up whatever pennies she could and sent him to America. He left on a ship in the middle of the night with only the clothes on his back. When he arrived in America and they asked him his last name, he told them Tedeschi. Knowing my father, this was probably his way of spitting in the eye of fate, by calling himself what he hated most."

Michael shook his head in sympathy.

"Man, I really feel bad for your old man, it sounds like he had it rough."

Angelo looked around the hospital room, almost seeing the horrible memories from the past that were never far away, then also shook his head. "Don't feel bad for my old man, 'cause he took out all his frustrations and pain on me and my mother . . ."

Angelo paused in deep thought, then quickly added, "Look Mike, I already said too much, and I don't wanna talk about it no more."

Michael understood. For him, whenever someone brought up his wife, it started the domino effect of bringing him back to a real ugly place. He turned to Angelo, and in his familiar serious tone, barked "Just because I'm leaving, doesn't mean I won't be watching you. If you step out of line, I will finally give you that beating I owed you since the first day we met."

Angelo laughed.

"Whatever you say, killer, whatever you say!"

Michael stood up on weak legs, leaned into Angelo, and the two men hugged goodbye. As he watched Michael walk gingerly out of the room, Angelo thought to himself, *Shit, I forgot to thank that little bastard for saving my life.*

On Angelo's fourth day in the hospital, and in defiance of his doctor's warnings, he decided to go to Bobby's funeral. Mia, along with Angelo's nurse, helped him into a wheelchair, and they headed to his truck that Mia had parked on the first floor of the hospital's indoor parking garage. When they reached the garage, Mia told Angelo and the nurse to wait and to make it easier, she would bring the Escalade around. As Mia drove up, the nurse assisted Angelo in standing, and handed him a pair of crutches.

The nurse opened the passenger side front door and, as Angelo hobbled forward towards the truck—WHAM— it exploded in a huge, orange fireball. Angelo was thrown off his feet by the blast and crashed into the concrete wall five feet behind him. The nurse, who was holding the car door open, was killed instantly by flying shrapnel. In fact, her body shielded Angelo from most of the deadly slivers of accelerating, burning metal. The Escalade bucked several feet into the air and almost flipped on its side, before righting itself. The vehicle's windows exploded outward, peppering Angelo's face and torso with hundreds of tiny shards of glass that embedded themselves up to a quarter of an inch into his skin.

As Angelo tried to recover from the hardest hit he'd ever experienced, he heard his old boxing coach in a distant voice, yelling *get up Angelo get on your feet before you get counted out.* In his altered state, he was somehow able to draw himself back to consciousness and get on his feet. He heard a slight ringing in his ears and everything else was deathly silent, as if someone had just pressed the world's mute button. This was despite the fact that at least twenty car alarms were blaring simultaneously, along with the hospital's emergency alarm. With blood oozing from his ears and nose, he willed his body to lurch forward through a heavy cloud of smoke and noxious fumes, towards the car. *I gotta' get Mia outta there.* When he ripped open the mangled driver's side door, he immediately knew that she and their unborn son were dead, and that he now had nothing to live for. For the first time in his life, Angelo gave up all hope and caring, and collapsed into a dreamless void. Exactly forty-eight minutes later, in the hospital's Emergency room, Angelo Tedeschi was pronounced dead.

Chapter 40

When Eddie was told the news of Joey's death, he flew into an uncontrollable rage, and destroyed several rooms in his house. Although his informant couldn't give him exact details on how Joey had died, it didn't matter, because he held Angelo fully responsible. Eddie remembered the phone conversation from one week earlier. Joey had called to give him his report on the deal with the Russians and Angelo's waning allegiance to the family. In that phone call, Joey told him with complete confidence, "Angelo's definitely turned on us."

In stunned shock, Eddie answered, "I can't believe it. I just can't believe it."

Joey continued, "It's been four months since you asked for the list of the other undercover officers, and where is it? Your own guys down here have reported he's been makin' big money on the side, and where's your tribute? He fucked up on that last shipment deal by not warning us his own under-cover guys were working the area! Pops, when I look him in the eye, all I see is a liar. He's definitely turned on us, and our way of life. Maybe 'cause he's a thousand miles away, he thinks he's his own boss. Maybe this cop thing got to his head, I don't know, but I say he's turned, and he has to go before he does something that hurts us."

There was a long pause on the phone, and Joey thought they'd been disconnected, until his father said in a very low monotone, "I can't believe I'm saying this. Okay, you have my authorization take out Ange."

Eddie slammed the phone down, agonized by his decision, going through immense feelings of rage and deep sadness. *I treated Angelo like a son, opened my home to him, and gave him every opportunity and this is his how he repays me.*

That final conversation with Joey replayed in his head, and reinforced for him that Angelo was solely responsible for his son's death. Once he was eventually calmed down by his bodyguards, he started to plan his revenge. He knew he had to hire an outsider, because the hit couldn't be authorized without the approval not only of his boss, but the other acting members of the Mafia council. To convene that type of meeting these days could take weeks, and he wanted Angelo dead now. He contracted an ex-Israeli Mossad agent named Mohti to take out Angelo. Mohti was used not only by the mob, but also by numerous governments, including Arab countries that wanted complete secrecy. Mohti answered to no one and had no living family. His family had been killed in a rocket attack and he blamed the liberal Israeli government for their weakness. As a result, he now applied his trade to the highest bidder.

When Mohti saw Angelo standing with his crutches on the hospital curb, he knew he was close to completing his mission. The security was way too tight for him to try to take him out in his hospital room. Mohti was a patient hunter and decided to utilize his time by following Mia. When he observed Mia enter the Escalade inside the hospital's garage, he activated the car bomb. Once activated, he would be one step away from pushing the detonate button. His plan was to follow the truck to an area where no civilians could get hurt and then detonate it. As the Escalade pulled up to Angelo, something went wrong with the remote. Possibly it received another powerful signal from some of the hospital equipment, and prematurely detonated. As Mohti slowly drove away from the now-chaotic scene, he made a mental note to remember the unreliability of that type of remote in proximity to hospitals.

Eddie watched the news of Mohti's botched hit and immediately knew he was in trouble. The news reported a nurse had been killed, alongside a pregnant female and an unnamed undercover cop. The reporter advised that, in order to protect the other officers in his unit, the name of the undercover officer would not be released. They only provided his age, and that the cause of his death resulted from extensive internal injuries suffered in the blast.

Eddie believed the bosses would understand his need for revenge. The problem would be that Angelo was a real cop, and two innocent civilians had also been killed. With all the media attention it garnished, the incident would bring a lot of unnecessary heat on the mob. For his part, Eddie had been clear with his instructions, and had specifically told Mohti to make sure he avoided any collateral damage. *Well, what's done is done, and now I will have to face my judgment.*

The day after Angelo's death, the F.B.I. and numerous other agencies started their investigations. The F.B.I. was familiar with the unique type of C-4 plastic explosive used on Angelo's truck. Only two weeks earlier, a high level Chicago mobster had been killed using the exact explosive and detonating device. Mob operations throughout the east coast were now disrupted and millions of dollars were lost by the ongoing local and Federal investigation. Local law enforcement also rounded up numerous lower echelon mobsters or "soldiers" on petty offenses, squeezing them for information. The heads of the Florida and New York Mafia families called an emergency council meeting.

When Eddie received the summons from the family, he was already working on his defense. He had only two choices on how to play it. He could deny he'd had anything to do with the hit and blame it all on the Russians, and hope that Mohti would never talk. The problem with that would be if Mohti was forcibly brought in and questioned on who hired him. With the Serbian interrogators the mob liked to use, even a man like Mohti would eventually talk. *Shit, he might talk if they just offered him enough money.* The last problem with lying to the council would be that even if he initially got away with it, he would have to live the rest of his life in fear. No matter how long it took, if they ever found out he would be immediately killed for lying.

His other option was to admit he'd ordered the unauthorized hit, showing that he was a man of honor and had nothing to hide. The downside to that was, he would be admitting he knowingly broke rules and that infraction alone could also be punishable by instant death.

After much thought, he chose to go with the latter. After explaining a father's need for revenge, he would then vow to punish Mohti for his unprofessional work. He believed the odds were in his favor that he would most likely walk out of the meeting alive, with probably only a demotion and a stiff fine. The meeting was scheduled in the basement of an unassuming two-bedroom Brooklyn house, located off Flatlands Avenue on East 57th Street.

As Eddie pulled up to the house, he saw at least ten guards in the street pretending to play a game of stickball. The meeting was only scheduled for thirty minutes, and Eddie was confident he'd be able to sway two out of the three bosses into seeing things in his favor. Indeed, having sons themselves, he figured two of the bosses wouldn't look too unfavorably upon his actions. By the end of the meeting, Eddie was told that, due to the complexity of his actions, the three elder patriarchs would rule on his fate over the next several days. Eddie was confident that he'd won the first battle, because if they were going to whack him it would have been done immediately. The only thing he figured they had left to discuss was what type of punishment he would receive, and at this point he was leaning towards something lenient, like a financial fine.

In the meetings that followed Eddie's testimony, Florida boss Frank Mezzanotte—who was taking the worst financial losses—argued for the strictest punishment. The other two bosses were more understanding of Eddie's decision, and leaned more towards imposing a stiff financial penalty. Mezzanotte argued vehemently, and by the second day a decision was finally made.

It was only four days after the initial council meeting, and a messenger was sent to Eddie's house to inform him of the decision. It was early in the morning, and Eddie was sitting on his patio deck drinking his coffee and reading the newspaper. The messenger, a large scarred man, walked out onto the patio. Eddie hearing his screen door open, Eddie turned his head, expecting one of his guys who he'd asked earlier to bring back freshly baked bagels.

The messenger walked out on the deck, and the two men locked eye contact like the opposing poles of a magnet. Eddie broke eye contact, and slightly nodded his head in complete understanding.

The messenger raised his gun towards Eddie's head and asked in a calm, monotone voice, "Eddie, did you see the sunrise?"

"Yeah, Angelo, I did."

Angelo Tedeschi pulled the trigger and Eddie Salerno was no longer of this earth. Oddly enough, Eddie's last thoughts weren't of rage or hate, but of contentment. *If it has to be this way, then I'm glad it's my son, Angelo, and not one of my sworn enemies that releases me from this life and gives me peace.*

The body of Eddie Salerno was wrapped in a thick carpet roll and removed by two of his trusted bodyguards.

Chapter 41

Ten minutes after Angelo's truck exploded in the hospital parking lot, he slowly regained consciousness. He found himself back in the same E.R. room he was brought to only four days earlier. Miraculously, he only suffered a concussion and numerous lacerations. As his eyes started to focus and he realized he was still alive, his first thought was a deep sense of disappointment and betrayal. Death was the one thing in all his years he'd never asked for and now when he'd finally embraced it, even death turned its back on him.

Twenty-five minutes after the explosion, F.B.I agents along with the Chief of Beachside P.D., were at his side. For his safety, it was then determined they would have the doctors announce he had died from his wounds.

Inside his new secure hospital room that night, Angelo removed all the bandaging from his lacerated face and got dressed. He focused on controlling the dizziness and immense pain, while he snuck out of the hospital. He somehow accomplished this despite the fact there were numerous patrolmen inside the hospital, working as his security detail. It helped that the cops were only concerned with people coming in, not going out. Lorenzo picked him up two blocks away and drove him to a secret meeting in a hotel, forty-five minutes north in Boca Raton.

Several hours earlier, Angelo had requested a meeting with the La Cosa Nostra boss of Florida, Frank Mezzanotte. The request was granted and the meeting was very brief. Only three hours after he'd snuck out of the hospital, he was back in his room. After the clandestine meeting, Frank Mezzanotte contacted the council and asked for an emergency session.

Two days after killing Eddie, Angelo was contacted at his New York hotel and summoned to a house in Howard Beach, Queens. Angelo directed the cab driver to drop him off several blocks away from the actual location. As he walked towards the house, his mind buzzed. *Maybe this is it. Maybe I'm the one that now gets whacked. Ah, fuck it, it don't bother me none. I had one a hell of a ride and with the greatest girl at my side. Maybe it's for the best I ain't no family man, and maybe I would have fucked up as a father, just like my old man. Not for nuttin', but I'd rather catch a bullet tonight by a made man than die by some disease in a hospital all by myself.*

Angelo entered the house from the rear door, and even though he was never told, he knew it would be in the basement. The basement was always where these meetings and other mob business occurred. As a kid, he remembered hearing the old timers talk about guys like the Chicago mobster "Mad" Sam, who kept a practical torture chamber in his basement, and was known as the master of the ice pick. He hoped that wouldn't be his fate because he believed torture was as dishonorable to the torturer as it was for the recipient.

As Angelo walked down the rickety stairs, he saw the same three bosses he'd met with earlier when he'd been given permission to take out Eddie. The bosses all welcomed him now and the ceremony began. Angelo's blood was drawn from his finger, and a card of a holy Saint burned in his hand. He swore to the oath that was presented to him, and was then inducted into the secret society of La Cosa Nostra. Angelo Tedeschi was now a made man in the Mafia.

After making his bones by whacking Eddie, he became eligible to become made. This was part of the agreement he'd reached with Mezzanotte a week earlier, at their meeting in Florida. Mezzanotte, who had been financially hurt most by Eddie's mistake, would now have Angelo in his crew, reporting directly to him. For Mezzanotte, Angelo was now the golden goose. It's one thing to have a made man with police connections, but Angelo was so much more. He wasn't just a regular cop; he was an undercover detective, privy to numerous ongoing operations. For Mezzanotte and his operation, it would be a source of priceless intelligence. It was for all these reasons that Mezzanotte "vouched" for Angelo as his sponsor, despite Angelo's tainted Italian bloodline.

Chapter 42

The following morning, Angelo called his two closest friends—Danny Phillips and Jay Gardner—from his hotel room. Angelo wasn't surprised when he heard Danny's nonchalant reaction. The voice of someone who was supposed to be dead and on his way to New York to be buried would rattle most, but not Danny Phillips. Angelo had a feeling Danny would somehow know he wasn't dead. *How would he know? I got no fuckin' idea, but nothing got past Danny.*

Jay, on the other hand, also acted exactly as Angelo had figured—by dropping the phone and screaming and crying with shock and happiness. When Jay finally calmed down, Angelo told him Danny would swing by his office and pick him up so they could give him a lift to LaGuardia airport in Queens, and see him off.

Two hours later, Danny and Jay arrived at Angelo's hotel. The three embraced, and Jay couldn't stop himself shedding more tears for his newly resurrected friend. Danny, on the other hand, was his cool and collected self, wearing a $2,000 Hugo Boss suit, and looking like he'd stepped off the front cover of GQ magazine. As Danny looked at his solidly-built, rough-looking friend, he noticed he was sporting many new scars. *Guys like Angelo are really hard to kill; they're too tough, too stubborn, and way too nasty to just die.*

On the ride to the airport, Angelo didn't say much and, to his friends, was understandably quiet. Danny and Jay gave their condolences about Mia, knowing full well not to pry for any details. He would tell them in his own time, or maybe not at all. That was just his way.

After dropping Angelo off at the airport, Jay suggested to Danny that they blow off going back to their offices in Manhattan.

Danny had a better idea, "I can't get my head back into work right now, either. How about we hit Coney Island and ride the Cyclone a few times, and then have some Nathan's hotdogs?"

Jay smiled and said, "Sounds like a plan."

On the drive back to Brooklyn, Jay looked to Danny for answers about Angelo and his future. Jay knew that Danny, of all people, would understand Angelo the best. Not just because they'd known each other so long, but because Danny also had the most uncanny ability to predict the future. Even with his high I.Q. and law degrees, Jay knew that Danny could always see the angles that, to Jay and most others, were blurred. Danny smiled to himself at both his friend's questions and faith in his clairvoyance. Danny couldn't predict the future. He wasn't "Houdini" or the magician his friends thought he was. He was simply excellent at reading people, and understanding who they really were. That was the real key to seeing all the angles and predicting people's behavior.

He tried to answer all Jay's questions about Angelo.

"What is Angelo going to do with his life? What will this life-changing incident of losing the only woman he ever loved and he himself cheating death do to alter him and the way he sees life? The answer is . . . absolutely nothing. Jay, here's the thing. Angelo isn't wired the same as most people. I've seen him deal with things that would have made most men completely lose their minds and throw in the towel. The only prediction I will make for you, besides that that particular leopard won't be changing his spots, is he might now be even a little nastier and more dangerous than he ever was before, and I would hate to be anyone he considered his enemy."

Angelo took his seat, 1D, in the very front of the JetBlue

plane on his flight back to Florida. He always sat up front in the section that had the extra legroom. First on the plane and first off—no waiting. He immediately re-positioned the air conditioning vent away from his head. Once comfortable, he folded his arms, leaned his seat back and closed his eyes. The last ten days of his life had been a chaotic rollercoaster ride he hadn't had a chance to reflect on. During that time, he hadn't thought too much about the hit man, Mohti. Mohti was just a tool or weapon utilized by people like Eddie. To want revenge on Mohti would be as stupid as vowing revenge on a gun or a grenade. If he did ever come across that weapon, however, he would immediately eliminate it. Not for revenge, but because it was a faulty piece of equipment that malfunctioned, and therefore served no sensible purpose in Angelo's world. And if or when the time came, he would dispatch it without malice.

When it came to Mia's funeral, Angelo followed all her wishes. After the Miami-Dade County Medical Examiner authorized the release of her body, he had her immediately flown to Newark, New Jersey International Airport. From there, the body was moved to the Buddhist Temple she belonged to in Cherry Hill, New Jersey. It was on the second night after she'd moved in with him that she told him her wishes if something ever happened to her. Angelo hadn't wanted to talk about it because he figured why talk about something bad like that when they were just starting new lives together? Mia explained that was exactly why it was the perfect time because, as a practicing Buddhist, she believed death wasn't the end but a part of an ongoing process. It was a transition into a new life, because she would be reborn.

Part of the tradition would also include having her body cremated. Angelo was against the cremation, but she'd smiled, gripped his hand warmly, and told him, "Burning of the body is essential in allowing the spirit to pass on to the next life, and just be happy I'm not a Tibetan Buddhist."

"Why, what do they do?"

"Sometimes, they dismember the body to feed to the vultures or other animals. In this way, the body eases the suffering of another being, and that is essential to the Buddhist philosophy."

Having heard enough, Angelo had said, "Can we get off this subject now, cause nothin' is going to ever happen to you while I'm around, and you know that."

Mia smiled and jumped into his arms, and said with utter conviction, "I know that, just like I know I will spend the rest of my life with you and that's a promise."

How right she was, Angelo thought. He felt a sudden chill and shifted uncomfortably in his seat.

As the plane landed at the Fort Lauderdale International Airport, a new emotion began to stir inside him . . . anger. His fists and jaw muscles started to involuntarily tighten as he thought about all the people who owed him money. These were the people who must have celebrated the news he was dead, believing they were now debt free. *I'm going to change that shit real fast, and get all the fuckin' money that's owed to me. No one's going to beat Angelo Tedeschi out of his money.* He also remembered Hagen had contacts with the test assessors in charge of the Sergeant's exam. He would bribe, threaten, or blackmail whoever he had to in order to get his Sergeant's stripes. With that type of power, who knew how high he might rise in the system? Maybe someday he could even take Hagen's seat as Lieutenant. Thinking about all his future plans, he couldn't wait to get back to Beachside and really start squeezing that city for every drop it owed him.

Epilogue

The Nikon D90 camera whirred as it took non-stop consec-
utive pictures of Angelo exiting the airport and hailing
a cab. Satisfied with his photos, Mark McPherson placed the
camera on the big file that rested on the passenger seat.

This was his new file, since the one he'd "liberated" from
Michael Frakes had somehow been stolen from his office.
For now, he'd put his hunt for the elusive white whale James
Hagen on the back burner. He was suddenly less interested
in going after Hagen—the real big fish, he now knew, was
Tedeschi. He put the car in gear and drove out of the airport,
a twisted grin on his face.

About The Authors . . .

David A. Yuzuk was born and raised in Brooklyn, New York and
 he always enjoyed being involved in
athletics. He played high school and
college football and has studied the
martial arts. Leaving Brooklyn, he
moved to South Florida where he has
been working as a Police Officer for
the last fourteen years. On his days
off, he works on his various creative
projects — writing, acting, and film-
making.

As part-time actor David Danello, he
has had speaking roles on TV shows
like Burn Notice, The Glades, and
America's Most Wanted. His movie
roles include Miami Vice, U.S.S. Seaviper, House of Bodies, I Love
Miami, Assumed Memories, and 5th of a Degree. He was nomi-
nated for Best Actor by the Miami Life Awards for his leading
role as David Ross in 5th of a Degree.

David's passion for writing started with screenplays and he has
IMDB credit as a co-producer and co-author of the film 5th of a
Degree (as David Danello). 5th of a Degree is the winner of the
2012 Golden Ace Award at the Las Vegas Film Festival.

David has also written an illustrated children's book The Legend
of the Smiling Chihuahua (www.smilinglegend.com).

I would like to thank the following people:

All the men and women who have served in the armed forces.

All the men and women of law enforcement.

My fellow police officers: Jaime Chalem, Harvey Arrango, Bryan Pegues, Michael Leoncini, and Former Marine Corp Staff Sergeant/P.O. Carlos Rivas. The men of the 2nd Battalion 1st Marines, 1st MARDIV 2004-2006.

Janeth "Tilly" Velasquez, Frank Musumeci, and Daniel Columbie.

My editor, David Antrobus, photos by Jaime Chalem of Nisso Studios and my formatting gurus, Zihong Gorman and Bryan Coker.

Neil L. Yuzuk was born in Brooklyn, New York. He worked in

sales and sales management before returning to college as a freshman at age 40. In 1987, he began working as a New York City Substance Abuse Prevention and Intervention Counselor, working in the high school SPARK Program.

After he retired, his full-time police officer/actor son David said, "Hey Pops, why don't you write a screenplay for me." He wrote a police procedural called, The Devil's Troll. "The experience of learning how to do research and creating characters and their back stories was an incredible learning experience." He then teamed up with David to collaborate on their first screenplay The Reluctant Knight. That screenplay eventually became the first book in the Beachside PD series — Beachside PD: The Reluctant Knight — and it was a Global eBook Awards finalist in the category of Suspense/Thriller.

Since then, he's co-authored the recently published Beachside PD: The Gypsy Hunter and he is currently working on the fourth book in the series, Beachside PD: Undercover (scheduled for December, 2012). The fifth book in the series will be, Beachside PD: A Captain's Story (scheduled for July, 2013) and the sixth book is projected to be Beachside PD: Special Weapons (scheduled for May, 2015)

Along with Daniel Columbie—an independent film producer/director—Neil has also co-authored another screenplay, Fade To Light. A family saga novel called Zaragossa: Fruit Of The Vine is scheduled for December, 2014. Zaragossa: Fruit Of The Vine is based in the research done for The Devil's Troll, and it will include that story—the hunt for a serial killer in the wine country of northern California.

Neil credits Robert McKee for teaching him the insights and skills of writing as well as his Thomas Jefferson High School English teacher, Harriet Epstein and his Brooklyn College Professor Martha F. Black.

I would like to thank the men and women, in the armed forces, who, through the years, have served our country, most especially my uncles who served during World War II: Harry "Buck" Yuzuk who was wounded and a decorated Forward Artillery Observer, European Theater;

his brother and my uncle, William "Velvul" Yuzik, U.S.N. who served on an aircraft carrier in the Pacific theater; my uncle, William "Willie" Pruce, whose ship was torpedoed in the English Channel, landed supplies on the D-Day beaches and transported them inland. It is rumored that he liberated Paris by trading his cigarette allotment for nylon stockings.

And my father Victor "Vic" Yuzuk and his brother Nathan "Nat" Yuzuk, who served on the home front, like millions of others, in support of our troops and our country. To all who served after that great conflict, from 1950 Korea to 2012 Afghanistan, your sacrifices have allowed us to be a free and open society.

On a more personal note, to my police officer contributors who have shared their stories and allowed me to tell them: Bryan Pegues, Marc Frieder, Jaime Chalem, Michael Leoncini, Harvey Arrango, et al.

To my friends, family, and former students — Thank You for your time, information, and patience in helping me do my research.

To all of you — Thank You for your support and for helping me keep it real.

And, most especially my technical support people, Leo Streit and Zihong Gorman — you are both an unending source of support — Thank You for letting me drive the both of you crazy!

Harry "Buck" Yuzuk, born c. 1922

<u>Medals and Commendations</u>
Good Conduct Medal
Army of Occupation
Presidential Unit Citation
Rome-Arno Campaign
D-Day Invasion Arrowhead
D-Day European Campaign
Bronze Star, Valor (Anzio)
Sharpshooter, Carbine
Marksman, Garand
V-E Day Victory in Europe

2012

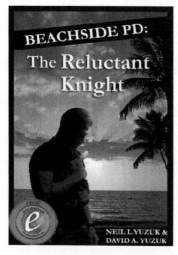

4.8 Stars on Amazon Reviews   5 Stars on Amazon Reviews

**The Beachside PD series books are
available both as Print books and eBooks at:**

WEBSITE:
http://www.BeachsidePDBooks.com

The website also offers the free BONUS CHAPTERS to Beachside PD: The Reluctant Knight, as well as information on,
and introductions to, all of the Beachside PD Books.

FACEBOOK
http://www.facebook.com/#!/BeachsidePDBooks

TWITTER
@beachsidepdbook

BOOK TRAILER ON YOUTUBE
http://www.youtube.com/watch?v=20e_i39GaQA

PLEASE NOTE: The authors are available for read-
ings, book signings, and other events. Neil is in the Greater
New York area and David is in southern Florida.

PROLOGUE to Beachside PD: Undercover

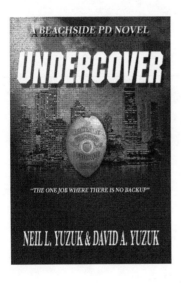

A BEACHSIDE PD NOVEL

UNDERCOVER

"THE ONE JOB WHERE THERE IS NO BACKUP"

NEIL L. YUZUK & DAVID A. YUZUK

The building was a beacon of light amid the storm-darkened Beachside, Florida. The Cadillac Escalade pulled up to a covey of police cars whose flashing lights lit up the hospital's windows like a psychedelic pinball machine.

The rain followed Anna and Elysa as the wind blew them through the ER door in a rush. Hurricane Evelyn was pounding Beachside, Florida — but mother and daughter were oblivious to the pools of water that followed them as they approached the group of police officers. Chief of Police Joshua Chamberlain saw them, separated from the group and went to greet them. He was quickly followed by his two Road Patrol Sergeants, Kaylia Ramirez and Lesli Sabon. The other officers trailed behind.

"Where's Danny?" Anna shouted. "I want to see him."

"He's still in surgery," the Chief said.

"What happened to him? You were supposed to keep him safe."

"I know. I shouldn't have let him stay in so long, but he wanted to see it all the way through . . . all the way to the end."

To an unknowing eye, Anna seemed unaffected. For the moment she wore the armor of a police veteran. Her facade of calmness maintained by the officers who were now surrounding her.

"How bad is he?" she asked.

"He was shot three times . . ."

Elysa swayed and was caught by Kaylia who brought her to a nearby bench. Anna stood next to her. Lesli brought them some towels. Anna let her colleagues tend to her daughter.

"Keep going," she ordered the chief.

"He was shot in the head, the chest and the leg. One of the nurses said that they were able to remove the bullets and they were sewing him up."

"How did this happen?"

"Danny called me and said that SPLAT was going to do an interception on a cocaine smuggling ring—two tons of coke was being brought in under the cover of the hurricane, but he said that something didn't seem right and we should be there as backup. When we arrived there was a firefight in progress. I thought Danny was dead until he called me on my cell and I found him in the weeds, bleeding badly. I called an ambulance and as we were rushing him here he gave me a full statement."

"Where did this go down?" Anna asked.

"On the old lighthouse Pier . . ."

Anna's facade cracked and she attacked the chief beating at him with her fists. He quickly hugged her trapping her arms, effectively pinning them. He was a big man and as hard as Anna tried to squirm out of his grip, the tighter he held her.

"God damn you," she screamed. "You're supposed to keep him safe. How could you fuck up like that?"

The chief spoke to her trying to calm her down, but she continued to scream her curses at him, at Danny, and at the fates that had brought them to this moment. Elysa came up behind Anna and started talking to her, it took what seemed to be an eternity. Anna went slack in the chief's arms and he released her. Anna turned to Elysa and they held on to each other crying.

The chief leaned over with his hands on his knees. Lieutenant Robert Zaragossa asked the chief if he was alright and the chief, breathing hard, straightened up and nodded, "I'm okay."

Two of the hospital security force had witnessed the attack on the chief and were approaching Anna when a blue wall cut them off. The chief pointed at them and waved them away. They backed off.

"Chief Chamberlain?" a doctor called out as he approached the group.

"Over here," the chief called.

"I'm Dr. Heinz. I did the surgery on Danny Phillips . . ."

Anna turned and grabbed the doctor's arm, "Is he alive?"

The surgeon pulled his arm away and asked "Who are you?"

"I'm his fucking wife. Is my husband still alive?"

"Missus Phillips, I need you to calm down."

"Calm down?" Anna grabbed the surgeon's blood splattered surgical tunic with both hands and pulled him close, nose-to-nose.

"Tell me if he's still alive, damn you." With that she released his shirt and pushed him back. He would have fallen if Zaragossa hadn't caught him. Elysa grabbed her and whatever she said calmed Anna.

The doctor was in shock—this god of surgery wasn't used to be manhandled, especially by a woman. He turned red and began to shake.

The chief recognized the symptoms and ordered him, in his most authoritative voice, "Doctor Heinz, your report."

Heinz straightened up and looked at the chief and then Anna. "Mr. Phillips is alive." With that everyone seemed to let out their collective breath.

"Chief, I'm not going to lie to you," he continued. "He was shot three times. The leg wound missed the femoral artery, but it took out a good bit of tissue, mostly muscle. If it was just that, six months of rehab and he would be fine. The second bullet came in the armpit of his vest on a downward angle. It bounced off of a rib, passed through a lung and created a pneumothorax. That means that it collapsed the lung. We re-inflated the lung and he has a chest tube in to monitor his recovery.

"That bullet then hit the small intestine. By itself, easily repaired. The only danger might be sepsis, an infection of materials that spilled from the internal wound. We're treating him with intravenous antibiotics.

"It's the third bullet that's the most life threatening. He was shot in the head, but the bullet didn't penetrate the brain itself, only the Dura. However, the trauma caused the brain to swell so I performed a decompressive hemicraniotomy." He looked at them and realized he needed to explain. "I opened his skull and removed a piece in order to give it room to expand without it damaging brain function or causing death."

Anna started to speak, but Heinz gestured her to wait.

"Here's the issue, his body was shot three times and the trauma is synergistic. That means that one plus one plus one equals four, or maybe five. It's going to be touch and go for the next seventy-two hours. If he survives that, he'll probably walk out of here."

"Thank you Doctor Heinz," said Anna, "when can we see him?"

"Give the nurse about ten minutes to set him up, but three minutes only — that's all for the first two hours. We'll see how he's doing then. And no beating up the nurses, understand?"

"Yes, Doctor Heinz," a chastened Anna said as the surgeon started to leave.

The chief stopped Heinz, "Before you leave . . . and every-one listen up." The blue wall moved closer. "When Angelo Tedesci was on the force many years ago, we had to fake his death in order to protect him. As far as we are concerned, Danny Phillips died on the operating table tonight without regaining consciousness. The head wound was deliberate and I don't want anyone getting a second shot at him. Does every-one here understand me?"

There were nods and yes sirs from the group.

Heinz shook his head, "Chief, we can't do that . . ."

Now it was the chief's turn to grab the surgeon by his shirt.

"Doctor, there is no can't here. There is only do. The story will be that Anna passed out when she heard of Danny's death and is being held for observation. You will put her in a room with him. Got it?"

"Yes sir."

"Good, now go make those arrangements. I'll clear them with your administration."

Heinz quickly left.

"Now as for the rest of you, Sergeants Ramirez and Sabon I want you and your officers back out on patrol. We have a hurricane and people who need help. Remember, Danny is dead . . . God forbid and I don't want to hear any chatter different from that on the radios. Use your cell phones for updates; now go."

They saluted the chief, rounded up their road patrol officers and went on their way.

"The rest of you go to your emergency stations. Lieutenant Zaragossa, I want you to call in your undercover officers, Andy Bello and Valerie Gordon. I want Andy in a hospital security uniform outside the intensive care unit and I want Valerie to be there dressed as a nurse. Call Bret Paden and have him assign Sam Perkins and Cynthia Outlaw to spell Andy and Val—rotating six hour shifts."

Robert Zaragossa moved quickly to follow orders. "Yes sir," Zaragossa said and as he turned away he was calling out on his department radio.

"Fitz," the chief turned to his Major Case Detective Chief Inspector Aidan Fitzpatrick, "I want you to take charge of our part of the shootout investigation and coordinate with the other departments. Call all of your people in."

"Yes sir," the older grey-haired man said. "You'll keep me up to date on Danny?"

"Of course. Wait up."

"James," he said to the Lieutenant of Detectives, James Outlaw, "I want you to call all of your people in and assign three of them to Fitz. I want the other three to work with Jenny Kuo and her forensics team. Then I want you to take over road patrol while McCafferty is away."

Outlaw, an older black man whose two daughters also were part of Beachside PD, put his hand on the chief's shoulder. "Josh, Danny's a tough kid. You stay here and hold down the fort, I'll make sure the department keeps running smoothly."

"Thanks Jimmy."

With everyone gone, the chief gathered Anna and Elysa. "Let's go see Danny."

Made in United States
Orlando, FL
22 March 2025

59717732R00139